Praise for THREADS

Great fun. It goes at a cracking pace and girls will love it.
JACQUELINE WILSON, AUTHOR

. . . the next Princess Diaries – *only hotter.*
AMANDA CRAIG, THE TIMES

A magical tale . . .
BLISS MAGAZINE

. . . a must read . . .
INDEPENDENT ON SUNDAY

Miss it, miss out.
MIZZ MAGAZINE

Bang on trend, with some hilarious fashion faux pas . . .
TBK MAGAZINE

The fashion story everyone's talking about . . .
SUGAR MAGAZINE

A treat . . . elegant and funny and has real narrative verve.
DAVID ALMOND, AUTHOR

The perfect stocking-filler for the girl who knows her Marni from her Matalan . . .
EVENING STANDARD

. . . upbeat and thoroughly entertaining.
BOOKS FOR KEEPS

A MESSAGE FROM CHICKEN HOUSE

The girls are back! I can't wait to hear what happens next! If *Threads* made you laugh and cry, helped fashion make sense, and inspired your wardrobe and your conscience, then prepare for a bumpy ride. Our friends are in action again, but the future seems to be coming unstitched. Sophia Bennett just gets better . . . and better.

BARRY CUNNINGHAM
Publisher
Chicken House

Beads

SOPHIA BENNETT

Chicken House

2 Palmer Street, Frome, Somerset BA11 1DS
www.doublecluck.com

Designer, Brand and Fashion House names used in the text are the international trademarks of their owners and are not used with permission and their use is not authorised, associated with, or sponsored by the owners of the trademarks.

The characters portrayed in this book are fictitious and any similarity to real persons, living or dead, is coincidental and not intended by the author.

First published in Great Britain in 2010
This edition published 2015
Chicken House
2 Palmer Street
Frome, Somerset BA11 1DS
United Kingdom
www.doublecluck.com

Cover design and interior design by Helen Crawford-White
Typeset by Dorchester Typesetting Group Ltd
Printed and bound in Great Britain by CPI Group (UK) Ltd, Croydon CR0 4YY

The paper used in this Chicken House book is made from wood grown in sustainable forests.

1 3 5 7 9 10 8 6 4 2

British Library Cataloguing in Publication data available.

ISBN 978-1-910002-95-7
eISBN 978-1-909489-96-7

To E, whose kisses are
SO not ew

Also by Sophia Bennett

Threads
Stars
The Look
You Don't Know Me
The Castle

Chapter 1

I've never seen Crow look so scared. And this time, she's got a point.

We're standing in Miss Teen's flagship store in Oxford Street. The shop floor is huge and shiny and practically empty. For now. The perfect shopping opportunity, you might think, but oh no. We're not shopping, we're waiting. And we're not the only ones. There's just one very large pane of glass between us and the biggest, loudest mob I've ever seen. It's been building up for hours. It can see us. It's shouting our names and it's counting down until it can reach us.

One pane of glass, that is, and a SUPERMODEL.

Svetlana Russinova is posing in the window. She's wearing one of Crow's little gold embroidered corset dresses with a flirty skirt that shows off her legs. I remember Crow designing that dress last spring.

Every now and again Svetlana looks back over her shoulder at us three girls, huddled together in the shop, and says something helpful like, 'There's thousands of them. Really. Oxford Street is full. Are you sure they'll fit inside?'

No, frankly, we are not. We're not at all sure we'll fit even half of them inside. Or that we'll survive the process. Or, more to the point, that we'll have enough of Crow's new high-street collection to sell to them when they get here.

Andy Elat is the only person who seems even vaguely relaxed. He's the man who owns Miss Teen. He said, 'We'll do a big launch for the new collection before Christmas. Everyone's talking about it. It'll be huge. You'll love it.'

If he'd said, 'It'll be like being in the middle of a natural disaster, with sequins,' we'd have got the picture. But he didn't. So here we are.

Crow looks the most terrified, but she's got her brother Henry for comfort. She's clinging on to him for dear life. I've got my friend Jenny and I'm sort of clinging on to her, but to be honest, she's more clinging on to me.

'They look angry,' she whispers. 'Are you sure we should let them in, Mr Elat?'

'They're just excited,' Andy says calmly. 'OK, Svetlana. You'd better come down now. Thanks, love. Two minutes, lads.'

The security guards nod. They are big and scary-looking and they'll probably be OK. We are small, teenage and unarmed. I'm trying to remember why I ever got involved with Crow. Or why I thought launching a high-street collection would be a cool idea. Or why I didn't decide to do it from A MILLION MILES AWAY.

'Three. Two. One. Open the doors, lads.'

Scream scream scream scream. And the next thing we know, they're coming straight for us.

This is it. My friend Crow is now officially a high-street designer. Stella McCartney's done it. Christopher Kane has done it. Now it's our turn.

I watch as the crowd run over us and through us and past us, anxious to get their hands on their favourite pieces before they go. Thank goodness Andy overruled me about Jenny. As Crow's official business manager (yes, really!) I had originally wanted Jenny to be the face in the window, posing in Crow's stuff and looking amazing. Jenny's red-headed and curvy and funny, and she'd be a great advert for the fact that Crow's dresses can look good on anybody. Plus Jenny was the first sort-of famous person to wear Crow's stuff in public, before there even was a label.

But Andy thought it would be better to have an internationally famous supermodel for today, rather than a slightly chubby sixteen-year-old who's been in one movie. And looking at Jenny now, in her 'vintage' (last year's) Crow prom dress, positively shaking with fright, I have to admit he had a point.

Svetlana comes back to join us. She's changed into poured-on skinny jeans and a hoodie with the hood up, so she looks like any other tall, blonde, thin, gorgeous person and doesn't get spotted by too many people in the crowd.

'It's going well,' she says. 'They're loving it. Look!'

If by 'loving it', she means throwing pieces in the air, grabbing them in large piles, fighting over them and crying, she's right.

The petal skirts are going quickest. They're made out of soft, jewel-coloured silk that catches your eye straight away. And when you're wearing them, they wave and flutter as you walk. It's like wearing a little piece of silk sculpture that moves. The jumpers will take a bit longer to be successful because you have to try them on before you realise how incredible they are. They just look a bit lumpy on a hanger, but on a body they turn even a short, rectangular teenager like me into a sex kitten.

The tee-shirts are a surprising success. They're just tee-shirts, after all. Although admittedly, Crow spent weeks and weeks getting the shape exactly right so they'd make anyone look curvy and lovely. That's the thing when your best friends are a beanpole, an hourglass and a midget. You learn to cut cleverly so the pattern will flatter everybody. Crow makes it look easy, but it isn't.

They've got crystal embroidery that glitters under the shop lights. Crow's best known for making couture dresses for famous actresses to wear – as you do when you're nearly fourteen – and the red-carpet stuff is usually scattered with Swarovski crystals, so the tee-shirts are, too. It's December and I think there are going to be a lot of crystal tee-shirts and petal skirts at Christmas parties this year.

The factories have been busy making this stuff for weeks. I was horrified when I saw it all arrive. Boxes and boxes and boxes of it, from India and the Philippines. I couldn't imagine how we could possibly sell it all and now I'm wondering if they've made enough.

I look around for Crow to see how she's getting on, but she's disappeared. Uh oh. I nod to Jenny and we form a search party. Eventually we find her taking refuge in the shoe section at the top of the sweeping stairs, which is totally empty apart from her and her brother.

Henry is, as usual, reading a book. He seems to have got THE HOTTEST SHOP IN LONDON mixed up with a public library, but Crow looks happy to tuck herself under one of his arms and sit quietly. Strange to think that a couple of years ago, he'd have been in Uganda, holding a machine gun, instead of sitting here, holding his sister and a poetry anthology. Not that he wanted to do the whole machine gun thing. He's much more comfortable with his book.

He smiles at Crow and her wide eyes flicker uncertainly back. It seems mean to make her go back into the maelstrom downstairs. After all, there's not much she can do right now. It's not as if she can work a cash till or anything.

Recently she's grown a lot. She's as tall as me now (which I suppose isn't saying much, even if it feels a lot to me), but she's all arms and legs, and she reminds me of pictures of baby colts struggling to stay upright on their long limbs, which is maybe why I feel this need to look after her. That and her dreamy brown eyes and slender fingers, which suggest that she's a fragile, delicate creature. Although I suspect that really she's tough as Doc Marten boots.

'Fifteen minutes,' I say, pointing at my watch and then pointing towards the lifts to the offices above us. Henry sees me and nods. He knows the schedule.

Jenny and I take a deep breath and prepare to dive back down into the human tsunami.

'By the way, what's happened to Edie?' she asks.

Good question. Edie is our other best friend and a total super-genius, who was supposed to be here an hour ago. I'm about to reply, when my phone goes. This is a surprise. I forgot to charge it last night and I thought the battery was dead. Edie's name is on the screen.

'Nonie? I'm on my way. But they've hacked my website. They're saying I'm a liar and it's all about Crow. They're saying . . .'

Well, I don't know what they're saying because my phone battery chooses this moment to die for good. It cuts Edie off and the screen goes dark, just to make a point.

Across the hordes of over-excited shoppers, Andy Elat

catches a glimpse of my face and obviously doesn't like what he sees.

'Everything OK, Nonie?' he mouths.

'Fine,' I mouth back, with a thumbs-up sign for extra reassurance.

I'm used to lying to grown-ups. It's a habit I've got into. It simplifies things.

Chapter 2

Normally on a Wednesday our schedule would be assembly, double history, break, English Lit. But today it's launch, interview, party. Then massive homework sesh, then train to Paris.

I'd like to pretend it's always parties and publicity, but it's not. We needed special permission to miss our GCSE classes for the Miss Teen events, then more special permission to go to Paris. And that's for a funeral tomorrow, so it doesn't really count.

I've always known tomorrow was going to be a bit tricky, but I've been really looking forward to today. Instead, I've got a knot in my stomach that isn't going to go away. On top of the whole crowd thing, Edie sounded really panicked on the phone. And Edie isn't the panicking kind. If there was an earthquake, Edie would be the one organising people and finding blankets and shelter. Something really horrible must have happened to her website to make her so upset.

When I say website, I don't mean Edie's got a page on MySpace or Facebook. I mean her very own WEBSITE. With its own internet address and logo and everything. She uses it to talk about all her do-gooding projects, her plans to go to Harvard and save the world, what we're all up to at school (featuring my latest outfits and, for extra laughs, what my mother said on the subject) and also what's happening with Crow.

Loads of people look at it. Literally thousands every week. There are the ones who want to know about how ex-child soldiers from Uganda, like Henry, are getting on, and the ones who want to know if Crow's doing her famous petal skirts as part of the new collection for Miss Teen. Guess which types of pages get the most views.

I can't imagine anyone calling Edie a liar. In fact, NOT lying is her biggest problem. There are times when you really hope she'll tell a little white one ('That coat looks great on you, Nonie'; 'That new haircut really suits you'; 'I'm surprised you got such low marks in your geography exam last year'), but she doesn't. She tells it like it is, every time. Whoever's done whatever it is to her website has got the wrong girl.

In front of me, two Miss Teen customers are fighting each other for an emerald-green petal skirt – the last in its size. It's only half an hour since the launch started and the cash tills are already besieged. In less than two years,

Crow's gone from being a little Ugandan refugee with reading difficulties to a cross between Vivienne Westwood and the Olsen twins. The Jewels collection is going to be massive and you can see the pound signs in Andy Elat's happy, crinkly eyes.

Finally, as the racks are being stripped of clothes, I spot Edie near the doors, looking flustered. She's wearing her tee-shirt embroidered with pink crystals saying 'Less Fashion More Compassion', which is our catch phrase. Two pounds from every tee-shirt goes to help children in Africa who've lost their parents to war and AIDS. Guess who had *that* idea. Edie also thought up giving a discount to people who brought reusable bags today.

The tee-shirt makes her look unusually fashion-conscious. Normally, Edie thinks 'special occasion' means a nice pleated skirt and a co-ordinated top, with possibly a jumper slung over her shoulders. EW EW EW. Even knowing me for most of her life hasn't made much of a difference, and if you ever see me with a jumper slung over my shoulders you can just kill me.

I smile and give her my quizzical look. The noise of people shopping around us is pretty deafening ('Have you got this in a size 14?' 'Can I have another bag?' 'That was MINE!' Beep beep beep from the cash tills), so talking is hard.

She comes over and gives me a hug.

'Oh Nonie!'

Tears start cascading down her cheeks.

'They said that I'm a fake and a hypocrite. On every page. They said that Crow's collection was made by sweatshops and people mustn't buy it and I'm just pretending to support good causes when really I'm just a . . . a . . . a . . .'

She sobs into my shoulder some more.

'A what?'

'A *slave-driver*!'

I goggle. Slave-driver? Edie is the type of girl who goes round picking up litter after people AND PUTTING IT IN THE RECYCLING. (If it's appropriate. She checks.) This is weird.

'Who *are* they?'

'This group called "No Kidding",' she hiccups. 'They're an ethical campaign group, based in California. They've put pictures on my site to look like graffiti. They say young children were used in India to sew the collection. And they've got this thing against me. They say I just want to be famous and I'm using Crow to get rich.'

Apart from that, they sound really nice. Not. In fact, the only good news is the bit about them being based in California. Otherwise, they'd be outside with placards, shouting.

I give Edie an extra hug. She manages to stop the tears from flowing and attempts a brave smile.

'Sorry I'm late. I've been on the phone to my hosting

service for ages, getting them to take the site down till I can sort it out,' she says.

Even when she's hot and flustered and positively tearful, Edie still can't help sounding like an internet whizz kid.

Chapter 3

'Right, girls. Sam Reed's waiting for you. Are you ready?'

Andy Elat's daughter, Amanda, who runs Miss Teen for him, is hovering nearby. She gestures up the stairs. I nod. Edie goes white.

'The interview?' she whispers.

'Yup,' I nod again.

'You don't think she's . . .? She won't've looked at . . .?'

'Sam won't have had time to see your website,' I reassure her. 'She won't even be thinking about it. Don't worry. It'll be totally fine.'

This isn't lying, because I'm making myself believe it as I say it. We collect Jenny, who's been stuck on the stairs for the last five minutes, squashed in by eager shoppers, and Crow and Henry, who are still in the shoe section, looking like something out of a local reading group. Amanda shepherds us all into the lift and up to the office floors of Miss Teen, where the hard work really happens.

Before the lift doors close, I catch one last glance of a sea of faces with expressions ranging from ecstatic (full shopping bags) to hysterical (empty shopping bags). The racks are empty. Completely bare. Apart from one sad-looking jumper. What's wrong with it? I wonder. But I can't find out, because it's time to go and tell a famous journalist what a lovely, jolly time this has been.

A tall woman with mad red hair, a leather dress and biker boots is waiting for us in a high-up office overlooking Oxford Street. Sam Reed has interviewed rock stars and film producers, writers and actors. She was recently on tour with Britney Spears, which must have been interesting. Right now, she's writing a piece about Crow for a Sunday magazine. She's spoken to Crow and me a few times already, but for her final interview she wanted Edie and Jenny too.

'You're obviously a team, you four,' she said to me when she was setting it up. 'Edie's got her website. Jenny wears the clothes. And Nonie, you mention the others every few seconds, regardless of what we're talking about. I want to get you all together. See how you work as a group.'

This made me nervous. We're friends. We don't 'work as a group'. We bicker as a group. Occasionally we have serious arguments. We drive each other nuts as a group. Mind you, I'd be kind of lost without the others around to annoy me. I promised Sam that I'd ask Jenny and Edie about joining us, assuming they'd say no, but they both went, 'Ooh, *The Sunday Times*? Yes please!' Which is why all four of us are perched on black swivel chairs, sipping tap water, while we answer questions about ourselves and our 'amazing fashion moments'.

This is going to be a challenge. Crow's life *is* a fashion moment. She's sitting here in sky-blue satin dungarees, a purple tie-dye tee-shirt, platform flip-flops and a raspberry-pink plastic anorak she picked up from a charity shop in the summer. Her hair is her usual oversize Afro, which means she can fit three mini paper lanterns on it, in a collection near her left ear.

Whereas, apart from her tee-shirt, Edie wouldn't know a fashion moment if it hit her over the head with a stiletto. This is the girl who wore *beige culottes* to school last summer. Luckily, she's sitting next to Jenny, who's been on a fashion rollercoaster. Jenny's been the one all the fashion editors make fun of in the 'what not to wear' pages, *and* the girl who gets to choose a Chanel dress for the red carpet, so maybe she and Sam can chat about all of that.

What Sam will make of me, I can't imagine. I don't really care what's in fashion, although I can't help knowing every designer's latest look. I just love finding unusual stuff, and the daily challenge of coming up with something new and original and just this side of 'go home and change, young lady'. Today, for example, it's crushed velvet leggings, a vintage ra-ra skirt, an old school blazer (not my school) and a fedora. My fashion nightmare is walking into a room and finding someone else dressed exactly like me. It's probably Edie's dream, come to think of it. She'd be great in a job with a uniform, like a policewoman or something. I'd go insane.

'Crow,' Sam says, kicking things off while we fiddle nervously with various bits of our outfits. 'Tell me how it all began. Take Edie, for example. How did she come into your life?'

Crow looks up and grins her broadest grin. As always when Crow smiles, the room suddenly lights up, as if someone's opened a curtain.

'Like an angel,' she says, quietly. There's a pause. Sam waits for more, but Crow seems to think she's covered it.

Jenny decides to fill in the details. 'Crow needed help with reading practice. Edie volunteered.'

But Sam isn't looking at Jenny, or Edie. She's still watching Crow.

'She saw me,' Crow says eventually, looking down at her lap, trying to explain. 'Lots of people didn't. See me, I mean. Not good people, anyway. Until Edie came. Oh, and she found Henry.' She sits on her hands at this point and clams up completely. But Sam's scribbling as if she's just dictated a novel.

The room's gone fuzzy and I realise my eyes are welling up. So are Jenny's. Sometimes you need a *Sunday Times* journalist to remind you how great your friends are. And when it comes to noticing people, and helping them, Edie can be super-amazing, despite the whole beige culottes thing.

I sneak a look at her. She's white as a sheet and biting her lip. This is turning into an emotional day for her. We all sort of assumed that Crow just took us for granted really, which was fine. She never said anything. But then, we never asked.

'And how about Jenny?'

Crow thinks for a minute. 'Jenny's my favourite girl to dress,' she says with another grin. Again, this is news to the rest of us. We thought Crow just made dresses for Jenny out of friendship. But she makes it sound like it's a real treat.

'She has a beautiful shape,' Crow continues. 'Perfect for couture. And I love her skin. It always glows against the right fabric. And her hair. Look! Ten different colours.'

So are Jenny's cheeks, right now. Her hair may be copper/auburn/whatever, but her cheeks are red, red, red. She's grinning fit to bust, though. She can't help herself.

'I didn't know dresses even existed to fit me before Crow came along,' she bubbles happily. 'I spent most of my life in changing rooms not being able to do the zips up. Putting one of Crow's red-carpet dresses on sort of changes you. It makes you look the way you *think* you look. You know, in your head. Before you see yourself in a mirror.'

Sam Reed nods and scribbles. 'Not a fan of mirrors, then?' she asks lightly.

Jenny flushes again and goes quiet. It all comes back to

me. Her misery at her boobs and spots, her red-carpet disasters. Sam can tap into these moments without seeming to try. I dread to think what she got out of Britney Spears.

'And Nonie?'

I jump. But Sam isn't talking to me. She's asking Crow *about* me. This is embarrassing. We've known each other for a year and a half. We see each other every day. Crow practically lives in my house, which is where she makes her stuff when she isn't doing a couture collection. She knows how fast I can eat popcorn while watching *Project Runway* – and what the sofa looks like after I've finished. What on earth is she going to say?

She draws breath. I'm on the edge of my seat, but in the end she just shrugs. She looks around at all of us, and out of the window at the grey, wintry sky. Then she holds up her hands and shrugs again.

I'm used to this. If your business partner is a natural shrugger, you learn to expect it. But after 'Edie is wonderful' and 'Jenny has nice hair', I was expecting a little bit more. I'm not sure whether to be disappointed or relieved.

Jenny jumps in again. Unlike Crow, she's not the strong and silent type.

'I think what Crow means is that Nonie takes care of everything. Nonie's brilliant with details and organising stuff.'

Crow nods, which is good. I'm glad that's what she meant.

'Tell me about it,' Sam says, with a smile in my direction. So for the next five minutes I describe the total, total pleasure of organising Crow's first catwalk show, even though it was the most difficult, complicated, stressful thing I've done in my life. And the fun of seeing the Jewels collection come to life and learning all about how you make high-street fashion and how amazing it is to be behind the scenes when it's happening.

'So it looks as if you've changed everyone's life for the better,' Sam concludes.

I assume she's talking to Edie, but when I check, she's smiling at Crow. Who's smiling back, in an embarrassed sort of way. Sam is scary the way she notices things. We all think of ourselves as looking after Crow on a daily basis. After all, she's younger than us, she's hopeless at school and we're her best friends. But it's totally true. We all find ourselves nodding, and then Jenny has to go even further and say, 'Oh yes. I *absolutely* wouldn't be here today without Crow.'

Which is so unbelievably obvious on the day of the Miss Teen launch that we all find ourselves giggling, while Jenny goes, 'What? *What?*' Even Sam Reed can't resist a smile.

We can hear movement outside. Sam checks her watch. 'One more question, girls. OK?' We nod.

She leans forward, and the look in her eye changes slightly. 'Edie, I was looking at your website this morning and I noticed there were some rather serious claims about the making of the new collection. How do you all feel about that?'

Oh, dear. Not good.

Crow and Jenny look totally mystified, because we haven't had a chance to tell them about it yet. Edie instantly goes white and tearful again. I feel as if it's my job to say something – after all, I'm the one who agreed that Sam could talk to us today – but my mind has gone blank.

At this moment, the door opens and Andy Elat is framed in the doorway, beaming confidently, with Amanda hovering nervously behind him.

'How's it going, kids?' he asks.

Does he have magical powers? Is the room bugged? A part of me is really confused by his perfect, perfect timing, but mostly I'm just relieved.

'I was just talking about Edie's website,' Sam says. 'And the No Kidding thing. I assume you've seen it?'

'All sorted now,' Andy smiles. 'Good work, Edie, love. But I've just been shown what they were saying a couple of hours ago. Terrible, unjustified accusations. Against a schoolgirl, too. I'm horrified. We all are.'

He grabs a spare chair and sits beside me. Sam Reed gives him a long, hard look, which is supposed to hint that Andy is not part of this interview, and would he please leave us in peace? However, Andy simply smiles back and ignores the look, and the rest of us are clearly grateful that he's here. Sam gives in.

'So, Andy, what's your reaction to No Kidding's claim

that some of the clothes in this collection were made by children working up to sixteen hours a day without a break in Indian sweatshops?' she asks. She sounds less 'kindly analyst' now and more 'hard-bitten journalist'.

'I can categorically deny them,' he says confidently. 'Categorically. You can quote me on that. They're rubbish from start to finish.'

I take a breath to say something, but Andy wiggles his fingers subtly in my direction. It's his version of the Look that we give each other when we want someone to SHUT UP. You learn it pretty quickly when you work with Andy.

I shut up.

'Were the girls aware that this was an issue?' Sam continues, looking across at all of us. We madly shake our heads, except for Crow, who looks too shocked to even move.

Sam notices Crow's stillness even more than our head-shaking. She obviously believes her and takes pity on us.

'That's it then, everyone. I think I've got enough. Thanks. I'll give you a call, Nonie, if I've got any follow-up questions. Great collection, Crow. Good luck!'

The way she says 'Good luck' makes me more nervous than if she'd just said goodbye.

Do we need luck? And what is her article going to be about? The fabulousness of the sold-out petal skirts? Or the rumours about how they were made?

Chapter 4

After Sam leaves the room, Andy's aides rush in to brief him on his next meeting. But Edie leaps out of her seat and grabs him first.

'Are you sure?' she asks.

'About the children in India?' he says. 'Absolutely.' He reaches out to put a friendly hand on her shoulder, then realises she's now taller than him, even in her ballet flats, and turns it into a pat on the arm.

'How can you know?'

'Regular checks. You can't be in my business and not be certain about this stuff. We monitor it all the time. Trust me.'

He looks at her expression. It's obviously not trusting enough.

'Look, my reputation would be in the dirt if I used child labour. And besides, I like children. Look at you lot. If Crow insists on working into the night to finish something, I can't stop her. But I don't make her do it. And I pay her.' He sighs. 'No children were harmed in the making of this collection, OK?'

'OK,' we agree, in slightly wobbly voices.

But Andy didn't get to be such a successful businessman by always believing people when they pretend to agree with him. Despite the fact that his minions are standing behind him, jiggling with frustration that he's late for his next appointment, he doesn't move. He looks straight at Edie.

'I've got a report,' he says. 'Several. From the people who go out to the factories and check this stuff for me. Get one off Simon here. Read it. Put it on your website if you like. Good grief, girls. You should be thanking me for providing so much employment for people in Third World countries. I thought that was your sort of thing.'

Finally, he moves on. Edie touches 'Simon here' on the shoulder and gives him her email address so he can send her the report.

Crow didn't wait while we had our chat with Andy. She dashed straight out of the room to find Henry, who was waiting outside, admiring the crowds on Oxford Street from a safe distance of about six storeys up.

She looks at us now from under the crook of Henry's arm, her eyes still wide with shock.

'What did he say?'

Edie describes our conversation.

'Is he right?' Crow whispers.

'Well, he should know,' Edie says uncertainly. 'He seemed very sure. Don't worry. He's sending me a report. Hopefully it'll explain everything.'

Crow's shoulders relax and she switches off. She trusts Edie totally and if Edie says, 'Don't worry,' she doesn't. I really wish I could be that way. It would make my life so much easier. The thing is, Crow needs all her brain space for creative ideas and new designs. The bits that are normally assigned to 'maths', or 'shopping', or 'what they did on *Gossip Girl* last night' in other people's heads are assigned to 'what *exactly* is that shade of blue?' in Crow's head. And the bit that was starting to worry about No Kidding instantly reassigns itself to thinking about jacket collars, or armholes, or whatever it is she's working on right now. If Edie tells her to worry, she'll worry. But until then, she won't.

Jenny is made differently. Jenny has lots of spare space for worrying. She can even use the *Gossip Girl* bits for worrying, if necessary. She wants EVERY DETAIL about what No Kidding said, and how they made it look, and how Edie felt when she first saw what they'd done, and what we think, and whether we should trust Andy, and whether we should start boycotting Miss Teen RIGHT NOW, just in case.

I'm in the middle of pointing out that Andy Elat is effectively my boss, because he pays for Crow to do her design thing, and for me to help her, so boycotting him might be rather rude, when Jenny starts patting the hip of her prom dress. Is this a new code for something, like the Andy hand-wiggle? She has also stopped listening to me.

After a minute of fumbling in a hidden pocket, she pulls out her phone and checks the screen.

'Text from Mum,' she says. 'I've been waiting for this. YES!' Then she reads it a bit more carefully. 'Oh no.' She turns to Crow. 'I'm really sorry. It's tomorrow. I'm going to have to miss Paris.'

'*What's* tomorrow?' we ask.

'Oh, a thing,' she says vaguely. 'I don't want to jinx it. Tell you later. Oh, look!'

We look. Three women are bearing down on us. Amanda Elat, Edie's mum and mine. They're all tapping their watches, to remind us that we have a strict schedule to stick to, and we're running late.

I think back through the schedule. Launch at Miss Teen, tick. Interview for *The Sunday Times*, tick. That leaves party, MAJOR Shakespeare essay and packing for a funeral. All in the next six hours.

Welcome to my life.

Chapter 5

I can't believe it. I'm sitting in a first class carriage on the Eurostar. I'm on my way to PARIS, the night after a party for the FASHION LABEL that I help to run. And all I'm feeling is tired and sad.

Edie and Crow are opposite me, looking how I feel. Edie's thinking about her website and Crow's thinking about the funeral tomorrow, like me.

Crow's friend Yvette, who taught her to sew, died last week. She was ninety-four, so fair enough, but it'll still be awful. Yvette was the coolest grown-up I've met and she pretty much saved Crow's life when she came to England by teaching her to cut patterns and knit warm jumpers. She worked for Christian Dior. Yes, the real one, in Paris. And she came to London to live with a GIRLFRIEND. How cool is that? We're going to miss her loads.

Until Edie came along, Yvette was the only person Crow knew in London who actually talked to her, apart from her aunt. Not only that, but Yvette completely understood what was going on in Crow's incredible head, and how talented she was, and she taught her how to turn her ideas into beautiful, beautiful clothes. Yvette was Crow's link to the great days of couture. As the lights of the Kent countryside rush by, I can see them reflected in Crow's over-shiny eyes, and I know she's wondering how she'll ever fill the gap. So am I.

Only Jenny is remotely happy and now she's not even here. She finally explained that the text from her mum was about a playwright friend of theirs called Bill something. He's asked if he can meet up with her tomorrow and apparently he's a big cheese and you kind of say yes, unless it's your own funeral you were supposed to be going to.

'Ooh, Nonie, I can't imagine what he wants to say to me,' she bubbles over the phone. Someone at Miss Teen gave me two new batteries for my mobile, and a spare recharger, so I can always stay in contact for those crucial calls. It's the kind of thing that happens when you help run a fashion label, along with stress and free clothes.

Jenny spends the next ten minutes imagining what Bill wants to say to her.

'He mentioned to Mum that he was really upset for me when Dad talked about me to that paper.'

Her dad used her two minutes of fame last year to talk about himself to a Sunday paper and embarrass Jenny in every other sentence by mentioning all her hang-ups and calling her a 'troubled, talented teen'. She's hardly spoken to him since.

'Bill saw me in *Kid Code* and he admitted that I was hopeless, so it can't be about acting. I wondered if it was something to do with Dad, but Bill's one of Mum's best friends and he knows she hates Dad's guts now, so it can't be that.'

'Maybe he wants you to introduce him to someone from Hollywood,' I suggest. Jenny is New Best Friends with half the Hollywood A-list since she made her film. Or at least, she knows people who know their phone numbers.

'Oh no. It can't be that. Bill *hates* Hollywood. Everything about it. That's one of his big things. He's into live theatre, small venues, the smell of the crowd . . .'

And on and on and on until finally the Eurostar enters the Channel Tunnel and cuts her off. I'm going to need both of those new batteries by the time we get to Paris at this rate.

I put the phone away and wait for Edie or Crow to ask me what that was all about, but they don't. Not even a flicker of interest. Edie's started doing Brain Teaser on her DS. If there's a super-mega level, she'll be on that.

Crow's got her notebook out and is sketching something. I look over her shoulder and see that it's a series of black cloaks teamed with high boots and floppy hats. Chic funeral attire, I'm guessing. Not what we'll be wearing tomorrow, but what we would be wearing if we were the sort of It-girls and movie stars who wear Crow's expensive stuff on a regular basis.

'That was Jenny,' I say eventually.

'Oh,' Edie manages. Crow just shrugs.

'She's fine, by the way.'

I give up and get out the French *Vogue* that I bought with most of my spare cash at the train station. Why I did that, when I'll be able to buy it for half the amount in Paris in a couple of hours, I'm not entirely sure, but there's something about French *Vogue.* See it. Get it. Plus I speak the language because my dad's French, and it's the only thing I can do in Edie's company that makes me look vaguely intelligent.

I savour the moment. Me reading in a foreign language (OK, looking at the photos in a foreign language, but it still counts) and Edie doing a boring DS game. YES! Suddenly, despite everything, I don't feel quite so miserable any more.

As the train pulls in to Gare du Nord, Granny arrives. She's supposed to be chaperoning us, but she can't bear sitting in carriages where people are allowed to use mobile phones, so she's avoided us for the actual journey and sat in the quiet bit.

Granny is already in her funeral gear. Black cashmere and fox fur over Balmain boots. Granny thinks fur is WONDERFUL and very practical for cold winters. Getting her and Edie talking on the subject is very funny.

I secretly love fur but I would never wear it, unless I was an Eskimo or something. You can't, can you? Except – Granny can.

'Are you ready, girls? Ah, French *Vogue*, Nonie. Well done. *C'était bon*?'

I don't answer. Granny's French accent is truly horrendous and the only way to discourage her from using it is to ignore her. She thinks I'm being rude, but it's for her own good.

We gather our stuff and get ready to get off the train. I catch sight of Crow and for once, she's not dreamy or frowning. She looks . . . different.

'Are you OK?' I ask.

She nods and whispers one word, like it's a magic wish: 'Paris!'

Of course! Paris is the centre of her fashion universe. It's the home city of her favourite designer of all time – Christian Dior – and now she's about to step into it, having imagined every detail since she was eight. I only hope it'll live up to her expectations.

There's the Eiffel Tower, of course, and the River Seine and the Louvre and Notre Dame and the boutiques. But there's also the dirt and dog poo and mad taxis and tourist menus, and some pretty impressive rudeness from Parisians if you do the wrong thing. But then there's the Pompidou centre and the croissants and the crêpes and the hot chocolates and the cafés and the *other* boutiques.

She'll be fine. Whatever she's expecting, she'll be fine.

In the middle of the station concourse, a short guy in an ancient Burberry mac is standing alone, looking a little bit lost.

I drop everything and rush towards him, launching myself into his arms.

'Papa!'

It's a shock to realise I'm finally as tall as him. A little bit taller, actually. He really is microscopically small. I guess he must have stood on a step to kiss Mum when they were dating. I quickly check for thinning hair on the top of his head, but luckily what Dad lacks in height he makes up for in hair follicles. Loads of them. They add at least an extra two centimetres.

'Nonie! *Trésor*!'

Lots of big hugs. The others join us and Dad finds a hug for Edie and Crow as well. He came to Crow's first show, so he knows how amazing she is, even though he sounds like he's coughing when he tries to pronounce her name. She almost wraps him in her poncho when she hugs him. Wow. Even Crow's as tall as Dad now. Poor Dad.

With Granny, Dad exchanges a nervous smile and a nod of the head. Granny thinks Dad is a sad, artistic loser and Dad thinks Granny's an elegant, posh headcase with a bad accent. Luckily, she's off to stay at the Ritz, so they won't have to see too much of each other.

'See you tomorrow, girls,' she says, gripping her suitcase handle tightly. 'Eleven-thirty. Get as much sleep as you can.'

She heads off for the taxi queue, fox fur trailing, and Dad guides us towards the Métro. Dad doesn't have a car, doesn't drive and doesn't see the point of taxis when Paris has underground trains and buses. He brandishes white cardboard Métro tickets for us all and I feel a sudden glow. Paris Métro tickets are in my top ten most romantic things in the world.

As Dad leads us through all the gates, stairs and corridors to the right underground platform, I give Crow a nervous glance. I mean, the Métro's great, but it's not exactly the Eiffel Tower. However, I needn't have worried. Her mouth is slightly open and she looks as if her brain is elsewhere, but I happen to know that what she's doing is processing every image around her.

Crow has a photographic memory. She'd be brilliant in a crime scene.

'Miss Lamogi, at what angle of tilt was the trilby worn by the woman you saw for two seconds behind the victim two weeks ago last Thursday?'

'Thirty degrees, Your Honour.'

Well, she wouldn't know to say 'thirty degrees', but she'd be able to draw it.

She's mentally recording every step, tile, poster, light, every expression and outfit on all the passers-by. I don't think Crow sees stuff as good or bad. Just interesting or boring. And the Métro is definitely interesting. When we get to Dad's apartment she'll start jotting down her favourite impressions. Soon we'll be seeing little glimmers of these images appearing in her designs.

In fact, she starts drawing as soon as we sit down in the train. So far we've been in Paris for half an hour and she hasn't said more than its name and a whispered '*Bonjour*' to Dad. I catch his eye and shrug. Most people find Crow a bit strange to start with. But he's an artist. He gets it. He just gives me a grin and turns to Edie.

'Nonie says you 'ave a . . . website. That is so marvellous. 'Ow's it going?'

Oh dear.

Or, as we say in Paris, *zut alors*.

Chapter 6

It's eleven-thirty on the dot and we're in the Église Saint-Roch, not far from the Ritz. This is the church where Yves Saint Laurent had his funeral last year. It is SO classic and beautiful and glamorous and French.

It's my first funeral and I'm not sure how I'm supposed to look. I mean, I know I'm supposed to be upset and I AM upset. Very. But I'm also surrounded by famous fashion people and I'm kind of impressed and overawed. And Crow is a bit of a fashion star, even in Paris, so people keep staring at all of us like they're impressed to see us too. I keep wanting to enjoy myself, then remembering I can't.

Yvette's coffin is amazing. It's shiny and black but you can hardly see it because it's smothered in white lilies. Big, small, star-shaped, bell-shaped. I had no idea you could get lilies in so many shapes and sizes. But the fashion crowd have obviously decided that they are the ONLY flower worth having this season.

When we first heard about Yvette, we thought she was a figment of Crow's imagination. How was it possible for anyone who had worked with the master, the great Christian Dior himself, to still be alive, even, never mind to know a little girl from Uganda who lived with her aunt in a flat in Kensington? Then Granny met her and it turned out they'd sort of known each other in the old days, when Granny used to be a Dior client and came in for fittings. Then, thanks to Crow, all these London fashion types met her, and we realised she was practically a goddess.

Yvette was a genius with silk. At Crow's level, designers mostly make their couture designs themselves, but in the big fashion houses there are specialists. The designer chooses the fabric and does a bit of a sketch and it's taken away by these incredible women to be turned into a real outfit. The women are called *mains*, which just means 'hands'. You'd think that would be pretty rude, but they seem OK with it.

Balmain spent years trying to poach Yvette from Dior's *atelier flou*. So did a young Valentino. But instead, she fell in love with a young seamstress from the *atelier tailleur*, who did wizard things with jackets and trousers, and they moved to London to live a quiet life together. Which they did for years, running an old furniture shop and generally being happy.

I love this story. It has a happy beginning, middle and end, which is how things should be, in my opinion. And because Yvette taught Crow to be so super-amazing at sewing, Crow managed to become a designer about ten years earlier than normal, and I got to meet all my fashion heroes – or most of them, anyway – before my sixteenth birthday. I've already decided that my first child is going to be called Yvette. Or Yves, if it's a boy, after Saint Laurent. I've got the whole thing totally worked out.

The funeral is packed with fashion royalty. People who really knew Yvette, people who wish they'd known her, people who work for people who knew her, and people who just want to talk to the people who knew her.

Everyone is wearing an Outfit. Black or grey. Chic. Expensive.

Almost everyone, that is. My outfit is white. Very white. Very short. Very Sixties. Very original Mary Quant. I AM SO LUCKY I FOUND IT IN A CHARITY SHOP LAST WEEK; IT'S PRACTICALLY A MUSEUM PIECE. True, a couple of extra inches on the hem wouldn't have done any harm. I'm wearing safety knickers and super-thick tights, just in case I have to bend over. But it goes perfectly with my white plastic lace-up boots, which are completely irresistible. Yvette would understand.

Edie looks like the President's wife, all grey coat and tiny hat and soulfulness, so she makes up for me. Crow, naturally, has ignored the black/grey thing and is in a purple and blue printed dress with a crimson poncho. All clothes that remind her of Yvette, because they made them together. I can sense some of the other designers wishing they'd thought of something like that. Crow can't help standing out.

We get to the hotel where they're having the reception afterwards and Crow's besieged. Normally I have to save her from moments like this, because she hates talking to strangers. But this time it's different. People want to talk about Yvette, whom she adored, or about how to make clothes really, really well, which is Crow's passion, so suddenly she's the one having all the interesting conversations and Edie and I are left talking to each other.

Granny's supposed to be looking after us, but she keeps bumping into people she used to know forty years ago, or people who knew my mum when she was a model here, and for a woman at a funeral she's giving the strong impression of having the time of her life.

I'm back to thinking about Yvette and how much we'll miss her. I'm not having the time of my life, but talking to Edie is better than moping by myself. Edie's still thinking about her website, or more to the point, about these Californians she's never met who seem to hate her so much.

'They live five thousand miles away. Why did they pick on me?'

Ignoring the fact that she knows California is five thousand miles away (how does she pick UP this stuff?), I point out that she's constantly interfering in the lives of – sorry, helping – people she's never met.

'You go on about what's happening in South Africa. That's not exactly close. And Uganda.'

'Well, Crow's from there,' Edie says, hurt.

'Yes, but she lives in Kensington now. *You've* been to Uganda more recently than she has.'

Edie went this summer, to say hi to Crow's parents and her little sister, and to check up on the school she's been raising money for.

'But that's taking an interest,' she protests. 'Not being nasty for no reason.'

'What I mean is,' I say, 'for some people, the world's a tiny place. You taught me that. Crow gets fan mail from Japan. It's weird. I guess people can be angry long-distance too.'

'But what have I *done*?'

'I don't know! You just got a tiny bit famous, I suppose, so they noticed you.'

'Well, I don't *want* to be. And do you realise your dad hasn't got wi-fi? Or any kind of internet connection? So I can't do a THING about it till we get back to England.'

Edie's mouth keeps moving and I can tell she's going on about my dad's lack of technology, but I've just noticed that, behind her, a boy with blond floppy hair is looking at me. And has been for a while. And he's EXTREMELY CUTE. If Robert Pattinson had a blond, floppy-haired, younger brother, this would be him.

I smile at him. Then I remember that Edie's life has been RUINED by hackers and go back to being 'worried friend'. Cute guy gives me a grin and winks at me.

I look at Edie for a while, pretending to listen, then flick my eyes back up for a moment to check out cute guy again. Still looking at me. Winks again. Mouths something. I do my quizzical look. He mouths it more slowly.

I think it's 'Like the boots.'

He's flirting! Cute Robert Pattinson-lookalike hunk is flirting! With me! At a funeral!

This is sort of cool. I should feel really bad about it, but I can't help smiling some more. He sees me smiling and trying not to and grins at me again.

Gorgeous, gorgeous smile.

'Are you listening to me AT ALL?' Edie demands.

'Oh. I was,' I promise.

'Sorry. Am I boring you?'

'A tiny bit, to be honest. And look. Cute guy over there likes my boots.'

'I am telling you about the MOST STRESSFUL MOMENT OF MY LIFE and you're staring at some guy who LIKES YOUR BOOTS?'

'Yes.'

I decide to make a stand. 'I know about the most stressful moment, Edie. Honestly. You told me yesterday. And last night. And this morning. I can't possibly feel more sorry for you than I already do. But he's really cute.'

Edie sighs deeply and turns round. Then she turns back, all pink.

'Ooh. He *is* cute. He reminds me of someone.'

'Robert Pattinson.'

'Mmmm.'

I'm not sure if she's agreeing, or just daydreaming. RPattz is her only secret vice.

She turns around again for a second look but by now he's come over and he's standing right behind her. She makes a sort of shrieking sound and goes the colour of Crow's poncho.

'Hi,' he says. 'I'm Alexander.'

Gorgeous voice too. English, but with the faintest French accent. Maybe he grew up here. And totally confident. It's quite possible he's aware of his effect on girls, but the twinkle in his eye stops him from seeming too smug.

'I'm Edie,' Edie says, holding her hand out.

He shakes it with a serious sort of smile, then leans over to me and kisses me on both cheeks.

'Hello, Boots,' he says.

'Nonie,' I squeak.

'Boots,' he insists. 'Are you two busy this evening?'

'Well, actually, I was going to try and find an internet café,' Edie starts.

I give her the Look. She sighs and gives up.

'Can I show you Paris?'

Now he's starting to annoy me slightly, despite the gorgeous voice.

'I've known it since I was a kid,' I tell him. 'My dad lives here.'

'Not *my* Paris,' he continues, with his wicked, self-confident grin. 'Bring your dad, if you like. I promise I'll look after you. And definitely your pretty friend.'

'Oh!' Edie's poncho colour had died back down to pink but now it ramps back up to crimson. I wonder if she's about to have a feminist moment and say something extremely rude, but instead she simpers like one of her Jane Austen heroines and starts fiddling with her coat buttons.

'And my granny?' I ask, cheekily. 'And my friend Crow?'

'The designer girl? Wow! Definitely her. Which one's your granny? Cool lady in Balmain? Sure. Her too. We'll make it a party.'

I breathe a sort of a sigh of relief. He's almost too gorgeous and probably too old for me, but he's obviously gay, so that's OK.

What straight boy would instantly know that Granny's boots were Balmain?

Chapter 7

After the reception, Edie, Crow and I make our way back through the streets of Paris to the Île Saint-Louis, in the middle of the River Seine, where Dad lives. His apartment is beautiful, romantic and tiny, with amazing views over trees and water. The ceilings are high, the walls are covered in tatty old peeling silk panels and there are piles of books and half-painted canvases everywhere. It looks extremely messy, but the clutter never changes. What some people might call piles of old rubbish (Mum does) turn out to be carefully collected knick-knacks from famous arty friends. The place has been photographed loads of times for magazines.

There's a sitting room and a studio overlooking the river, next to a kitchen so small you might mistake it for a cupboard, and a bedroom and an antique shower room at the back. At night, the three of us are in sleeping bags wherever we can fit. It's why poor Henry had to stay in London: nowhere to squeeze him in, sadly.

Dad's in the middle of an experiment with paintings that look like photographs taken too slowly, where the subject has moved and gone out of focus and left a sort of trail of light behind them. His model is a woman with dark hair, who can't be much older than Alexander and who I suspect is Dad's latest girlfriend, but he's not saying. There are canvases of her all over the place. In the studio, propped up in the kitchen, even in the shower room, behind the towels.

'What do you think, *trésor*?' he asks, pulling one out from under the basin.

'*Chouette*,' I say.

Chouette is sort-of French for cool. It's also a word you can say very quickly and hopefully Dad won't notice that I'm not being entirely truthful when I say it. Sometimes his experiments are brilliant works of genius and sometimes they're not. But you never tell an artist that or they go all moody and can't work for weeks. Art appreciation is ten per cent honesty and ninety per cent ego-massaging. It can get quite tiring if you're not used to it, but luckily Mum does it for a living, so I am.

'*Merci*,' Dad says, putting an arm around my waist and looking at us both in the mirror. We're weirdly alike, in a vertically challenged, no-cheekbones, curly-hair sort of way. 'Champagne?'

He has a bottle open in the kitchen. Not that I've seen him open it. It's just that he *always* has a bottle open in the kitchen. Like milk. It's so tempting to say yes to a glass, but I can feel Mum's presence looming over me. She saw me once after a couple of sneaky glasses at a fashion party and she SO wasn't impressed. And I really don't want to be tipsy tonight, what with my sort-of-date and everything. So I decline and wish I was about five years older.

Luckily Crow takes my mind off my very boring Orangina, by talking at me through the open shower room door. Crow hasn't stopped talking since the funeral ended. This is unheard of for her. She's normally too busy dreaming up designs to actually *say* much. But not today.

'I spoke to so many ladies from the workrooms. They all said Yvette was a legend. But they're *all* cool. Can you imagine? There's this lady called Gina who specialises in making lace rosettes. That's it. Just lace. All day. But she said it's great. And she had this high-necked lace shirt on and a contrasting lace jacket she made and it should have been . . .' Crow struggles for the word. Not a good one, obviously, and flutters her hands to relay the potential fashion disaster. 'But she was *gorgeous*.' Crow sighs and stifles a yawn. It's been a busy couple of days.

I grunt a reply while trying not to jiggle my face too much. We spent ages meandering back here and now Edie and I are in a bit of a rush. Edie's getting changed and I'm focusing on major eyeliner issues in the shower room mirror. In the end, Granny put her foot down about Crow coming out with us this evening. Underneath all the excitement she's obviously exhausted. But she doesn't seem to care. She's too busy gushing about the *mains.*

'I met the lady who makes the trimmings for Chanel suits. And two people who do embroidery for jewelled shoes. Just . . .' She flutters her hands again, but this time in a good way. 'Did you know, they have these rooms full of pearls and beads from all over the world? And one full of feathers. Just feathers – in drawers. Some of them are seventy years old. The birds they came from are extinct.'

I decide not to point out that the feather collection and the bird extinction might be connected. Edie does, though, of course. Crow sounds a bit crestfallen for a minute, but soon she's off again, talking about the difficulties of working in silver thread.

Even when we're all dressed and made up and Alexander arrives (and my tummy does a mini-rollercoaster ride), Crow keeps on going. She's rethinking trimmings and embellishments. She wants to work with lace and tweed. She's realised she hasn't scratched the surface of jewelled embroidery.

Alexander sits down in Dad's only chair in the sitting room that isn't piled with canvases, stretches himself out and enjoys the excitement in Crow's voice as she talks. Which gives me a good opportunity to watch him from my perch on a rolled-up sleeping bag on the floor. He really is extremely beautiful. Long legs. Long fingers, which I really like. Cheekbones, which my mother (ex-model) would approve of. And he's fit. To look at, obviously, but also he must work out a lot. Lots of muscles. But not bulgy ones. Just nicely . . .

Oh no. He's turned round and caught me looking at him. He gives me that smile again.

'How are you, Boots?'

'Fine,' I squeak. 'So, what do you do, er, Alexander?'

He laughs out loud.

'You sound like the Queen. But *much* cuter. I dance, Boots. I dance.'

'Oh.'

Pole dancing? Is he a Chippendale? The only thing this tells me for sure is that he is definitely, definitely gay. I'm even more relieved.

'At the Royal Opera House. I joined last year.'

'OH!'

Edie, Crow and I all say it together. A ballet dancer. Wow. Totally wow. And based in London. Interesting.

'I'm going to design for the Royal Ballet one day,' says Crow, as if she's already got a contract. She hasn't spoken to them yet, but it's just a question of time.

'Well, they could do with a bit of help in the tights department,' he says with a serious expression and a sly glance at me.

I've gone poncho colour, I know it. And I'm so hot I want to fan myself. Which is SO not the effect I'm going for.

After that, the evening goes surprisingly well, though. Granny arrives and we head off together, leaving Crow and Dad poring over his collection of art books and comparing notes on favourite painters. Meanwhile, Alexander is totally sweet and polite and doesn't try anything on with anybody. He takes us to a jazz club in a cellar somewhere cool and is a fabulous dancer, *naturellement.* He dances equally with Edie, me and Granny. After we've boogied away for a couple of hours, he politely escorts us home, via a lovely walk along the river.

Granny is charmed.

'Such a shame about him,' she says, as he disappears off towards the Left Bank, where the taxis are.

'You mean the whole "ballet dancer" thing?' I ask, with a look.

She gives me the look back.

'Yes. Exactly, darling.'

'What thing?' asks Edie.

I promise I'll explain it to her one day, when she's old enough.

After some pretty ineffectual eyeliner removal in Dad's mirror, I slip silently into my sleeping bag next to Crow on the sitting room floor.

Not silently enough, as it turns out. Crow opens half an eye and asks how it went. I tell her it was fine and she gives me a sleepy smile.

'Are you OK?' I whisper back. After all, it's not every day you launch a collection, go to a funeral and leave behind the one member of your close family who's on the same continent as you, because there's no floor-space for him.

'Of course!' she says. 'Did you know it's bad luck to sew in a label until the very last moment? The *mains* are really superstitious about it. I never heard that before . . .'

Her voice trails off and I realise she's asleep again.

'*What* did she say?' Edie asks in a hoarse whisper through the door of Dad's studio, where she's curled up in her own sleeping bag.

'She's muttering about labels,' I tell her.

'She would be!'

There's the sound of distant rumbling from somewhere. I assume it must be a Métro train until I realise it's Dad snoring. He's a totally impressive snorer. It must have driven Mum bananas the short time they were together. Edie starts giggling and sets me off too. Then she asks me again what Granny meant about the ballet dancer thing, which leads to a bit of a chat, and next thing we know it's four in the morning and we're still awake.

There's only one thing for it. Hot chocolate in Dad's kitchen, made with real melted chocolate and the remainder of his milk. It would be *so* much easier if the recipe required champagne.

'I've decided something,' Edie says thoughtfully, balancing on her rickety stool with her chocolate and looking out at the lights rippling on the river, and the dark blue of the sky before dawn.

'What?' I ask nervously. She's going to win the Nobel

Peace Prize? She's doing Further Maths A-level next year?

'Paris is *totally* the most romantic city in the world. I have to come and live here one day.'

I'm amazed. I don't think I've ever heard Edie use the word 'romantic' before, unless she's discussing Jane Austen in an essay. She's right though, of course.

In the morning, Dad finds us both asleep with our heads on the kitchen counter, and won't let us move until he's done a quick sketch of us, and laughed his head off.

Now I get what Mum meant about living with artists being a nightmare.

Chapter 8

Back in London, Crow gets straight to work on her new couture designs. She has loads of clients with parties and awards ceremonies coming up and she's fizzing with ideas.

Other nearly-fourteen-year-olds might spend time messaging their friends and checking out YouTube and watching TV. I'll admit I did a tiny bit of that when I was fourteen. OK, I did mostly that. But Crow isn't normal that way. She doesn't own a computer. Never uses her phone, except for taking photos. Hates reading. Hates typing. Isn't interested in TV.

She loves movies and galleries and arty parties and anything that fires her imagination. Mostly, though, she just sits in her workroom after school, or wanders around the streets of London, designing things in her head, or working out new techniques for making them real on tailor's dummies.

Lots of girls have written to Edie's website saying how

jealous they are of Crow since she got famous, but I'm not sure if they'd love her life. She adores it, but like I say, she's not totally normal. In a good way. Edie writes back and tells those girls they can have Crow's life when they've done ten thousand fashion sketches for practice and can recreate a Dior dress from scratch, like Crow can. Edie's tough that way.

Right now, Edie's in talks with her internet people about website security (at last), and I'm supposed to be finishing my Shakespeare essay. But instead, I really need to catch up with Jenny.

It's Saturday morning and time for our usual rendezvous at the Victoria and Albert Museum café. I've just been to Paris and been sort-of romanced by a ballet dancer. I can't wait for her to ask me how it went.

'It was amazing,' she says.

'What was?'

'The meeting with Bill. I have to tell you EVERYTHING.'

'Can I just—?'

'Well, first, I didn't think he was going to talk about acting at all, and I didn't really want him to, because, you know, it wasn't so great last time, but it turns out I may have to think again.'

She looks at me expectantly. Like I'm supposed to have guessed something. I just want to tell her about Ballet Boy. I breathe in to say something and she takes that as a desperate need to know more.

'It turns out, Bill's written a play. Sort of about me. Sort of for me. One of the characters is this girl whose father has let her down and she has to rebuild the relationship with him and this stepmother character. She's quiet at first, but she gradually becomes the soul of the piece. And he said he wrote it with me in mind. What my dad did, you know, selling that story about me, and imagining if I had to go and live with him afterwards. There was a girl who was going to play me. My role, I mean. But she's just backed out. And they start rehearsals in January. And Bill thought of me. I might not get the part, obviously. Probably not, in fact, but . . . are you listening, Nonie?'

'Yes. You said you might not get the part.'

'Which part?' She's looking at me suspiciously.

'The part he wrote for you.'

Phew. I wasn't actually listening, but luckily the words just sort of stuck in my brain and came out at the right moment.

'Exactly.'

She takes this as an excuse to go on and carries on chatting about it for another ten minutes. Something about the play being staged in a small theatre in Hammersmith that used to be a boathouse for rowing crews. Perfect for her to practise acting properly in a low-key venue where she wouldn't be under the pressure she was under in Hollywood, where her performance was – and even her mother would admit this – painful.

I notice that someone at a table nearby is pretending not to stare at us. Is it Jenny they recognise, because she was in a blockbuster last year and she's still wearing her Louis Vuitton scarf 'disguise'? Or me, because I've been in a couple of magazines recently, talking about the Miss Teen collection?

Then I realise it's a girl who goes on Edie's charity fun runs, and who's seen us both looking sweaty, in tee-shirts and sports bras, jogging in Edie's wake. This is what it's like to be not-quite-famous.

'And so I'm doing it next Thursday. I can't believe I am, but I am.'

What Jenny's doing next Thursday, I have no idea. Something to do with this play, obviously. An audition?

'Good luck,' I say, hoping this is roughly appropriate.

'Thanks,' she smiles. 'Anyway, how about you? How was Paris?'

At last! So I tell her about the funeral and the reception afterwards and the fact that there was this guy who happened to notice me . . .

'AHA! I KNEW IT! Tell me EVERY DETAIL!'

Hooray! This is what I've been hoping for all along. So I tell her about Alexander and the beautiful hands and the fact he calls me Boots and the is-he-isn't-he-gay thing, and she does a much better job of listening to me than I did of listening to her.

'Well, I think he's toying with you,' she says eventually.

'*Toying*?'

Only Jenny uses expressions like 'toying'. She not-quite went out with an EXTREMELY FAMOUS MOVIE STAR during the blockbuster thing, so this makes her an expert on men. Expert, and world-weary. Her man abandoned her, so all men are vile. They toy, apparently.

'Don't you think he's just using you to get to Crow?'

'Crow? Why?'

'So she can design something for him? I don't know! He sounds dangerous.'

This is typical Jenny nowadays. Sad, but true.

I show her a picture of Alexander from Google Images that I just happen to have in my handbag. It's a bit dog-eared, but it gives the general idea.

'Oh. My. God. He's gorgeous.'

I nod.

'*Definitely* dangerous. Have nothing to do with him, Nonie.'

'Well, I'm not likely to, am I? He hasn't called me or anything. He doesn't even have my number. Plus the whole gay thing.'

When I get home, my brother Harry's in the kitchen, smooching with Svetlana. He's been going out with her since Crow's first show, which is nearly a year ago now. He's in the final year of his art degree at Central St Martins, but he spends most of his time DJing at parties and fashion events, so he gets to see more of her than many boyfriends would. This doesn't stop them being disgustingly clingy in public, though.

'Get a room,' I say, throwing my bag down and making myself a hot chocolate.

He laughs.

'Oh, by the way. Some guy called while you were out. Alexander? Said you met him in Paris. Says there's this performance for rising stars on Thursday and did you want to go? He'll meet up with you afterwards. I've written down the details.'

'Thanks.'

I continue whisking in the chocolate. I'm a top hot chocolate maker and my method is elaborate. Plus, it takes my mind off how shocked I am. And gives my cheeks a chance to go back to their normal colour.

'So, come on,' Harry says. 'Who is he?'

'A dancer,' I tell him. 'Don't worry. He's gay. He just liked my outfit.'

'Alexander Taylor?' Svetlana asks. 'The new guy from the Royal Ballet School?'

'Er, yes.'

For a moment, I'm surprised Svetlana's heard of him, but then she goes to about ten parties a day and she probably knows everybody interesting in London, New York, Paris and Milan.

I sit down opposite them. They're not smooching quite so badly now. Svetlana has unwound most of herself and is perched delicately on Harry's knee.

'I thought he was dating Lulu Frost,' she says

thoughtfully. 'I worked with her in New York a couple of months ago. She's doing Gucci at the moment. He's younger than her, but so persistent. And confident. He's SO not gay, darling.'

She gives me a wicked grin.

'Oh,' I say.

And drink a LOT of hot chocolate. Which I hope will explain why my cheeks have gone poncho colour again.

Chapter 9

'She looks like a horse,' Jenny says loyally.

We're in my room. Supposedly doing French homework. Jenny's going on and on and on about this meeting she's got on Thursday with the director of Bill's new play. I've briefly mentioned Lulu Frost. Jenny insisted on seeing pictures.

Lulu happens to be advertising a coat in my copy of *The Sunday Times* magazine, featuring the piece on Crow. (*Petal power: fashion's new girl starts to blossom*. Only a tiny bit at the end about slave labour. Big relief.)

Lulu has glossy black hair, sapphire-blue eyes and long, long lashes. Despite the lashes, she definitely doesn't look like a horse.

'She looks great,' I point out.

'Her nose is too big.'

'She's a SUPERMODEL.'

'No, she's not. Not like Svetlana. She's just in a lot of ads at the moment. She's a model. That's all.'

'THAT'S ALL?'

'Look, if he's gone off her, that's not your fault, is it?'

'I thought you said he was dangerous and I wasn't supposed to see him again.'

'He is, and you shouldn't. I'm just saying you're more beautiful than her. I can quite see why he fancies you more. I just think you should ignore him.'

'Oh, *thank* you, Jen.'

I give her an enormous bear hug. She really is the nicest possible friend. I know for a fact that I am a flat-faced midget with wonky hair, but Jenny says all the right things.

'So? What are you going to do?'

She's looking quite severe now. I know I ought to say that she's right and I'm not even going to return Alexander's call. But he's gorgeous. And fit, in every sense. And he looks a bit like Robert Pattinson. And his voice is pure honey. And he definitely fancies me. And he was really nice to Granny and perfectly charming all evening that night in Paris. And he makes my insides do really impressive arabesques when he catches me looking at him.

How can I possibly NOT go on one teeny, weeny date with a hot young ballet dancer who appreciates decent footwear? I'd be crazy, right? And to think our children would be athletic AND beautiful AND they'd probably have that floppy hair . . .

'I'll be very good. I promise. I won't let him even kiss me.'

'Noooooo.'

Jenny tries a bit more, but I think she's realised she's not going to persuade me. She makes one last, desperate effort.

'What does your mum say?'

'She'd had a string of boyfriends by the time she was my age. She says to respect myself, not drink anything with an open top and be back by eleven. She knows I won't do anything naughty.'

And she's right. I have SUCH a clear idea of how my first night of naughtiness should be, and a quick meal with a guy I've just met who used to go out with a model isn't even close. I may watch *Gossip Girl*, but I don't intend to live it.

I feel totally virtuous and confident. In fact, the more Jenny tries to talk me out of it, the more virtuous and confident I get.

On the way in to school on Thursday morning, I'm feeling pretty good. It's the last day of term. My hair has been de-wonked by Granny's hairdresser, who is a miracle worker. I've just received an invitation to an intimate Christmas soirée by Stella McCartney. A hot ballet dancer fancies me instead of a model. And, to top it all, I spot two sixth-formers in pieces from Crow's collection for Miss Teen, and looking great in them.

I walk into the classroom radiating goodwill, despite the fact that it's geography in two minutes. I smile happily at all my friends. I sit down next to Edie and give her my broadest grin.

She ignores me.

I ignore her ignoring me and concentrate on unpacking my pencil case. I'm still a six-year-old at heart when it comes to my pencil cases. This one is customised with Swarovski crystals I've 'borrowed' from Crow's stash. Crow has doodled her famous dancing girls in ink all over the lining for me. I'd like to think of it being left to the V&A when I'm dead and famous . . .

> *This was the actual pencil case that Nonie Chatham* (or Nonie Taylor?) *used at school the year she masterminded the launch of the most successful fashion collection ever to reach the UK high street . . .*

It's only when I hear a tear splash on to the desk that I realise that Edie is not only ignoring me, she's crying. The lesson's supposed to be starting, but that tear demands attention. I whisper as quietly as I can.

'Is it those Californians again?'

She nods. More splashy tears.

'Have they done more stuff to your website?'

She shakes her head and sniffs.

'No. Actually, they apologised. One of them did, anyway. This boy who manages their communications – Phil. He said they got a bit carried away. I told him that Miss Teen's really careful about who makes their stuff. Mr

Elat's always going on about how good they are, but the No Kidding people won't back down. Phil says they've got pictures of kids working on pieces from Crow's collection in these horrible back rooms in Mumbai. He says it's not just Miss Teen. It's happening all over.'

That's the trouble with wanting to save the world. There's an awful lot of world to save.

Something's confusing me, though.

'How did he tell you all of this?'

'Phil? By email.'

'They hacked into your website and you gave this boy your EMAIL address?'

'Only after he apologised. He left lots of comments on my blog saying how sorry they were.'

'Edie, for someone so clever, you're completely bonkers.'

She nods. She's not feeling particularly proud of herself right now.

'So what are you going to do?'

'What *can* I do? I don't know what to do.'

This isn't like Edie at all. Edie always knows what to do. It isn't always the right thing, but she knows anyway.

'Have you talked to Crow?'

'Yes,' she says. 'Last night.'

'And?'

'Crow says if I'm not happy, she won't work with Mr Elat any more.'

'But he's funding her red-carpet dresses. She can't

work without him!'

'I know,' Edie says. 'But she said she'd just make the clothes herself. If she just made one dress a year, and it was perfect, that would be OK for her. You know she felt guilty about designing anyway, when she thought Henry might be dead.'

'What did you tell her?'

'I told her to keep going. I said not to worry again. I told her I'd do all the worrying.'

'And this is you worrying?'

She nods again.

'Well, there's only one thing to do,' I decide. 'Get proof. They say they've got these photos. Have you seen them?'

'No,' she admits, sniffling.

'Ask for them.'

It's so easy when it's someone else who's got the problem. If I had to stand up to these people myself, I'd be terrified, but telling Edie to do it feels fine.

'You're right,' she says. She sits up a bit straighter and flashes our geography teacher a smile to show her that we've been paying total attention.

Chapter 10

Crow adores the Royal Opera House. She loves the thick red velvet curtains and the gold embroidery and the plush seats and the little girls with their mummies, all dressed up and on their best behaviour.

In the little girls' honour, she's worn a new set of pink fairy wings over her gold satin dungarees. And four purple velvet bows in her hair. It should look weird but she wears her clothes as if everyone dressed that way and actually, she's gorgeous.

It seemed natural for Crow to use the spare ticket. Edie has orchestra practice and Jenny's busy with the thing she's got to do with her playwright, whatever that is. And Crow enjoys the ballet more than them anyway. Yvette used to save up and bring her occasionally and she loves everything about it. The scenery, the costumes, the choreography, even the sound of the ballerinas' block shoes rapping across the floor when they do something complicated *en pointe*.

I love it too. Even when I'm not PERSONALLY INVITED by one of the dancers. Mum used to bring me when I was one of those little girls on their best behaviour. We used to sit at the back, because Mum liked to see the patterns made by the *corps de ballet*. And it's cheaper. It's where all the die-hard ballet fans sit, so you get to hear the gossip about who's not dancing so well this week and who's about to get promoted.

But today, Crow and I are in a box, at the side, right up close to the stage. Because I *have* been personally invited by one of the dancers and these are the tickets he left for me. You can practically hear the dancers breathe from here. It's scary. I'm not sure I wouldn't rather be at the back.

There are three short ballets tonight, featuring the company's rising stars. Alexander is in the first and last. The opener is famous for its athletic jumping and I'm guessing he uses the middle one to get his breath back before lifting a bunch of ballerinas round the stage at the end.

As the curtain rises, Crow nudges me and hands me something – red opera glasses – so I can admire the dancers even more close up.

Wow.

They really are very athletic. All of them. But Alexander most of all.

They don't muck about in the first ballet. They start as they mean to go on, with lots of leaping about everywhere and showing off their tights and incredibly muscly legs. Alexander leaps beautifully. He takes off and then seems to hang in midair for about twenty minutes, before landing delicately with a flourish and a smile. Then he whizzes round the stage doing pirouettes just to show how much energy he's still got.

My insides are pirouetting too. It seems that every third smile is aimed at our box and I'm guessing he's not directing them all at Crow, although she's certainly grinning at him fit to bust.

'He's amazing, isn't he?' she whispers cheerfully.

I nod. I'm not actually capable of speech right now. I can't really believe this is happening. Cute guy in the tights, the best dancer on the stage of the ROYAL OPERA HOUSE, is flirting with me FROM THE STAGE.

I must be dreaming. I keep waiting to wake up. But whenever I open my eyes, I'm still here, Crow's still grinning and Alexander is still rushing about, smiling straight at me whenever he's got a spare moment.

The first interval comes as a relief.

'Oh, by the way,' Crow says while we're queuing for ice creams (the Royal Opera House does the best ice creams in London, needless to say), 'Miss Teen want me to do another collection for next winter.'

WHAT?

'Sorry?' I mumble. 'I wasn't concentrating.'

So she says it again. The same words, in the same order.

Miss. Teen. Want. Her. To. Do. Another. Collection.

OH. MY. GOD.

My brain parks Alexander in the 'deal with later' section, and switches from being incredulous to excited to a bit confused. Crow normally needs *me* to tell *her* information like this, because she's rubbish with things like phones and letters and emails.

'How did you find out?'

'Amanda Elat rang after school today,' she explains. We usually work with Amanda. We only see her father on big occasions, like launches. 'You were busy getting ready so I picked up the phone.'

Thank goodness she did, for once.

'That's fantastic!' I say. 'They must really believe in you.'

Then I remember the bit where Edie said Crow might not work with Andy any more and my insides crunch themselves into a knot so tight I'm not sure they'll ever pirouette again.

'What did you say?'

'I said OK,' Crow says simply.

'What about Edie? And the No Kidding people?'

Crow obviously hasn't thought this one through.

After a minute of deep contemplation, she shrugs.

Great. Another problem for her business manager, then. I'll talk about it with Edie later, and see if we can think of a plan.

We get our ice creams and go back to our seats. I really

don't notice the middle ballet at all. My brain is much too full of new collections and retailing supremos and child labour accusations.

Then it's time for the final ballet, which opens with Alexander centre stage, smiling straight at me before carrying a whole flock of ballerinas round the stage, one-handed.

My brain retrieves him from the 'deal with later section' and passes instructions to my insides to react accordingly. And to my surprise, it turns out that they're still fully capable of pirouetting after all.

Afterwards, Henry is waiting outside, as arranged, to take Crow home.

'How was it, Crow-bird?' he asks, with a smile for both of us.

'Good,' we say together. Crow is a girl of few words and I'm still a bit speechless.

He grins and guides her off towards the Tube. Which leaves me on my own to wait for Alexander. He's suggested a place nearby with a bar and a restaurant, so I go in and try to look as old as I possibly can and sit at a table by myself, pretending that I do this sort of thing all the time.

Luckily, someone has left a newspaper lying around at a nearby table and I grab it and bury my head in it. It's one of the free ones they give out on the streets, full of gossip interspersed with interviews with the Prime

Minister. Even more luckily, Alexander arrives while I'm still on the gossip pages, so I'm not reduced to finding out any more about the Prime Minister than I strictly need to know.

'Boots!' he says, and smiles that smile again.

I get up and he kisses me on both cheeks, before looking me up and down.

'Nice dress.'

It's not a dress, really. More of an overgrown tee-shirt. One of Harry's, from an old band tour, which I've smartened up with a belt and leggings and one of Mum's waistcoats that she doesn't actually know I've borrowed. And hopefully won't.

'Drink?'

'Er, yes,' I say. 'Coke, please.'

Great. The one time I could ask for champagne and get away with it and even look a bit sophisticated in the process. And it doesn't even occur to me until it's too late.

But Alexander grins again and orders two Cokes and a large bowl of chips.

Now he's sitting still, I realise that he hasn't taken off all his makeup, which is probably why he was so quick getting changed. He's still got foundation on and there's a definite hint of eyeliner. It's strange, but not in a bad way. When he kissed me hello (on the cheeks, like I said), he smelt of sweat and lemony aftershave. He's got a huge linen scarf wound round his neck and, a bit like Jenny doing 'actress in disguise', he definitely looks 'dancer off duty'.

Robert Pattinson-lookalike dancer off duty. Talking to me about Paris. Asking what I thought of his performance tonight. Playing with his Coke straw with those long-fingered hands of his.

Am I in heaven or what?

Actually, I'm not totally sure. The chips come and Alexander tucks in like a man who's just carried a dozen ballerinas round the stage in a hurry. I'm quite peckish myself, but there isn't a fork for me and I don't know if we're supposed to be sharing. He didn't say. And for some reason I don't dare ask.

So I spend the next few minutes watching his beautiful hands and talking about Paris and feeling extremely grown-up but also getting increasingly hungry and wishing I could nick a chip or two but not daring to.

And then someone comes into the restaurant with a group of friends and notices me and waves.

No. No no noooooooooooo.

It's my brother Harry. I hang my head in shame.

'Hi, sis,' he says, coming over. 'Is this your dancer? Hi. I'm Harry. Happened to be passing. Mind if I join you?'

MIND IF I JOIN YOU? Is he UNHINGED?

'Course,' says Alexander, smiling his usual smile and indicating the nearest chair. 'Have a chip.'

Oh great. So the chips *were* on offer. I grab several. But I'm still furious with Harry.

'Oh look,' he says, casually glancing at his wrist. 'Ten to eleven. Got to get you home in a minute, little sis.'

'I have taxi money,' I hiss through my teeth.

'Don't waste it,' Harry says. 'I'll pay. Big brother treat.'

He's enjoying this. Every minute of it. He's not even pretending this was a coincidence. And at one minute to eleven he gets up and shrugs his shoulders in a 'time to go' sort of way.

Alexander gets up too and gives me a regretful smile. 'Bye, Boots,' he whispers in my ear as he gives me a goodbye kiss ON THE CHEEK again. Because my BROTHER is watching. I'm so angry I could dance all over Harry in Doc Martens.

'What was *that* all about?' I practically spit at him, once he's bundled me into a black cab.

'Mum had a rethink,' he says. 'Just wanted to make sure Alexander knew where he stood.'

'Well, it's a very long way away from me, isn't it?' I point out. Pointedly.

I fold my arms and face away from him for the rest of the journey. And try to pretend I can't hear him sniggering to himself on the other side of the cab.

Chapter 11

Jenny, of course, thinks Harry saved me from a fate worse than death. She thinks the whole thing sounded hilarious. I assure her it absolutely wasn't. Anyway, she'd think anything sounded funny at the moment. She's in such a good mood.

We're all in Crow's workroom, in my basement, watching her drape fabric on tailor's dummies. She's working on a couple of dresses for her stall in the Portobello Road market, where stars and It-girls do their shopping. Jenny has loads of ideas for new styles, which Crow politely ignores, but luckily she's soon too busy talking about acting to pay much attention.

It turns out Jenny's 'thing' *was* an audition, and she passed it. They told her there and then. They were pretty sure they wanted her already for Bill's new play and they were just making sure. She's practically playing herself, so it's not going to be too much of a stretch.

She starts rehearsals at the end of January. She's very,

very excited and if I wasn't a humiliated little puddle of shame, I'd feel pleased for her too. As it is, I just fake enthusiasm as well as I can. Fortunately, she's thrilled enough for both of us and doesn't notice.

Edie is still trying to understand Alexander, like he's some sort of maths problem.

'I don't get why he didn't offer you a chip,' she says. 'Or order for you. Or ask you what you wanted. I mean, he obviously *likes* you, so . . .'

I point out two things: one, he's a boy, and two, he's a few years older than me, so obviously he's going to do loads of things I don't understand. It's part of the deal. The excitement. The thrill.

'Yes, I see . . .' she says, the way she says she trusts Andy Elat when she doesn't.

'He's a really good jumper,' Crow adds. 'He can leap for miles.'

This is true, of course, but not totally relevant. We all nod anyway.

At this point, my phone goes. It's a text from an unknown number.

Hi Boots, it says. *Touring Cuba for a bit. See you Jan 23rd? Your brother's DJing. He can keep an eye. Look after those legs. A xxxxx.*

We spend the next hour and a half analysing it. Our Eng. Lit. teacher would be proud of us.

What do five kisses mean?

What legs?

Does he *want* Harry to keep an eye? Or is he being ironic? Or sarcastic, Edie wonders. We spend ten minutes arguing about what the difference is. Edie knows, but can't explain it very well.

What does 'touring Cuba' mean? Is it code for 'Your brother is such an idiot I can't bear to see you again for the foreseeable future'?

In the end, we Google him.

Turns out, 'touring Cuba' is code for 'touring Cuba'. With a bunch of other dancers, in a bid to build relations with their amazingly good ballet schools.

That bit, at least, I can understand.

Chapter 12

Christmas last year was a bit rushed. Crow was busy preparing her first couture collection for London Fashion Week. This year, because she's been working for Miss Teen, she's not doing one. But she's still doing her normal party dresses, *and* she's been asked by a couple of actresses to do their dresses for the BAFTA awards, *and* she's got her new high-street collection to think about. The first one was pretty small, but this time they want about forty pieces: tops, trousers, skirts, dresses, jackets, you name it. If I was Crow, my brain would probably burst.

Jenny is so excited about her new play she's just longing for the holidays to be over. I have January 23rd to look forward to. Harry's admitted he's doing a set at a club in Shoreditch that night, near where lots of the designers have their studios. He seems very relaxed about it, as normal. Whereas I'm terrified that I have less than six weeks to work out what to wear. Only Edie seems to want to get into the Christmas spirit.

Edie's the one who makes sure we get presents for all the right people, and do our holiday homework, and book tickets to see a pantomime. She even makes sure we go skating on the temporary rink outside Somerset House. We look like something out of a Victorian Christmas card. Except I'm in neon legwarmers and my old pink fake polar bear jacket, which isn't totally traditional.

Jenny and I must be the only girls in our school who fast-forward through the holidays so we can get on with interesting stuff. January comes at last and I can start counting down the days on Mum's calendar in the kitchen. Harry has threatened to draw a big pink heart round the 23rd, but if he does, he knows I'll kill him.

Crow, in the middle of everything, has offered to make me a dress for the Big Date. Harry has promised not to leave his decks or even glance in our direction, so hopefully things will go more smoothly this time. Crow and I spend ages choosing fabric and end up going for some silver lace made by our favourite fabric designer, Skye, who's always inventing new materials and doing clever things with old ones. I will look gorgeous and incredible. More so than ever before. Alexander will forget I even *have* a brother.

I'm in a fitting when Edie calls. Crow is perfectly used to adjusting things on clients while they have a mobile phone clamped to their ear, so she just sighs quietly and lets me take the call.

'They've sent them,' Edie says.

I sigh.

'Who's sent what, Edie?'

Then *she* sighs, exasperatedly.

'No Kidding. They've sent the photos.'

'What? Just now? It's taken them long enough.'

'I know. All through the holidays, I was starting to think they'd forgotten or even that they'd made this whole thing up about child labour. That's why I was having such a nice time. But they were just being inefficient. They sent them this afternoon.'

'And?'

Long pause at Edie's end.

'Are they bad?'

Sniffle at Edie's end.

'Yes,' very quietly. 'Yes, they are.'

Oh.

'Are they real?'

'I DON'T KNOW!'

I hold the phone away from my ear. Edie can be very loud when she's upset.

'What do they look like?'

'They look like CHILDREN! Tiny, exhausted children. In a room with no windows, no proper light. Sitting behind these things that look like drums, with fabric stretched over them. Sewing crystals on pieces I recognise from Crow's collection. On pieces I've actually WORN!'

I sigh again. So does Crow. Without a word, she helps me out of the silver lace dress.

'I'm coming over,' I say.

'Thanks, Nonie.' Another sniffle. Edie ends the call.

'It'll be all right,' I promise Crow.

'I know,' she says simply, looking at me with her totally trusting brown eyes like I'm Super-Nonie or something, which makes it worse. I'll just have to tell her when we've fixed everything.

In Edie's bedroom, we look at the photos on her computer screen. Some of the children are tiny. Others could be our age. It's impossible to tell. They're only wearing scraps of clothing because it's obviously hot in that room. They're sitting in a circle, with huge piles of crystals in the middle, all concentrating hard on what they're sewing. It's like something out of *Oliver*, except without the music, or the costumes, or the happy ending.

If the pictures have been faked, they've been faked very well. And why would anyone *want* to fake them? Nobody hates Crow, as far as I know. Or Edie. Or even Andy Elat. I can't see why they'd deliberately want to hurt us by making this up.

On the other hand, the reports by Andy's minions look very believable too. He sends people out three or four times a year to tour the factories he uses, and they don't just pop in for a quick visit. They spend several days there and talk to all the workers, and everyone seems to be reasonably happy and well-paid. And grown-up.

Somebody's lying, but who? And meanwhile, over Christmas the news has leaked out that Crow's been asked to do her second high-street collection. Even though Edie didn't mention it herself because it isn't official yet, her website is full of comments from all over the world asking if it's true, and what happened about the child labour claims that were mentioned in *The Sunday Times*, and what is Edie doing about it now?

'I don't know what to say,' she says. 'What do I tell them?'

Super-Nonie considers this for a while. Super-Nonie gets every little grey cell in her brain working on the problem. Super-Nonie gives up and plays with a stray thread in her jumper.

'You don't know either, do you?' Edie asks.

I shake my head.

Super-Nonie could do with a few more little grey cells.

Chapter 13

Pointless asking Jenny for advice. She's busy learning her part and being happy. It's like four years ago, when we were twelve and she was Annie in the school musical. She's not being prima donna-ish exactly. But unless we want to talk about vocal exercises, or projection issues, or the inner struggle of her character, she's not really interested.

She's been to visit the Boat House Theatre and she says it's perfect. It's close enough for her to get to quite easily for rehearsals after school, but far enough away that lots of people won't even notice that the play's on, and she won't have to worry about scary reviews like last time.

It wasn't her fault, but last time one critic said, 'In a movie of true stars, Jenny Merritt's performance was so wooden I was tempted to make a dining table out of it.' Which was pretty accurate, unfortunately. Then her father sold that 'troubled, talented teen' story. Then Joe Yule, the boy she thought she loved, abandoned her for the Queen of Evil, as we call her. You'd know her as Sigrid Santorini, super-starlet and fashion cutie, who wore one of Crow's dresses to last year's Oscars. Apart from that, 'last time' went very well.

Because of all of that, even though I have other things on my mind, I'm determined to be nice to Jenny. So I go over to her house and pretend to be the crazed ego-maniac father in the play so she can practise her lines. And I don't say anything when she begs me to tell Alexander I'm busy on the 23rd and never see him again.

I don't even try to find out her thoughts on child labour. I don't think she has any, unless it's to do with the trials of young actresses trying to combine GCSE home-work with rehearsal schedules.

'Honestly, Nonie, you wouldn't *believe* the nightmare. I'll have to have special deadlines and permissions from *all* the teachers.'

OK. She can be a bit prima donna-ish sometimes.

On the morning of the 23rd, Crow and I have a meeting to talk about the new Miss Teen collection with Amanda Elat.

'What's your plan?' Edie asked me, when I told her about the meeting.

I don't know why she bothered. There is no plan. I'm going to wing it like I usually do. I was about to lie and tell her something impressive-sounding when she saw the look on my face and just said, 'Oh. Good luck, then.'

Which was kind of her. I'll need it.

One thing is certain, though. It's going to start well. Before we get on to all the dodgy stuff about factories, Crow will completely wow the Miss Teen team with her new designs and hopefully they'll all get so excited they'll agree to pay everyone double and the problem will go away.

Crow's work over Christmas has paid off. Her designs are always astonishingly amazing, but she's given me a sneak preview of the new ones and they're even more extraordinary than usual. Dancing girls in tweed and lace and sequins, jewels and feathers, prancing all over the place like 1920s society queens crossed with exotic birds. You can just see all her conversations with the *mains* in Paris being translated into teenage party gear, with an incredible twist.

We get to the offices on Oxford Street and everyone is super-friendly, which helps my nerves, and Crow's too, I think. Someone arrives with a tray of hot chocolates and a large plate of biscuits. Amanda comes in, dressed in a Miss Teen sweater dress with an antique shawl over her shoulders, and gives us a warm smile.

Amanda is like your favourite aunt. She drives her little Mini like a maniac, can beg clothes off all the best designers and is an expert on Top London Burger Joints. She works too hard, making sure that Miss Teen is always ahead of the fashion trends. This makes her pale and thin, despite her impressive appetite for burgers and biscuits, so sometimes you just want to wrap her up and tell her to calm down. But then she tells you about what Miuccia Prada said to Tom Ford on Valentino's yacht last summer and you realise her life is OK, actually.

Today, she's full of enthusiasm about how quickly the first deliveries of Crow's Jewels collection sold out, and how much coverage they got for the launch, and how pleased they are. I feel like I'm in a warm bath of fashion loveliness. Then Crow gets out her incredible sketches and everyone huddles round to have a look.

Nobody says anything for a while. And I feel the temperature get colder.

'Interesting,' Amanda mutters eventually.

Amanda never says 'interesting'. She says 'amazing' and 'wonderful' and 'gorgeous' and 'beautiful'. Never just 'interesting'.

'I like this lace bit,' says Kazuko, a girl on the design team who's going to help with choosing fabrics and trimmings to turn Crow's vision into reality.

The lace bit is a very small part of a very big outfit.

Another girl breathes in to say something, then doesn't say it.

'Well,' says Amanda after a very long pause indeed. 'I think we have a problem.'

My tummy contracts into a teeny, weeny ball and I can hear a sort of ringing in my ears. It's like being in double maths when you haven't done your homework and the teacher's just asked a question and everyone's looking at you.

'Really?' I ask. 'What?'

Amanda sighs.

'For a start, these designs are very adult. I can't see them working on the average teenager.'

I glance at Crow. She looks a bit shocked and hurt, but doesn't say anything. I reach across and squeeze her hand under the table. She squeezes back. This hasn't happened before. We're not sure what to do.

'We need something . . . fresher,' Amanda goes on. 'And I don't want to worry you, but we need to get a move on. Soon our lead times will be getting quite tight.'

I nod wisely. We business managers understand all about lead times. And tightness. Talking of which, the neoprene mini-skirt I chose for today was a definite no-no, on reflection.

You'd think the process would be: design dress, make dress, sell dress. Which doesn't necessarily take much time at all. But when it comes to a new high-street collection, it gets more complicated. Crow's bit is OK: design dress. But then the Miss Teen people have to make pattern for dress, choose fabric for dress, get sample of dress, check fit of dress in several different sizes, get new sample of dress, order production of dress, advertise dress, put dress on their website, and a whole bunch of other stuff that explains why their headquarters looks as if it's designed to run an airline, or a small country, rather than some shops selling cute stuff for teenagers. This is why they need 'lead times'.

But Amanda hasn't finished yet. She's still looking at the designs and sucking her teeth.

'Also, they're not as commercial as I was expecting. They're just too . . .'

'Busy?' suggests Kazuko.

'Complex?' adds one of the boys.

'Undoable?' sighs another.

'They've got zips,' I point out, feeling a bit lost. 'And buttons.'

'Lloyd means we can't *do* them,' Amanda says. 'Not in vast quantities. Not at the right price points.'

I nod wisely again. We business managers understand all about price points. Actually, I really do. I'd forgotten, but Crow's designs have to retail for very specific amounts. So much for a tee-shirt. So much for a dress. So much for a skirt. And that's what the shop *sells* them for. They have to be *made* for a fraction of that. Which can't be done if they're covered in sequins, lace and feathers.

Everyone just sits around the table, looking at each other, sighing.

Crow squeezes my hand again. She looks dazed and deflated – even the butterflies in her hair seem to be drooping slightly – and for once she doesn't seem to have any bright ideas to fix the problem.

Now doesn't seem the ideal time to bring up the whole

child labour issue.

'And by the way,' Amanda adds, through the sighing, 'we've also got to deal with this child labour issue.'

Oh help.

'Really?'

'Yes, really.' She's starting to look less like a favourite aunt and more like my headmistress. 'We're already getting lots of questions about our ethical policy. And most of the people mention No Kidding, or that *Sunday Times* piece, or Edie's website, or all three. They actually believe these rumours about children being used to sew.'

'I see,' I say. 'It's really difficult. I mean, I know you've got people who go and visit the factories to check and everything, but—'

Amanda cuts me off.

'We have. And they do a good job. Can you get your friend to say so publicly and put an end to this nonsense? Our clothes are made by adult workers who are paid a proper wage.'

I gulp. Amanda doesn't usually sound like this. Where are the amazings and wonderfuls and gorgeouses? Where did 'nonsense' come from?

'We'll see what we can do,' I whisper.

For the first time in ages, she smiles again. 'Thanks. I'm sure you'll be brilliant. And I'm sure Crow can rethink the sketches and come up with something a bit simpler and more workable in a week or so. Can't you, Crow?'

'Yes,' we say. 'No,' we think.

This is SO not amazing and wonderful.

Five minutes later, we're standing back outside Miss Teen on Oxford Street and I can't believe it all just happened.

'Are you OK?' I ask Crow.

She shrugs and frowns and hesitates for a moment, before shrugging a bit more.

I know what she means.

Chapter 14

'Price points? Let me get this straight. PRICE POINTS?'

'Yes,' I say nervously. 'You see, if they can't sell them for the right amount of money, people won't . . .'

'Children are being used as SLAVES. Working SIXTEEN-HOUR DAYS. In filthy back rooms. No breaks. No play. No school. And you're worried about PRICE POINTS?'

'Not me. Amanda.'

Edie isn't taking this as well as I hoped. I thought I'd phone her as soon as she got in from her latest chess tournament. Now I'm wondering if it was such a good idea.

'You haven't exactly got any proof that children are being used,' I say.

'Yes I have. You've seen the photos.'

'They could be faked.'

'So could that note from Roksanda Ilincic you've got framed on your bedroom wall. But it's not.'

I'm impressed she's remembered it's Roksanda Ilincic. Her stuff is *soooo* romantic and Crow's a real fan. But that's not the point.

'We agreed that we didn't know who to believe.'

'We agreed we didn't know what to *do* about it. But I do now. I've been thinking.'

I sigh. It's always dangerous when Edie's been thinking.

'It's not just Crow's collection, anyway. It's happening all over the place. Every time you buy some cheap jeans in a supermarket you have to ask yourself how they got so cheap. Who made them? How much did they get paid? Was it fair?'

I have to say, she lost me at the 'cheap jeans in a supermarket' bit. I just don't wear jeans. And I don't often buy clothes from supermarkets. I make my own stuff, mostly. Or buy it from charity shops. Or 'borrow' from Mum. OK, when I don't get it free from Crow and Roksanda and people, but that's just part of my job . . .

'*Nonie?* Are you concentrating?'

'Yes,' I lie. 'You were saying it's happening all over the place.'

'Exactly. I'm going to start a new campaign. Phil's right. We have to take action.'

'Phil?'

'From No Kidding,' she huffs. 'Remember?'

'Don't tell me. You're going to make tee-shirts. With slogans on. And sell them.'

She's done this before. I know the procedure.

'Yes I am, actually. Fairtrade ones that we've paid a good price for. Made out of Fairtrade cotton by people who aren't exploited. I'm just working on the slogan now. I was going to do "No More Fashion Victims", but Katharine Hamnett's already thought of it.' Edie sounds very fed up about Katharine Hamnett. 'Instead, I'm thinking of "Cheap Clothes Cost Lives".'

Edie certainly doesn't muck around when it comes to slogans. I imagine myself telling Amanda Elat about it at a price point meeting. Not a good image.

'Er, I don't suppose you could wait until Crow's done her second collection and Andy Elat isn't so . . .'

'Yeah, sure,' Edie says. 'No problem. I'll just hang about while the CHILDREN run up some more nifty little numbers for fashionable teenagers to wear, in their SLAVE FACTORIES.'

'I'll take that as a no,' I say.

She sighs. 'Besides. There's something else I ought to tell you.' Her voice changes and goes low so I have to strain to hear her. 'I've been nominated for this ethical blogging award. I mean, I can't exactly ignore the photos now, can I? Not when they're saying I'm a "teenage role model for engagement with issues of world poverty and injustice".'

'Wow! Edie? An AWARD!'

She sounds sheepish. 'It's just a nomination. The other people are really amazing, though.'

She describes them to me. They are a law student from Brazil who's saving the rainforest, a high-school student from Arizona with a record-breaking IQ, an Indian nun (yes, really) and some kid from Ukraine who is *radio-active* as a result of the Chernobyl disaster years ago, and is bound to win. God, Edie lives in an exciting world. I mean, Marc Jacobs is a hero to me, but even he can't claim to be radioactive. Not that he'd want to, I suppose.

'And it's not the top award or anything,' Edie continues. She really is *so* embarrassed about this. 'It's just the "rising star" category.'

'OH MY GOD!'

'Nonie? What's happened?'

It's what's *about* to happen. The words 'rising star' have reminded me: I have a DATE with my nearly-boyfriend in TWO HOURS! What have I been *thinking*?

'I have to go. Alexander . . . but well done. And good luck. And do the tee-shirts, of course. I'll even buy one. And Crow'll be fine. I'll just . . .'

'Oooh, Alexander!' she yells at me, excitedly. 'Shut up and get going! We'll sort it out later. Just have a good time, OK?'

It's how we stay friends. She can switch from Saviour Of The World to normal person, just like that. And she totally understands how cute my nearly-boyfriend is.

Ninety minutes later, I'm in Crow's workroom, staring at myself in the mirror. Crow's staring at me too, needle in hand, just in case I need any last-minute adjustments.

She gives me one of her rare, incredible smiles.

'I think we're done,' she says.

We are. I have been transformed from wonky-haired midget into glamorous fashion queen. I'm in a gorgeous, silver knee-length dress that makes me look at least eighteen. I have proper, grown-up tights on without any patterns, sequins or holes. I have not only high heels but PLATFORMS that give me ten precious extra centimetres in height. Designer platforms by Prada that I shall probably leave to my children in my will.

I'm wearing enough eyeliner for an emo convention and individual fake eyelashes, for extra oomph. And possibly a tiny spritz too much perfume, but it's too late now.

I have never looked like this before and I probably never will again. I'm a hot babe, basically, and Alexander is going to adore me.

'Jewellery?' I ask, panicking suddenly.

Crow shakes her head. She's probably right. There's enough going on already.

I grab my jacket and my vintage bag from a little pile on the workroom floor (I'm not *totally* careful with my clothes, I admit), and I'm ready to go.

Mum's standing in the hall, waiting.

'Wow,' she says. 'You look . . . different. Go gently on him, darling. He won't know what's hit him.'

Different good or different bad? It's too late to find out, so I give her a quick kiss and head out of the door before she realises quite how much of her perfume I've borrowed.

'Back by midnight, don't forget,' she shouts after me.

SO Cinderella. I've been given an extension because Harry will be there.

'And don't let him . . .'

Yada yada yada. I can't hear because I'm rushing into the taxi and concentrating on not doing a Naomi Campbell in my platforms down our front steps. They're not quite as easy to walk in as I'd hoped. Especially for a girl who lives in Converse.

Harry's doing his set in a posh members' club, which is on several floors of an old East End warehouse building. I've been sort-of hoping Alexander would be in the reception area, waiting for me, but he's not. I guess real, proper grown-up boyfriend types don't behave like your friends and meet you as soon as they can. But this club is big, and he could be anywhere.

By the time I track him down in the bar my insides have already performed several ballets and my ankles are starting to hate Prada with a passion I didn't know they were capable of. I'm feeling hot in more ways than one. I hope I look cool and sophisticated.

He's sitting on a bar stool, relaxed and glamorous. I pause and flutter my eyelashes in his direction. One of them comes off and gets stuck to my eyeball. I have to pick it out with a finger.

Meanwhile he comes over and kisses me on the cheek again, smiling. He looks me up and down and the smile fades slightly.

'Where are the legs, Boots?'

'Er, still here,' I say.

I wait for him to say something nice about my dress or my makeup or my hair or something.

'Want a drink?' he asks.

'Yes!' I gulp. 'How was Cuba, by the way?'

'Stop sounding like Her Majesty!'

He says it with a laugh, but I'm just trying to be polite. I can't help it if the Queen's polite too. What else do you ask someone who's just come back from Cuba? If you can't bring yourself to ask if they like your dress?

We go over to the bar and I order champagne. YES YES YES!

It's a bit of a surprise when the barman eventually passes me a smoothie. I look at it through my droopy fake eyelashes, confused. The barman grins. 'Your brother was round earlier. He told me how old you are. And that this is your *second* favourite drink.'

'Did he tell you how much I loathe every millimetre of him?'

'Yup,' the barman says, still smiling. 'He did.'

'Cheers,' says Alexander, clinking his glass against mine. 'So. Tell me about school.'

This quite simply has to be The Worst Date In History. I'm wondering whether to just leave my smoothie and find my taxi money and go. But luckily Alexander sees the look on my face and leans forward and brushes a lock of hair away from my face.

'Only joking, Boots,' he says, a bit huskily. 'I missed you. Tell me all about *you*.'

The next hour is nice. We sit and talk. He tells me about performing in Cuba and helping young kids from the streets who might become future stars. I tell him about Crow's new party dresses and the agonies I went through choosing these shoes (although not the agonies I'm going through now, wearing them). I watch his long fingers playing with the rim of his glass. His sky-blue silk shirt tucked into designer jeans. His blond hair curling slightly over his collar.

Then we hear the thump thump thump of Harry's music and go through to a room where you can hardly move for dancing bodies, grooving the night away. Alexander miraculously finds an empty spot and whirls me around, making me look like I'm some sort of trained dancer myself.

Even in this confined space, he is the best possible dance partner. Totally concentrated, totally cool, totally brilliant at thinking of the perfect move at the perfect time, whisking me out of the way just in time to avoid being whacked by a stray limb from some other dancer who's not quite so together.

I completely lose track of how long we dance for. I even forget that I'm wearing impossible shoes and in severe danger of breaking an ankle every time I move. It's impossible to talk, because the music's so loud, which means I don't even have to think of any intelligent conversation. So I'm a bit disappointed when eventually Alexander nods his head towards the seating area at the back of the room.

I hadn't really noticed it before. Lots of dark velvet armchairs around low tables with little candles on. Lots of couples sitting around, chatting and . . . snuggling. Etc.

Quite a lot of etc., actually.

Alexander finds one empty armchair and guides me towards it. But where's he going to sit?

Oh. He flings himself into the armchair in front of me and deftly sits me on his knee, so our faces are level. Then he puts one of his beautiful, long-fingered hands on my thigh. I look at his angular cheekbones. Even in this low light, I can see little beads of sweat forming on his upper lip.

So there he is, looking at my face. And I'm looking at his. And getting quite obsessed with the little beads of sweat. I get the sense that his upper lip is going to be moving closer to me any time now, so I'll get to see them from even more close up. I try to find them sexy.

I don't.

My insides are impossibly confused. They're doing a major finale now, full of arabesques and grand jetés and multiple pirouettes. But they're also seriously wishing that the upper lip would stay where it is and not come any closer to mine.

It does, though.

At the last moment, I drag my eyes away from it. Alexander kisses me properly. And guess what, the sweat rubs off his upper lip onto mine. NO NO NO NO NO.

The kiss itself is OK. So-so. I've had better practising on the back of my hand, to be honest. And certainly with a French exchange boy last year, and that was in a Eurostar duty-free shop and lasted about three seconds.

By now, Alexander has started poking the tip of his tongue between my teeth. I can't help myself. I clamp them shut. YUK! I'm not up for the whole tongue-in-mouth-kissing-in-public scenario.

EW EW EW EW.

I let the kiss last as long as it needs to, but my jaw stays firmly shut.

When Alexander pulls away at last, his eyes are closed. He seems not disappointed, as I'm expecting, but dreamy.

Then he opens his eyes and smiles at me in a 'How was it for *you*, baby?' sort of way.

I smile back and pretend I've got another fake eyelash in my eye. I use the opportunity to wipe my lip.

EW EW EW EW.

How am I ever going to admit this to Jenny? I'll have to lie and say it was wonderful.

And just as I'm thinking this to myself about Jenny I could swear I spot the Queen of Evil, Sigrid Santorini herself, disappearing through a door in the far corner of the room. Sigrid, the woman who stole Jenny's first nearly-boyfriend. Sigrid, the woman who stole the star piece of Crow's first couture collection. Sigrid, who lives in California and couldn't *possibly* be in a club in Shoreditch where my brother is DJing.

I'm confused. My *brain* is doing pirouettes now. This must be some sort of nightmare mirage, brought on by the stress of the First Proper Kiss.

I put my arm around Alexander's neck and secretly check my watch. Ten past eleven. Only twenty minutes to go until I can ask him to get me a taxi.

'Fancy another dance?' he asks.

I nod with relief. Dancing I can handle.

'By the way,' I ask. 'What's through that door over there?'

I point to the far corner of the room.

'That's the VIP section,' he says. 'Where the stars go. I know the guy on the door. Want a look?'

I shake my head violently. 'No. Definitely not.'

'Rather dance, hey?'

He gives me a confident wink, certain of my complete adoration of his every move.

Nineteen minutes left. I follow him onto the dance floor.

Chapter 15

'It was incredible,' I say. 'He was *such* a good dancer.'

'And?'

'And?'

'Did he kiss you, you idiot?'

I nod.

'*And?*'

'It was lovely.'

Jenny gives me a very suspicious look.

'Are you sure?'

'Totally sure. It's just, you know, hard to describe.'

She should know. She made a rubbish job of describing her first serious kiss to me. And that was with a MOVIE STAR on the set of *Kid Code* and he KISSED HER FACE ALL OVER.

'Try.' She still looks very suspicious.

Instead, I tell her about the room and the velvet armchairs and Harry's set. I almost tell her about the Queen of Evil, but manage to stop myself. It must have been my imagination.

Jenny can see I'm avoiding the important stuff, but she doesn't push it. Instead, she smiles a quiet smile to herself and asks, 'So when are you seeing him again?'

'We haven't fixed a day,' I say. Which is code for 'He hasn't called or texted, so I have no idea.'

I ought to be devastated, but I'm sort of not. I'm more relieved, so far, but I wouldn't admit that to Jenny in A MILLION YEARS.

We're in the school cafeteria, having lunch. Edie's supposed to be joining us after a debating club session she does on Mondays. Edie does extra stuff most days of the week, but Mondays are the worst. She needs one of those Hermione Granger things that make you go back in time, but sadly we're not at Hogwarts.

When she does come, she sits down with a smile, takes a sip of her water and says something that has Jenny and me spluttering our lunch all over the table.

'Did you know, by the way, that Sigrid Santorini's in town?'

Oh. My. God. I was so sure I was wrong about seeing her.

But more importantly, HOW ON EARTH COULD EDIE KNOW? It's not exactly the kind of news they announce in the *Financial Times*. I've seen Edie less than a metre away from one of the most famous women on the planet and she didn't seem to notice.

'My mum told me this morning,' she says casually. 'She

thought I'd be interested. I wasn't, I have to say, but I thought you would be. There's some film festival Sigrid's going to. Mum heard her on the radio, talking about it.'

Straight after school, we go home together to my house, to Google Sigrid. We meet Crow in the hall. Her school finishes earlier than ours and she usually beats us to it.

'Sigrid's in town!' we say, all together, like some sort of stressed-out girl group.

Crow looks at us calmly.

'I know,' she says. 'She's just left a message. She wants another dress.'

For the next hour, we surf the web.

Eighteen months ago, Sigrid made a smash-hit comedy with Joe Yule, Jenny's heart-throb (and mine and half the female universe's – but Jenny got an actual snog out of him before Sigrid came along). The movie's being shown at a festival next week. Joe's busy being the New Teenage Sex God on a film set somewhere, so Sigrid is going along to greet the crowds. Meanwhile, she's staying in a chic little hotel in Soho, going to a couple of European awards ceremonies and generally 'catching up with all her old friends from previous visits to the ancient city of London'.

And some of her old enemies, apparently. Crow says she's due for her first fitting tomorrow.

'I have to go over to her hotel. She doesn't have time to

come here. Can you come with me, Nonie?'

At first I say yes, assuming it's straight after school. But then it turns out Sigrid can only do an appointment at nine pm. And for once, I'm accompanying Mum to a private view by one of the artists she represents. She doesn't ask me very often and I can't possibly turn it down.

Jenny can't go, with rehearsals starting in a few days and lots of advance homework to do. And hating Sigrid's guts, of course. Which is how Edie ends up agreeing to keep Crow company. We don't think anything of it at the time, apart from the fact that Edie is very kind, which we knew anyway.

We think a lot about it later, but by then it's much, much too late.

Chapter 16

'It was fine,' Edie says.

We're back in the school cafeteria. Edie has promised to tell Jenny and me exactly how it went last night.

'And?' I ask.

'And?' asks Jenny.

Edie looks up from her shepherd's pie, surprised. She thinks that 'fine' is a perfectly reasonable description of a Hollywood starlet's fashion fitting in a posh London hotel.

'And WHAT?' asks Jenny at last.

'Oh,' Edie says. 'Well, Sigrid was very nice.'

Edie does this. If you ask her to describe someone in Jane Austen or Thomas Hardy she'll use about fifteen adjectives you've never heard of and you need a dictionary to keep up. But normal people are just 'very nice'. I think Edie spends most of her time thinking about chess club or orchestra or going to Harvard and hardly notices real people at all.

Not that it's a surprise to hear 'nice' associated with Sigrid Santorini. Despite being the Queen of Evil, this is how she comes across when you first meet her. The thing with Sigrid is, she doesn't *know* she's the Queen of Evil. She thinks she's an adorable cutie and the rest of us just can't wait to be a part of her fabulous world. She bounces around, smiling at everyone and radiating joy. It's only later that you find she's ripped your life to pieces, stabbed you in the back, stolen something precious and disappeared.

And she seems to think even *that's* OK, because simply being in the presence of somebody so famous will make everything better for you. What's worse, she's often right. The night she stole Crow's star catwalk outfit last year she said to me that she'd wear it on television and we'd get loads of publicity out of it and we'd be really grateful. Well, she wore it to the Oscars and Crow became an overnight sensation. But she didn't *tell* me she was saving it for the Oscars and in the meantime Crow had to make another one and I nearly died. So I'm not as grateful as I might be. And I still think she's the Queen of Evil.

'Nice HOW?' asks Jenny. Jenny likes detail.

'She offered us loads of stuff from her hotel suite. They had five kinds of juice and this massive fruit bowl and some really interesting biscuits I hadn't seen before . . .'

Jenny jiggles with frustration.

'What was she wearing? What kind of dress did she

want? What was the fitting for? How long is she staying in London? Did she say anything about . . . anyone?'

Jenny says this as one very long word, but Edie gets the gist.

'Well. She was wearing her hotel bathrobe. I think it was white with a pocket and . . . oh, all right. She wanted a dress to wear to an awards do in Italy in a few days. She knows all the Italians are going to be in amazing stuff so she's after something special. And she's only supposed to be in London for a week or so, but she just heard her next film's been cancelled or something so she's not sure what she's doing exactly. She was on the phone about it a lot while we were there. Actually, she said a lot of rude things for someone so nice. And – what was the other thing?'

'Did she talk about anyone we know?' Jenny asks.

'Oh. No. Not exactly. She asked after both of you, of course. Well, sort of all of us in general. But mostly she just looked at the dresses Crow brought along and said how she'd need them adapted to show off her legs. Oh, and I told her about the new collection for Miss Teen and the play and everything.'

'Right,' Jenny says.

All she really wants to know is whether Sigrid had anything interesting to say about Joe Yule, the boy who broke her heart, but she's too shy to ask and Edie is too dim about these things to work it out for herself.

'To be honest,' Edie goes on, 'I'd been starting to wonder about Sigrid a bit. I mean, she said some *very* rude things on the phone. But she was so interested in the new collection. And the play. She wanted to know about the actors and the theatre and the director and everything. I couldn't tell her much, but it was nice to see she cared.'

Edie goes back to her shepherd's pie. Jenny and I are both pondering something. Perhaps it's the use of the words 'Sigrid' and 'cared' in the same sentence. Something definitely doesn't feel quite right, but we're not sure what.

'Oh, and I told her about my website and she gave me these,' Edie adds suddenly. She scrabbles around in her backpack and pulls out a red silk purse, which she lays on the table. Inside is a pair of pearl and silver dangly earrings, each about the size of my hand. 'Sigrid said she doesn't need them and I can auction them for charity. When I auctioned off Jenny's shoes last year they made loads of money. These might make even more.'

Jenny and I explain to Edie that they were not 'shoes', they were Louboutins. And that it's rude to suggest that one actress's earrings may be worth more than another actress's shoes, even if the second actress is your friend and not *very* famous. And we don't point out Edie's *other* fatal error, because we still haven't spotted it.

Chapter 17

It's Friday evening. Jenny's rehearsals have just started. They're in a studio south of the river and she happily heads off most days after school, singing show tunes at the top of her voice and frightening passers-by with the high notes.

Crow's due back from an art show opening with Henry and some design student friends so she can finish a dress, but meanwhile I'm borrowing the workroom because I'm making a dress of my own and the good part is, it's homework! After much begging, pleading and tearful sulking (in French, which is the best language for sulking in by a million miles, just so's you know, and also makes me sound vaguely sophisticated), I got Mum to let me do textiles GCSE. Yes!

You'd think if your child was good at something – and sorry to brag, but in the normal world where everyone isn't a fashion designer, my stuff is 'surprisingly impressive, Nonie'. Anyway, you'd think if you were good at something your parents would *want* you to do an exam in it, so you'd get a decent grade at least once in your life, but no. Mum said it was too easy! Repeat after me, TOO EASY! Much better to cram my schedule with geography and history and science and things that make my head hurt. But she came round in the end. I think Dad helped persuade her to give me a break. Plus, a part of her actually *does* want me to get a decent grade for once.

So I'm doing textiles. And I have to do this project linking clothes with art. Which is just total heaven to me. I can't draw for toffee, but I can cut out pictures and stick them in scrapbooks like a pro. Yves Saint Laurent was influenced by painters like Picasso and Mondrian (see, on my specialist subject I sound really cultured and informed!). I'm doing a dress based on Cézanne, who I discovered when I first started helping Crow. And it's fabulous. Trust me, it is.

There's only one problem. When you're sitting at a worktable pinning and basting, listening to your friend's jazz collection, you have lots of time to think about stuff. Great if you want to get your head round Shakespeare's tragedies (I don't, particularly), but rubbish if you keep wondering when your I-thought-he-was-my-boyfriend is going to call. And wondering. And wondering.

It's been nearly a week since the club in Shoreditch. I know that wasn't exactly my best experience ever, but still. Things are supposed to happen after a first proper date, and they're not.

When is Alexander going to text me? At first, I was cool and laid back about the whole thing, like a Woman Who Has Regular Boyfriends. But now I'm back to my old self, and a bit of a wreck. What happens on the second proper date? Will there ever be one? Is he busy or is he just deliberately making me wait, for some bloke-reason that I don't understand? Was the first proper kiss, in fact, as bad for him as it was for me? Am I a Seriously Bad Kisser? Have I put him off for life?

I've asked Crow's opinion and she just said Alexander was probably too busy dancing to call. As if.

I really want to ask Harry. As an older brother, Harry's job is to explain to me about men so it's all slightly less confusing. But he was so mean to me after my first nearly-date that I can't talk to him. I've even considered asking Svetlana, but as Alexander was supposed to be going out with a friend of hers, I can't really talk to her either.

In desperation, I put the Cézanne dress down and go and ask Mum.

I catch her in the kitchen, grabbing a quick glass of wine between phone calls.

'Er, Mum. How long are you supposed to wait to hear from someone? After . . . you've seen them. About something.'

I hope I've been vague enough.

'Has Alexander not called?' she asks. Then she says a word in French that isn't particularly complimentary to my possibly-already-ex-boyfriend. I assume this means he should have contacted me by now.

'You've been a bit quiet, darling,' she goes on. 'How was the date? I never really asked.'

'Lovely,' I say.

Lovely is my new word, I've decided. Lovely means 'back off and leave me alone, I'm confused'.

Mum gives me a pitying look, which is worse than anything she might have said.

Then she adds, 'Well, he brought you back on time, so that's good. But listen, if he does anything to break your heart, you'll tell me, won't you? And I'll get Harry to bop him on the nose.'

Throughout my childhood, Mum has threatened to get Harry to bop people on the nose for me. As I'm five years younger than him, normally the people in question are also younger, smaller and slightly scared of him. They are not tall, fit dancers with *very* developed muscles and sweaty upper lips. I think, in a bopping contest, Alexander would win hands down. He could probably do it with one leg wrapped around his head.

'Thanks, Mum,' I say. She tries.

Back in the workroom, I try and concentrate on getting the overlapping panels of my bodice to line up properly. I also try not to look at my phone every thirty seconds, waiting for a text.

Then one comes and in my excitement I drop the phone and the cover comes off and it makes a worrying, sad beeping noise. SO not good. When I've finally put it back together and discovered that it still works after all, the text turns out to be from Jenny. It's a smiley face and a question mark.

Aaaauuugghhh!

I text her back anyway. A series of question marks, rather than the 'Leave-me-alone-you-are-not-who-I-need-to-talk-to-right-now' that I *wanted* to send. She calls me and I can hear her breathy, actressy voice, which means she's just been talking to lots of her theatre friends and life is suddenly a big DRAMA, darling. I hope there isn't a fashion equivalent of this, and that I don't do it if there is.

'Caroline's gone!' Jenny breathes.

This would be incredible news, if I had the faintest idea who Caroline was. I tell Jenny as much.

'The stepmother! Well, the actress who plays her. You know Caroline. She was in *The Smiling Detective* last year. And she was Keira Knightley's mother in that thing.'

I dimly remember Caroline from 'that thing'. It was a costume drama thing and we spent most of the time wanting to be Keira Knightley's younger sister, who had the most stunning silk dresses you can imagine, but unfortunately died of some horrible, old-fashioned disease about halfway through.

'Why's she gone?'

'We don't know!'

Jenny says this as if it's an answer to my question,

rather than just a really annoying comment.

'So why are you telling me this?'

'It's a big mystery! The producer says she's got family problems, but she was telling me this morning how much she was looking forward to the run. We're supposed to start in just over two weeks.'

Oh. This sounds bad. 'They're not cancelling the play, are they?' I ask, suddenly concerned.

'That's the strangest bit. The producer said they're looking at putting it on at a bigger theatre. He says we might get a transfer after we finish at the Boat House.'

I'm not sure what to say now. To most people, the idea of a bigger theatre would be great news, but the whole reason Jenny wanted to do this play was because the Boat House was small and out of the way.

'Er, congratulations?'

'Thanks,' she says, in a wobbly sort of way. I can picture her biting her lip.

I think she called me because she wants to believe it's good news, but she needs to hear someone else say it. Now that I know what I'm supposed to do, I spend ages telling her how perfect she'll be after a few weeks performing at the Boat House, and how she'll be ready for anything they throw at her. She gets less and less wobbly and by the end she sounds like she's almost looking forward to it. Thank goodness for Mum, and her 'How To Talk To Creative People' lessons. You never know when they're going to come in handy.

* * *

Strangely, I have to do it all over again two minutes later.

Edie calls to say that her mum and dad, who are teachers, both have to attend a parents' evening tonight. This is mildly interesting, but not worth a phone call, in my opinion. Then she says her little brother Jake's on a sleepover and am I busy?

I am, of course – after the dress, I've got geography to do and I've recorded an episode of *Britain's Next Top Model* – but this is clearly code for 'Please can I come over?' so I invite her over.

She arrives fifteen minutes later in the strangest of moods and I take her to the kitchen for a hot chocolate. If I didn't know Edie better, I'd say she was on a caffeine high. She's all jittery and can't sit down and keeps wandering round the room, touching delicate stuff from Mum's art collection and making the pictures wonky.

'Everything all right?' I ask.

'Fine,' she says, looking goofy.

The answer to my next three questions is 'Fine', or 'OK, I suppose'. This is going to be tough.

Meanwhile, Harry's in his bedroom, trying out the playlist for his next set. He can only really get into the mood if he plays it EXTREMELY LOUD, so the whole house is shaking. The next-door neighbours hate us. Edie tries a few dance steps. Something *very* strange is happening.

Then suddenly I remember. The ethical blogging

awards. They must be happening around now. Are they tonight? Does she need me to hold her hand while we watch radioactive kid win a prize?

'Er, is your website going OK?' I ask. I sense she's in too strange a mood for direct questions.

'Fine,' Edie says. But in a 'please ask me more' sort of way.

'The awards must be soon,' I prompt.

'Oh, they've happened,' she sighs. She runs her fingers over a pile of unframed photos that must ON NO ACCOUNT BE TOUCHED.

'Why don't we go to my room?' I suggest. 'And what happened? Did radioactive kid win?'

We start to head upstairs.

'No,' she shouts, over the sound of some Icelandic pop group that Harry's recently discovered.

She's not making it easy for me. Then I realise the obvious. We're at the door of my room. I turn to look at her.

'Did *you* win?'

'Yes!' she squeaks. 'Yes, I did!'

And we both do a jig round the landing. Or as much of a jig as you can do to Icelandic pop. More of a pogo.

I turn on my laptop and make her show me the ethical blogging website, where it says 'Winner' in flashing letters next to Edie's name, and there's a whole page about *her* website, and how much the ethical blogging people admire it for being 'informative and committed, but also fun and in tune with teen culture'. You can tell they haven't actually *met* Edie.

'And there's this,' she says. Now that she's finally admitted winning, she's desperate to show me more.

She does some rapid typing on my keyboard and up comes the most boring webpage I've seen in my life. It's a series of graphs. It's like homework. Ew. But apparently it's her 'web stats' – how many people actually look at her site – and on the biggest chart is a line that's just taken off, showing that she's suddenly got hundreds of new readers. And the number's growing by the minute.

'The ethical blogging people warned me this might happen if I won,' she said. 'But I was so sure I wouldn't.'

'*Warned* you? Isn't this a good thing?'

'I suppose so. But my site wasn't designed to cope with this many readers at once. It's in danger of crashing. I need to talk to my hosting service in the morning.'

There she goes, the internet whizz kid again. You wouldn't normally think that the idea of your site crashing would make you grin from ear to ear like a crazy person, but that's what Edie's doing right now. She's really proud of this award. And what's so sweet is, I really don't think she would ever have told me if I hadn't asked. Or rather, if she hadn't made me ask.

Edie just stands there, next to my desk, jiggling about and looking happy in a shocked sort of way.

'Come on,' I say, grabbing her hand. 'Party.'

Mum's back on the phone upstairs, but we hear the

front door opening and go down to find Crow in the hall. She instantly puts her satchel down and starts boogie-ing around the room in an 'Edie victory' dance.

'What about Harry?' she asks breathlessly, mid-boogie. 'Does he know?'

She's right, of course I may still be cross with him for sniggering at me, but it's time for a brief ceasefire. We all pile into his room and he grins at us as if nothing's wrong anyway. He's in the middle of some Memphis Soul by now and once he hears the news he turns his speakers up as loud as they'll go, which is very.

Memphis Soul, it turns out, is perfect for dancing around the room with your brother and two of your best friends, to celebrate their total amazingness.

'You're famous now!' I shout to Edie over King Curtis and his band.

'Only to ethical bloggers,' she laughs.

'Well, I'm going to check out your website,' Harry adds, 'so that's one new reader, anyway.'

'I always knew you were the best,' says Crow, in the same way she says she's going to design for the Royal Ballet one day – like it's a simple fact.

We carry on dancing, despite loud knocks from next door, and I lead a conga around the room. You wouldn't think you could conga to Memphis Soul, but if you try hard enough, you can. Then my phone goes in my pocket. Without thinking, I grab it and press the 'Answer' button.

'Yes?' I shout.

'Er, hi. Nonie?'

'Yes. What?'

'It's Alexander. Er, are you OK?'

I explain to Alexander that yes, I am indeed OK. I am also busy celebrating and I'll call him back later. Then I put the phone away and get back down to dancing. I mean, of all the stupid times to call.

It's only as I'm going to bed and it's suddenly all quiet that I realise what I've done, and what an idiot I am.

Except I'm not. He texts first thing in the morning, begging for another date as soon as possible.

Chapter 18

Sure enough, Edie's site crashes on Saturday morning. She gets it fixed and five minutes later, it crashes again. Apparently she's going to need another machine to run it on or something. Anyway, it's complicated and technical and expensive but she doesn't really mind because other people start blogging about the fact that it crashed and that gives her even *more* traffic and she's becoming really quite famous on the web.

I try not to think about the number of people who now get a daily update on what I'm wearing. If you do, you go mad. Especially if you're going through a bit of a 1930s phase and you spend a lot of your time in vintage bias-cut satin dresses that your mother thinks look more like moth-eaten nighties. Worn with your trusty old pink polar bear jacket – now a bit short and more of a shrug – and winkle-pickers.

Crow and I have our follow-up meeting at Miss Teen this morning. Before I started working in the fashion business, Saturday mornings were strictly for shopping and smoothies. Now they're also for meetings. Not our favourite thing, but no meetings, no collection. So we dress up nicely and smile bravely and go.

I don't wear bias-cut satin for this. Miss Teen people don't do 'moth-eaten'. I wear a lime-green gingham pleated mini-skirt, braces and one of Harry's shirts. And a new pair of Converse All-Stars that I've covered with bottle tops in an effort to recycle. I look perfectly respectable and business-like. Well, next to Edie I might look a bit relaxed, but I'm going for 'normal teenager', not 'aspiring member of the Royal Family'.

Crow's wearing her standard working outfit of tee-shirt and dungarees, with a floor-length tartan cloak. And a huge tartan scarf wrapped around her hair. Took her five seconds to do. Looks incredible. Sigh.

On the way to the Miss Teen HQ, I buy a celebrity magazine in a newsagent and flip through it. Two girls in Crow dresses – one couture, one high-street. Good. Interestingly, the girl in the couture dress has teamed it with pixie boots. PIXIE BOOTS? Is she crazy? But the more I think about it, the more I like it. Oh, and there's a picture of Sigrid Santorini falling out of a club with a man whose name I recognise. It takes the whole bus journey to remember why.

Then I realise. It's Jenny's director. Sigrid is stalking us.

When we get to the HQ we're shown into the board-room, not the design/chatting/everything room that we normally go to. This room is large and grand and full of wood. The walls are lined with wood. The table is made out of an enormous chunk of it. The chairs are wood-colour. Even one of the artworks on the wall is made of wood blocks. If Edie saw it, she would think of the rain-forests and weep. It would probably remind Jenny of her performance in *Kid Code*.

Hot chocolates are handed round, as per usual, with cappuccinos for the grown-ups. Amanda comes in, looking even more tired than usual (bad sign). Then the design team troop in behind her and sit in their chairs, staring at their cappuccinos and not looking at us (very bad sign). Then Andy Elat himself comes in, chatting to another man I haven't seen before and sounding very jolly. But he doesn't say hello. Extremely bad sign.

When everyone's settled, Andy finally pretends to notice Crow and me. He nods briefly in our direction. If he's trying to be scary and intimidating, it's working. Even Crow looks slightly unnerved. I have a feeling she's wishing Henry was here, to tuck her under his arm.

'This is Paolo,' Andy says. 'My new PR guru. I'm sure you're all aware of him, so no introductions needed.'

Everyone round the table nods except Crow and me. I've never heard of him, and an introduction would be really nice.

Paolo has one of those beards that is only a few millimetres long and reminds you of David Beckham. He's about the same age as Mum, with dark hair, light brown skin and very pink lips. I'm guessing he's Italian and that he probably has brown eyes, but I don't know because he's wearing impenetrable black wraparound sunglasses. To go with his black polo-neck jumper, baggy black flannel trousers and shiny black shoes. He looks like how I'd imagine a Russian bodyguard to look. If he had a pistol tucked into his trouser belt, it wouldn't seem at all out of place.

Paolo looks super-serious. He's turned his head in our direction, so I suppose he's checking us out, but I can't be sure.

'Great to meet you at last,' says the girl nearest to him, holding out her hand.

He says nothing, but stands up and leans forward a bit. The girl rightly guesses that this means he wants a kiss, not a handshake. So she gets up and air-kisses him on both cheeks, which is what you do in fashion. I wonder for a split second whether Crow and I are supposed to air-kiss him too, but one look at Andy Elat assures me that kissing is off the agenda for us today. We've done something terrible and we're about to hear all about it.

I realise that since our last meeting with Amanda, we haven't made quite as much progress as we'd hoped. Crow's designs are still just as 'adult' and 'undoable' as ever, and I haven't exactly managed to get Edie to change her website. But we've been busy with dates and Sigrid Santorini and party frocks. And anyway, there are those photos from No Kidding, which we can't really ignore, and that reminds me – surely Andy will be impressed when he hears about Edie's amazing award?

I decide to start things off on a positive note, so I lean across to Andy and say, 'I don't suppose you've heard, but our friend Edie's just won a web award.'

He looks back at me without a hint of a smile in his crinkly eyes and says that yes, funnily enough, he *had* heard about that.

Wow! He already knows. Yay!

'Isn't it incredible?' I say. 'She's thrilled. Her site's got so many hits it's crashed twice. She's having to upgrade the server.' I can't believe I just said that. Sometimes the right words come to me when I'm least expecting it. I sound so technical!

I'm about to go into lots more detail when Andy does his wiggling fingers thing, so I shut up.

'Exactly,' he says. 'Paolo?'

Paolo strokes his mini-beard. Paulo pauses until he has the room's full attention. Then Paolo speaks.

'DISASTER!' he declares, glaring through the sunglasses. 'It has to stop.'

'Stop?'

'Stop! Cease! Desist! Every day this girl . . . this *schoolgirl* . . . gets more hits on her website. More publicity. And now the award. Thousands of people go to her site. Not just other girls now. Journalists. Bloggers. Fashion commentators. *Serious* people. They read about Crow. They read about Miss Teen. They read about Mr Elat and his brand. And they read this.'

He presses a button and some wood panels slide aside on a wall at the other end of the room, to reveal a screen that's already been set up to connect to the internet. Everyone turns to look. It's showing Edie's homepage and in huge letters across the top (above a picture of Svetlana in her amazing gold dress) is a banner advertising Edie's new campaign which says, 'Cheap Clothes Cost Lives', with a link to the No Kidding photos of children doing embroidery.

There's a gasp around the table from the design team. Oh dear. This moment wasn't great when I'd imagined it and it's even worse now I'm actually sitting in it.

Everyone looks at Crow and me. Not in a good way. We shrug. What are we supposed to do?

Paolo says, 'So. Disaster. First, the suggestion that Miss Teen clothes are cheap. They are not *cheap*, they are *reasonably priced*. Second, that Mr Elat and his brand might be in some way involved with bad labour practices. This is preposterous! It is unthinkable! It is an insult to the brand.'

Paolo stops. He has spoken. The room is filled with silence. Everyone goes back to staring at their cappuccinos. I feel a bit sick.

'Paolo's right,' Andy says. He sounds a tiny bit kinder now. Perhaps he can see how green I've gone. 'Edie needs to buck her ideas up, Nonie. I've shown her the studies. They prove I'm not involved in this stuff. But one minute she's talking about child labour and the next minute she's talking about Crow, and that means Miss Teen, and that means me. This could cost me millions. Millions.'

Amanda joins in. 'Edie's getting quite famous in her own right, because of this website. People trust her. She's got to come out and say once and for all that *some* people may be carrying out these practices, but that we don't. Because we don't. We've written this piece she could put on the website, explaining everything. Can you ask her to put it on? And to take down that "Cheap Clothes Cost Lives" banner? I'm sure it wouldn't be hard to do.'

I'm very tempted at this point to say yes. If I say yes everybody will smile and leave the table and this meeting will stop and I can go to the toilets and cry, which is what I really want to do.

But we'll only end up back here in a week. Because I know that even if I ask Edie, she won't listen to me. So I might as well get the worst over with now. I take a deep breath.

'The reason people trust Edie is because she says what she thinks. She'd love to believe that Crow's clothes are made by grown-ups working in proper factories, with good pay and healthcare and everything. But she can only talk about what she's seen with her own eyes. And you've seen those pictures from No Kidding. Tiny children making Crow's tee-shirts. They look very real.'

Amanda sighs. Andy sighs. Paolo sighs so hard his sunglasses nearly fall off.

'Fakes,' Andy says. 'Photoshop. I'm sure you've done

it at school. It's easy.'

I sigh.

Somebody is lying. We don't know who. *Please* can I just go to the toilets and cry?

Then Crow says something. We're all pretty shocked. It's standard procedure at these meetings that Crow draws and I do the talking. But she sits there, looking perfectly composed, and talks straight to Andy.

'If you don't want to work with me any more, Mr Elat, I understand.'

Dead silence. We're all too shocked to speak.

She stands up. 'But I can't make Edie change. She's just . . . Edie. Thank you for everything, though. You've been so kind and amazing to me.'

Then she walks over, GIVES HIM A KISS ON THE CHEEK – a proper kiss, not an air one – and walks out of the room.

Oh. My. God.

I get up as quickly as I can and follow her out. I don't kiss anybody on the way. I have a bit of a kissing phobia at the moment.

Outside the room, we look at each other, eyes wide, and I suddenly find I don't want to cry in the toilets any more. I want to go out in the street and laugh. So does Crow.

We're not quite sure what we've done. But, weirdly, it felt good.

Chapter 19

We meet in Edie's room.

It's full of baskets of chocolates and teddy bears, from people saying congratulations about the award. This is odd, as anyone actually reading Edie's blog would know she's not remotely interested in chocolates or teddy bears. Baskets of calculators or textbooks, or chess sets, would have been great. But there aren't any of those.

She turns to me. 'Tell me again,' she says.

I've explained all about Paolo and the brand and the wooden boardroom, but the bit she keeps wanting to hear is Crow walking out at the end. We've described it five times and she still can't get over it.

'You did that for me?' she asks.

Crow shrugs. Edie interprets this as a yes and hugs her so tight she can hardly breathe.

'Was it like this?' Jenny asks, mincing around the room and twirling on her heel with a flourish. Any excuse for acting, these days.

'No,' we say. 'It wasn't.'

Of course we haven't asked Edie to put up that message they wrote for her, or to take down her banner. We might as well ask her to run around London in her underwear. Besides, it's too late now. All these new people are checking her site out and they all know what she really thinks.

Plus, two of Edie's chosen charities have been in touch to say that donations have noticeably gone up overnight, and thank you. Our HEADMISTRESS has emailed to say well done. And Phil from No Kidding has practically sent an essay on how great Edie is, and apologising all over again for hacking the site before Christmas. I bet he's feeling silly now.

We're all busy 'wowing' at all the emails, but Edie still wants to talk about the meeting.

'So what happens next? With Mr Elat?'

I copy Crow's shrug. We don't know. The only annoying thing about walking out of a meeting with your head held high is that the meeting carries on without you and people decide all sorts of crucial things while you're not there and you have to wait for them to update you.

We all go a bit quiet. Nobody wants to say out loud what we're thinking, which is to wonder whether Crow and I still have a job in fashion. And hey, no problem. If we don't, that just gives me more time to worry about my GCSEs.

Edie's mum puts her head round the door and

thankfully breaks the silence.

'We're having a big family lunch tomorrow. Edie needs feeding up after all this excitement. Would you like to come?'

You might expect Edie to have a pushy mother who's constantly trying to make her come top in maths and set running records, but actually no. Her mum's really chilled and spends most of the time worrying that Edie's overdoing it and trying to feed her up and make her listen to pop music 'like your other nice friends'. Unfortunately, Edie's mum only has one speciality dish and that's pizza, and once you've tried it you start to understand why Edie might be so slim. But it's a nice thought.

Jenny says sorry but she has a special meeting about her play. Crow's in the middle of several dresses, including final adjustments for the one Sigrid Santorini wants to wear in Italy. Edie looks at me in desperation. So far she's managed to convince her mum that we all adore pizza and can't get enough of it. I'd love to help out, but actually I'm busy too.

'Er, I'm very sorry,' I mumble. 'But I have a date.'

I say this as quietly as I possibly can. With Jenny in the room, I really really don't want to have this conversation.

'Ooh, DATE?' asks Edie's mum. The good news is she believes me and she's not offended. The bad news is she desperately wants to know more. 'With a boy?'

'Er, sort of,' I mutter, even more quietly.

'Who? *Alexander*?' Jenny explodes. 'You're going back

out with him? You're totally barmy!'

Edie's mum is so fascinated by this news that she sits down on the bed to join in. For some reason, friends' parents think we really enjoy discussing our love lives with them, and we're just waiting to ask their advice and hear all their anecdotes about what happened when they were teenagers.

I listen politely while she runs through some of her dates with *her* early boyfriends. I'm concentrating on not showing that the story about her snogging spotty youths to the strains of Duran Duran in the 1980s is TOO MUCH INFORMATION. When she's finished, Jenny goes on at me about Alexander's 'hidden agenda', then Edie tries to be helpful by suggesting nice little skirt-and-top combos I could wear to impress him. Only Crow stays silent. I love that girl.

I ignore all Edie's advice on outfits, obviously.

Today, I'm going for 'you didn't comment on my fabulous get-up last time, so now I really don't care'. Which means pixie boots (I rushed out and got some), a bias-cut slip, frayed at the hem where I tore the bottom off, hand-painted leggings and one of Harry's jackets with the sleeves rolled up, because I spilled hot chocolate on my old pink polar bear and it looks like it's got some sort of disease. And no fake eyelashes, because we're going on the London Eye, where the view is incredible, and I want to be able to see it unimpeded.

Alexander meets me by the fairground carousel near the Eye, wearing his usual designer jeans/linen scarf combo, and looking gorgeous and Robert Pattinson-ish. He smiles when he sees me, comes over, gives me a quick, sweat-free kiss on the lips and casually puts an arm around my waist. He doesn't mention his earlier lack of contact. Neither do I.

'Nice leggings, Boots. What's on them?'

'Swear words,' I explain. 'Italian ones. I'm learning them from my pen pal. He has a large vocabulary.'

'Cool.'

He guides me across the open queuing space, towards the giant wheel with capsules all round it that looks nothing like an eye at all (but 'The London Sort-of-like-a-clock-without-numbers' just wouldn't have worked so well), and when we get there it turns out we have a capsule all to ourselves, with a bottle of champagne and strawberries laid out ready.

YES!

We spend twenty-five minutes going round the wheel, looking at all my favourite sights in London, taking pictures of each other on our phones and talking about fun stuff like his new ballet and Edie's amazing award and the fabulousness of my pixie boots.

Then we walk along the Thames to the posh restaurant he's chosen to take me to. It's not a brilliant day. Cold and cloudy, with a strong breeze coming off the river. But that just means that Alexander has to put his arm more tightly around me and I can smell his lemony aftershave.

For a while, that boardroom seems miles away. I am on a date! And I am having a good time! The only thing that would make it better would be for Crow, Jenny and Edie to be in a café somewhere along the South Bank, watching me enjoy myself so much.

We get to the restaurant, which is posher than I'm used to (Mum says why waste money on white tablecloths when I prefer burgers anyway?), and I have no idea what to choose so Alexander orders for me. We talk more about ballet and running a catwalk show and our favourite bits of Paris. The food comes and I hardly notice I'm eating it. There's Thing With Vegetables. Followed by Thing With Chocolate Sauce. Tastes fine. Don't care. I'm with the best-looking man in the room and he is SO flirting with me.

Then after lunch he's meeting up with some friends so it's time to say goodbye. The champagne has kicked in by now and I'm feeling wobbly and not totally well. I'm expecting him to walk me to the Tube, but instead he walks me to a bench overlooking the river. A cold, windy bench. Oh dear.

We sit down and he does that thing where he suddenly whips under me and I find myself sitting on his lap. I look across at his upper lip, hoping for the best, but no, they've started. The little beads of sweat are slowly appearing. He's half-closing his eyes, going in for the kill.

My whole body is screaming EW EW EW, but it's too

late now. He's bought me lunch.

We go through the whole rigmarole again. His lip is sweaty. He pokes his tongue around. I keep my jaw firmly shut. He keeps his eyes closed and looks transported. I wish he would be. And then, finally, it's over.

Am I allergic to kissing? Do I have some sort of medical condition? Is it only me?

'See you, Boots,' he says, with his confident smile.

And he's off. And I'm left alone on the windy bench, feeling dizzy and wondering where the Tube is.

I'm sure it's not supposed to be like this.

Chapter 20

Luckily, at school on Monday Jenny and Edie forget to ask me about the date. Unluckily, it's because we have other things to worry about.

Sigrid Santorini to make West End debut.

Hollywood actress hits London.

New play gets star treatment.

We're in the school library. Edie has fanned all the papers out. I'm giving Jenny a hug and she's crying as quietly as she can, so the librarian doesn't notice.

'That's what they called the meeting about yesterday,' Jenny explains. 'They wanted to share the "good news" before it hit the papers.'

Sigrid has 'graciously agreed' to step in at the last minute and take the place of the actress who was mysteriously sacked from Jenny's play. We know that 'graciously agreed' means that as soon as she found out about *Her Father's Daughter* from Edie, Sigrid set about cosying up to the director and setting herself up for a starring role. Something to keep her busy after her new movie was scrapped.

Poor Edie is upset too, for giving Sigrid all the information she needed about the play, but it wasn't her fault. Even Jenny has to admit this. Once a girl like Sigrid gets an idea, there's nothing you can do to stop her. And you never know what she's going to do next.

She's part of a trend. Some Hollywood movie stars aren't happy with earning gazillions and being on thousands of cinema screens. For a little while at least, they like to be 'simple acting folk' and earn a tiny amount of money appearing live on stage to a small audience. And some of their favourite stages to act on are ours, in London, which are as close to the stages that Shakespeare performed on as you can physically get. Although I don't think Shakespeare did *Phantom of the Opera*.

Mum takes me to see the big names sometimes, when we can get tickets, and they're mesmerising. It's kind of strange seeing them normal size, as opposed to three metres high and in Technicolor, but you get used to it.

We're not the only ones who enjoy going, of course. The plays usually sell out. Now, *Her Father's Daughter* will too. In fact, the Boat House isn't big enough. With a Hollywood name involved, especially one who's going out with the New Teenage Sex God, the backers have managed to get the play transferred to a major West End venue at the end of its run. *That's* why there was talk about a new theatre. Everybody is thrilled.

Jenny is devastated.

'It's not *her*, particularly,' she mumbles. 'I'm not in that many scenes with her and I'm supposed to hate her in the play, so that bit's easy. It's the whole publicity thing. Look!'

We look. Every paper has a piece about the play. Even the *Financial Times*, which is where Edie spotted it this morning, naturally. We know what Jenny's thinking. From now on, there will be paparazzi outside the rehearsal studio. It will be worse once the play opens. Everyone will have their picture taken on the way in, clutching their coffees, and on their way home, looking tired and drawn. Jenny's every spot breakout will be analysed in celebrity magazines. And if she's rubbish again, like she was in her movie, everyone in London and half the country will know.

Apart from that, it's great news.

'Was Sigrid at the meeting?' I ask.

Jenny nods. 'She was her usual, bouncy self. She said she was totally psyched to be working with us all, and just to treat her like any normal actress. She was wearing a mink jacket.'

Edie growls. I've never heard her growl before. It's quite scary.

Jenny goes on. 'They're giving us an extra week of rehearsals to let Sigrid get up to speed. The director says he's decided to make the stepmother character even younger, so she's twenty-two instead of thirty-two. He says it adds tension to the mother-daughter relationship. And they've decided to expand the part slightly, to give Sigrid more to do.'

'How slightly is "slightly"?' Edie asks.

I remember the picture of Sigrid and the director coming out of that club. Her dress was minuscule and he was looking extremely happy. I'm betting 'slightly' is 'really quite a lot'.

'She's coming to rehearsals tomorrow,' Jenny says. 'They've given us the day off while Bill does some rewriting. She's already texted me to say how thrilled she is to be acting with me, and that I must have a lot to teach her. I think she did that to everyone.'

Jenny says this with a straight face, but we all suspect that this is Sigrid-speak for 'how lucky you are to be working with me and you have so much to learn from me'.

'I'm sure it'll be fine,' I tell her, holding out my hand to touch hers. It's the best I can think of.

'Sure, as long as Sigrid has a personality transplant,' Edie adds glumly.

I give her the Look, but she ignores me. She's too busy looking surprised when Jenny starts crying again.

On Tuesday, Alexander texts me after school suggesting a club in Chelsea where I happen to know the cocktails cost £100. Mum says I absolutely categorically cannot go. This is a mega-relief, although of course I'd never tell her.

How many sweaty kisses is a £100 cocktail worth?

He texts back in the middle of my *Romeo and Juliet* essay, suggesting an evening viewing at the National Portrait Gallery instead. I happen to love the National Portrait Gallery. If you're obsessed with clothes it's perfect: men and women in some of the most incredible fashions through history. And I love evening viewings, when it's quieter, and the light's more interesting, and you come out into the London night afterwards.

I know how it's going to go. Great date. Lots of interesting conversation. Then a bench somewhere. I'm tempted to say no, but Jenny will be SO full of herself if I do that I can't bear it. I say yes and pretend to myself that I'm looking forward to it.

Two seconds later, the phone goes and I think, Oh no, he wants to talk about it. I answer warily. Even more so, when I discover it's actually Amanda Elat on the other end. What have we done now?

'Hi, Nonie,' she says brightly, in a sucking-up sort of way. 'How *are* you?'

'Fine,' I say cautiously.

'Oh, *good*. How's Crow?'

I think this is code for 'Has Crow said anything about the truly scary experience she had at our offices three days ago?' And she hasn't said much on the subject, so I say in code back, 'Er, fine.'

'Great!' Amanda bubbles. 'Fantastic!'

I wonder if this is code for 'I'm really sorry we gave

you both such a horrible time and please can we start again?'

But I'm not sure, so I don't say anything. There's a long silence over the phone.

'Are you still there?' she asks, eventually.

'Yes,' I say.

'Right.' She's panting a bit now. I wish I knew what she wanted so we could get it over with.

'Edie hasn't changed her mind about the website, I'm afraid,' I add, to speed things up.

'Oh, don't worry about that,' she says lightly.

Excuse me? DON'T WORRY?

We've just sat round a big, scary table with lots of people staring at their cappuccinos because what's happening is so awful they can't bear to look at us, and then we've walked out of the meeting with the super-terrifying supremo who runs the company, and she says, 'Don't worry'?

'We're working on it,' she says. 'And I'm sorry about Saturday. But something you said has given us an idea.'

I stare at the phone. It was weird on Saturday but this is weirder.

'I've got some thoughts I'd like to discuss with you,' she continues. 'Can you fit in a meeting? I could come to you, if that makes it easier. And Crow's finalising some party dresses, isn't she? I bet they're fabulous. I'd love to see them.'

Fabulous? What about 'preposterous' and 'disastrous' and 'lose me millions'?

We fix a time for Amanda to come round. When she rings off, I go back up to the top of the house and find Mum in her cubbyhole office, texting on her BlackBerry.

She sees the look on my face and pauses mid-sentence. 'What is it, darling?'

I explain the conversation I've just had. Mum laughs.

'Remember when you told Alexander you were too busy to talk to him? What happened next?'

Three offers of dates is what happened next. And a windy bench.

'You played hard to get. Without meaning to. This is the same story.'

'You mean the Elats are *flirting* with us?'

'Sort of. Crow's reminded them how valuable she is to them. She's just done an incredibly successful high-street collection for them. And what did they do? They invited you both in and made you miserable.'

'Andy said we might lose him millions.'

'He forgot to mention that you might *make* him millions. He was a clever man to find Crow and he's clever enough not to let her go.'

'But what about Edie? And the award? And "Cheap Clothes Cost Lives"?'

Mum smiles. 'Amanda said she'd fix it, didn't she? See what she comes up with. Just don't do anything you don't believe in.'

I give Mum a hug and go to my room and sit on my bed, trying to work things out.

One thing I know for sure: my mum is amazing and a very useful person to know at times like this. She may be slightly too addicted to her BlackBerry, but I love her.

Everything else is a mess. Why are people nice to you when you're mean to them? How does that work? And how can Amanda possibly fix the mess with Edie? And what exactly *is* it I believe in?

Well, I believe in Crow. I go down to the workroom, where she's fiddling with a ball-dress made out of green and gold ribbons that's so lovely you could just sit and stare at it for hours. I tell her what Amanda said, and Mum too.

'What do you think?' I ask her.

Crow ponders for a moment.

'I think I've unbalanced it by putting this corsage on the shoulder.'

She starts unpinning and hands the pins to me as she goes. You have to concentrate on this job, or it gets painful.

'I *meant* about Amanda.'

'We'll find out when she comes,' she answers with one of her shrugs.

'Yes, but what d'you think in the *meantime*?'

Crow turns to look at me as if I'm crazy and repeats, 'In the *meantime*, that corsage wasn't working. I'll do something more delicate. With wire, maybe.'

I'm about to flip out, but then I suddenly realise what she's saying. She means she's not going to waste that bit of her brain that could be thinking about corsages by worrying about Amanda Elat, when there's nothing she can do about it now anyway. As a plan of action, it's not as dumb as I thought.

In fact, how about if I used it myself? *I* could stop worrying about Amanda and use that part of *my* brain to think about Alexander. And how to manage the whole windy bench scenario. Which, come to think of it, is entirely avoidable if I . . .

I give Crow a big surprise hug and she screams. Oops. Forgot about the pins. Luckily there's only a tiny drop of blood on her arm and none of it goes on the dress. She sucks the wound better and glares at me.

'What?' she asks accusingly.

'Just that you're a genius, that's all.'

'Oh, *that*,' she says, and giggles. 'You think the wire will work, then?'

'I have no idea,' I call behind me. 'I've got to practise something.'

Chapter 21

Two evenings later, my National Portrait Gallery date with Alexander starts well. He is beautiful. He greets me with a smile and a gentle kiss on my forehead, as he sweeps my hair away from my face. His fingers are as long as ever and they gently touch mine as we walk round the paintings. He waits as I spend ages looking at the Elizabethans, admiring their ruffs and corsets and jewellery. I wait as he spends ages looking at the contemporary portraits of performers, including ballet dancers. I suspect he's partly planning his own portrait, for when the time comes.

We talk about ballet and fashion and the usual stuff and it's lovely. Then he takes me down the street to Trafalgar Square. I see him heading towards a fountain's edge, where we could possibly sit down in the moonlight. The time has come.

I initiate 'Operation Prada', which I thought up in Crow's workroom. I have deliberately worn my super-high platforms tonight, even though I suspect Alexander doesn't really like them. I pretend to twist my ankle and collapse in agony.

He calls me a taxi. I get in it and he gives me a quick peck on the lips goodbye, looking worried. I smile bravely.

YES!

'You're home early,' Harry says when I get in.

He's in the kitchen, making himself some toast and looking sorry for himself.

'I twisted my ankle,' I explain, putting more bread in the toaster. 'It's very painful.'

Harry looks down at my un-swollen ankle. I've forgotten that I cannot lie to my brother. I've tried over many years but it rarely works.

'Rubbish kisser?' he asks.

HOW DID HE KNOW?

'Svetlana said something,' he adds with a strange, lopsided smile. 'A rumour. Not to be repeated, of course.'

I look up at him sharply. I can't lie to him and he can't really hide things from me.

That look on his face when he mentioned Svetlana. And the way he said '*said*'. Like they're not talking any more. He's not looking too cheerful right now, either.

'Everything OK?' I ask.

'Yup,' he says.

We look at each other uncertainly over our toast and

then retire to the sitting room to watch reruns of our favourite programmes. But they're all about relationships or models, so we give up and end up watching something about police cameras, which is so boring we fall asleep in front of it and Mum has to wake us up for bed.

Chapter 22

The next Miss Teen meeting is very different from the last one.

For a start, it's in our kitchen, rather than the boardroom, and instead of staring silently at her cappuccino, Amanda starts by chatting in a friendly way about who we're all going to see at London Fashion Week this time around and how much she's looking forward to it.

Then she mentions how pieces from the Jewels collection are already becoming collectors' items on eBay. Versions of the dress Svetlana wore are being sold for hundreds of pounds – several times the amount they charged for them at Miss Teen. We talk about the magazines that have featured Crow's party dresses on actresses and It-girls, and how a couple of boutiques are thinking of selling the couture stuff.

Mum's right. Amanda's definitely flirting, in her own, strange way. But why?

Still with her polite face on, Amanda asks how the new

high-street designs are coming along. Crow brings out her sketchbooks and we look through them. They still haven't changed much. Each one is a riot of textures, colours and Paris-type trimmings and looks just as undoable as ever.

Maybe she was just lucky with her Jewels collection – that it worked so well for a high-street store. Maybe she can't really do 'commercial' and she should just stick to her normal dresses for party girls who can afford the amazing prices. Maybe I should just stick to helping her with those.

I asked Crow about changing her style to suit what they said at Miss Teen, and her shrug was almost painful to watch.

'This is what was in my head,' she said at last. 'I *can't* change it. I'd ask Yvette what to do, but . . .'

Yvette is now resting in peace in Père Lachaise cemetery in Paris and we miss her SO much. We both started getting a bit tearful at this point and changed the subject.

'When do you need everything to be ready by?' I ask Amanda.

'I'm afraid the original deadline's gone. We're too late for a winter launch. We could potentially do a summer one next year. But that means *completely* new designs. And we can't really finalise anything until we've sorted things out with Edie. Since that blogging award, a few people have actually returned the pieces they bought in December, saying they can't wear them because they're not ethical enough. We just can't risk that happening again.'

Great! I think, despite myself. Good on them.

'Oh dear,' I say out loud. 'What are you going to do?'

Amanda grins. 'Nothing! It's what *you're* going to do.'

She leans back and waits for us to ask her what she means, which we do.

'You're going to see the truth for yourselves. You said it, Nonie. Edie won't believe it until she sees it with her own eyes. We're going to send you to India.'

WHAT?

Is there a shop on Oxford Street called India? Or does she mean the country?

Crow and I both look very confused.

'Mumbai!' Amanda says. 'Dad's arranging for you all to go. You can stay for a few days, look round the factory, see for yourselves and do some sightseeing too. Crow's very first collection was inspired by the colours of India, wasn't it? It'll be good to see them close up.'

'What about school?' I ask. I hate to do this. It's awful reminding people you're only a teenager. But it will be worse to have to say we haven't got permission to go. And then it *really* hits me. I go cold and my tummy shrivels. 'We've got GCSEs next term.'

'We've thought of that. You'll go in the Easter holidays,' she explains. 'We'll talk to your parents about exams. Maybe we can get you some extra tuition. And in the meantime, good news! We have a very special client who wants a dress. A special dress for a major occasion and she wants Crow to make it. Dad's thrilled. This girl is pure publicity. *Good* publicity.'

AHA! *This* is the reason she's sucking up to us so much. I *knew* there had to be one. Then everything clicks together. I don't even bother to ask who it is. I know before she says it.

'It's Sigrid Santorini again. She's *such* a star. Lucky you!'

Chapter 23

It's February. This time last year, I was putting the finishing touches to Crow's Fashion Week catwalk show. I was surrounded by notes about models, hair, makeup, music, and requests to be in the front row.

This year, the invitations to other people's shows are jammed into the frame of my dressing table mirror – so many I can hardly see myself (which is good, given the total wonkiness of my hair right now). But the only notes I have lying about are revision notes for GCSE mock exams. I have a feeling it's not going to be as much fun this time.

We're planning to go to lots of shows, but going to one and organising one are two different things. I thought I would miss it a bit, but I don't. I miss it MASSIVELY. I miss it so much it physically hurts. I miss the near panic, the frantic phone calls, the certainty that nothing will be ready, the genius ideas for eyeshadow and shoes, the constant arrival of packages with props, the joy of seeing

Crow's incredible designs coming together into a story that will make people gasp with pleasure. The total, happy exhaustion when it's over. The feeling of being a working part of the fashion world, instead of on the side-lines, just looking at it.

Hopefully we'll get another go, but if we don't sort things out with Andy in the next few weeks, we can say goodbye to the kind of budget you need to put on a show. I feel shaky at the niggling thought in the back of my mind that it may never happen again. It's amazing how quickly you can get addicted to something if you're not careful.

It would be nice if somebody asked me how I was coping with being a spectator this year, but nobody does. Everybody seems to have something else on their mind right now.

Edie is busy making lists of shops we're not supposed to visit because of their doubtful ethical practices, and checking all the health advice about visiting India. She has ALREADY DONE most of the revision for GCSEs, even though they're months away, so she's not particularly worried about the exam part, just excited to travel. Weird. I think I know Edie so well and she surprises me every other day.

Jenny is busy calling or texting me every five minutes to say her play is changing out of recognition and she can't bear to talk about it. Sigrid is SO the Queen of Evil.

Alexander is busy trying to find out whether my ankle

is better so we can go out on another date. I've told him it's healing slowly.

Mum is busy stressing about my exams, but Dad has managed to persuade her that I really can't miss the India trip. He's suggested it'll help with my geography, which is quite funny. My geography is beyond help, but it was nice of him to try. Mum's also stressed about Harry, who's supposed to be planning for his degree show in June, but is 'moping about the house like a wet dishcloth' or playing soulful Russian folk songs very loudly in his room.

You'd have thought Crow, at least, would be missing Fashion Week as much as me, but if she is, she doesn't show it. Instead she's suddenly busy designing the most complicated, expensive dress she's ever produced.

Sigrid has been invited to a party in honour of the film industry at the Elysée Palace in Paris next month. The French President himself will be hosting it. And his wife, the ex-model, will be there. And enough paparazzi to fill the Eurostar. *That*'s the major occasion she needs the dress for.

It's in a different league from the Italian awards thing. Pictures of the guests arriving at the Elysée Palace will be on the TV news and in every paper and newsy fashion magazine, and half the fashion blogs on the internet. Fashion designers will be falling over themselves to dress the stars. John Galliano is probably doing a dress for someone. And Alberta Ferretti. And Alber Elbaz for

Lanvin, and the Valentino people (Valentino himself has retired to his yacht, as you do), and all my heroes. And Sigrid will be one of the prettiest, and one of the most photographed, people there.

For once, Crow can let her imagination run away with her. There is no such thing as 'undoable', or even 'unaffordable'. If Crow wants twenty metres of hand-dyed ultramarine silk so she can do some clever pleating, that's fine. If she needs amethysts and turquoises to sparkle on the bodice, that's great. If she has to hire a top professional French embroideress to complete the details on the waist and the train, fantastic.

The Sigrid dress can finally use her ideas from Paris and bring them to life. With Andy Elat's official approval it will have jewels. It will have sequins. It will have silver thread. The embroidery will be so complicated that it can only be done by one woman, who lives outside Toulouse and uses techniques handed down from the sixteenth century. It will cost so much to produce that Crow's whole village in Uganda could live on the money for a year. But hopefully the publicity will be worth a fortune and Andy Elat will be a happy man again.

One way of taking my mind off the shows is to go downstairs to the workroom and help. If I wear a padded bra and stand on a step, I'm about the same height and shape as Sigrid, and Crow can use me as a model to imagine her new creation.

My version is less exotic. I'm wearing the *toile*, which is made out of thin cream cotton and will make the pattern. Zero jewels. Zip embroidery. At the moment, I actually look as if I'm off to a toga party. But I get the idea of how it will be when it's finished and it will look as though Sigrid has risen from the sea like some sort of sparkling underwater goddess, picking up loads of precious stones on the way.

It will be incredible and will make the Swan dress she wore last year seem like a kindergarten smock.

I love to think of myself as a 'house model'. Normally that means 'design house', not 'your own house', of course. It sounds so romantic. I pretend the step and padded bra aren't required and Coco Chanel is fitting stuff onto me. Or at least I did until I discovered that Coco Chanel could be pretty mean on a bad day. Now we pretend it's Dior himself. Crow isn't the most perfect reincarnation of a middle-aged French bloke, but when she says, 'And now, mam'selle, please 'old still for ze mastair,' it makes me giggle so hard I end up with pin-pricks all over.

After the fitting, I do a mental calculation of the cost of the silk, plus the jewels, plus the embroideress, plus Crow's time to do it. It's an extremely large number. Needless to say, Sigrid isn't paying for this. We are. Or rather, Andy Elat is. Sigrid will borrow it and then, if we're lucky, we may one day sell it to a rich client. A VERY rich client. Or a museum.

* * *

'You're not worried, are you?' I ask. 'About working with such expensive stuff?'

Crow looks at me as if I'm completely bonkers. I don't know why I bothered to mention it.

'Nothing else will give the effect,' she says, wide-eyed.

Nothing except the most expensive silk in the world and a bucketful of gemstones.

'What if you spill something on it?' I don't mean to be negative, but I can't help thinking of my polar bear jacket, which is pretty much ruined.

Crow gives me another look. 'I don't spill stuff.'

This is true. I am the stuff-spiller in this household.

'Probably best if I don't pop by too often while you're working on the proper dress, then,' I say, assuming she'll laugh and tell me not to be silly.

She doesn't.

Chapter 24

Soon, Jenny gets pictured in two magazines slurping a smoothie on her way to rehearsals, alongside unfavourable comments about her jeans and unwashed hair and parka jacket.

'Where is the glamour-puss we knew last year?' they wonder sadly. As if she's supposed to go to a studio in south London dressed in Louboutins and a Burberry mac.

Somehow Sigrid manages to dress down for the same rehearsals and get universal sighs of appreciation. Her hair is always shiny. She's in jeans, but they're skinny, frayed and totally on-trend. She's in a biker jacket, but it's soft leather (not mink this time) and every fashionista wants one. She's in a tee-shirt, but it's a vintage one as worn by two of her friends in Hollywood and everyone loves it. She's not wearing makeup, but the fashion press find this 'authentic' and 'a sign of her dedication to taking acting back to basics'.

There are no pictures of her swanning around inside the studio, insisting on fresh, warm water with a hint of lemon every thirty seconds and wondering if it wouldn't be possible to have 'just a *little* bit more to say' in every speech.

Jim, the actor playing Jenny's father, hates her to bits. He is mostly left to nod and look amazed and adoring as Sigrid drones on with her new, expanded part. He and Jenny have completely bonded, which is strange since he plays a man we all find impossibly irritating in real life.

Everyone else, though, finds Sigrid adorable. The director dotes on her. The other actors want her autograph and love the anecdotes about Hollywood life and going out with Joe Yule, the Not-So-New Teenage Sex God. They even love it when she gets a text in mid-scene and STOPS REHEARSING TO READ IT, in case it's from Joe. And the stagehands and other backstage people keep going on about how thoughtful she is, arriving every day with a box of fresh doughnuts and asking after their pets. Only Bill, Jenny's friend, looks slightly grumpy each time he's asked to rewrite a scene to make the stepmother part younger, prettier and more centre-stage.

'The thing is,' Jenny says, 'they all know the play will be a success because of her. They all think I must be so incredibly grateful she wore one of my friend's dresses at the Oscars last year. They've all gone to see it at the V&A, you know. She took them there. It was like a little tour party. It was sickening. And because I know Joe, she thinks I'll want to hear all the lovey-dovey things he's doing, like sending flowers to her hotel every day and making playlists for her and tweeting about her on Twitter.'

'Ew,' I say. There is no other word. 'Ew' captures it exactly.

Despite ourselves, we look up the tweets.

Still missing darling @sigsantorini. Just sent her a little something to say 'Happy Monday'.

'What was it?' I ask.

'The letter S made out of twenty-seven diamonds on a platinum chain,' Jenny sighs. 'And a matching charm bracelet.'

We read on.

Thinking about @sigsantorini in London. Her play's in two weeks. She'll be dynamite. Check it out.

At this point, Joe gives the website of the Boat House.

'Their site crashed, obviously,' Jenny points out. 'Took a day to fix it. They were thrilled.'

We make ourselves miserable for a while longer, then Jenny remembers to ask me about Alexander.

'So? Is it true love?'

I was in fact just about to tell her about the fake swollen ankle, but her tone is so mocking that I'm instantly furious.

'It might be,' I say. 'We're going out again next week.'

Which means that unfortunately I have to text him

and suggest a date. He accepts instantly and sends round a big bunch of flowers to say 'Happy better ankle'. It must be a star performer thing. Now I understand how florists and jewellers stay in business.

Chapter 25

With Jenny's opening night just over a week away, Edie calls us to a lunch-break meeting in the cafeteria.

'I've made a list of all the main health hazards of visiting the Indian subcontinent,' she says, as if that's a perfectly normal thing to do, 'and it's not too bad. But the important thing is not to drink the water or eat salad.'

'Cool,' I point out. 'So we can live on burgers and Coke.'

Edie looks as though she'd love to disagree with me from a nutritional point of view, but is forced to admit that from a healthcare perspective, yes, that would be a good idea.

'Or what?' asks Jenny. It's always details with Jenny.

'Or bugs,' Edie says. Her eyes go so wide she looks like a bug herself. 'Bad ones. You spend your whole time on the loo.'

'Lucky I'm not going then,' Jenny smiles.

Edie looks shocked. 'Not going? Why?'

Jenny and I look shocked back.

'Because of her play, silly,' I say. 'It'll be transferring to the West End when we get back. Of course she can't go.'

Edie still looks amazed. 'But this is India. The chance of a lifetime.'

'So's the West End,' I point out. Jenny's still too shocked to speak. 'It's the biggest deal you can get. Huge. She needs all the practice she can get. Everyone in theatre will be watching. It'll be a major event.'

I've been thinking about Edie's dimness all this time, not about Jenny's nervousness. Then I notice Jenny's gone green.

'Excuse me,' she says, and rushes out.

It looks as though it's not only bugs that make you need the loo. Sometimes your friends can too.

After my quick text about going out, Alexander texts me back with lots of suggestions. One of them is going to see a comedy horror movie that's had great reviews. He says he's going with a bunch of friends. This sounds fun and bench-free, so I'm happy to say yes.

We meet up at a cool cinema in Notting Hill. I'm back in my pixie boots and remembering to limp slightly. All his friends turn out to be incredibly thin, pale and beautiful. They stand with straight backs and their feet turned out, or drape themselves elegantly on available surfaces. They are clearly ballet dancers and don't even need to wear linen scarves to prove it.

They are all very nice to me, even though I'm by far the youngest, and they like my new fake fur mini-dress (I miss the pink polar bear). One of the boys is from Belgium and insists on chatting to me in French while we queue for our tickets. So I chat in French back.

I am metropolitan and multilingual and totally amazing, basically. Once again I have made a good dating decision and I wish Jenny could be here to see me. All I need now is for the movie to be as good as everyone says it is and this will be a near-perfect evening.

But I never find out how good the movie is because I don't get to see it.

Just after the bit where they tell you to switch off your mobile phones, Alexander turns round in his seat and lowers his sweaty face onto mine. FOR FIVE MINUTES. Well, it might be a bit less but it feels like fifty years so it's probably about that. Then he breaks for air and I manage to watch a couple of funny set-up scenes until he turns round and DOES IT AGAIN.

Does the man have no shame? Do his friends not care? Am I supposed to come back and actually watch the movie some other time?

The third time, I open my teeth a bit just to see if the tongue-in-mouth thing is as bad as I feared. And it is. His tongue is hard and pointy and although I guess it can't be sweaty, it feels as though it is. This is so awful I'm suddenly living a horror movie of my own, except this one isn't a comedy and if you close your eyes you can't block it out.

At which point I finally realise that I DON'T FANCY ALEXANDER. I should have known ages ago.

I like the floppy hair. I like the Robert Pattinson overtones – anyone would. I like the long fingers and the muscly legs, but I don't like being called Boots and I don't like not knowing if I can eat chips or not and I don't like HIS FACE COMING ANYWHERE NEAR ME.

Which is not ideal in a boyfriend.

Suddenly I think of Crow and it's easy to know what to do. I wait for him to finish, trying not to picture the last horror movie I went to, where a giant spider landed on someone's face. Then I pull away, give him a gentle peck on the cheek and say, 'Sorry, got to go.' I get up and walk out of the cinema and don't look back.

It was a lot easier than I expected. And I feel so relieved, I know I've done the right thing. I'm also very glad that Jenny isn't here to see me on my date after all.

She'd be laughing so hard she'd probably rupture something and not be able to do her play.

Chapter 26

I make sure I'm not around when Jenny finds out. I tell Edie and Edie tells her, but Edie then tells me how hysterically funny Jenny found the whole thing, so I might just as well have told her myself.

Somehow the story gets out at home. Harry finds it so amusing he stops playing sad Russian folk songs for several hours. Mum tries to be sympathetic but you can tell she saw it coming.

I hate it when mothers can see things coming. It's a deeply irritating trait of theirs and they should pretend very hard that everything's a big surprise.

Only Crow is suitably shocked and sympathetic, so I talk to her about it for ages while she works on the new dress for Sigrid. She nods and doesn't say much, which is ideal (apart from reminding me not to come too close). Also, watching her work, it's occasionally possible to forget about Alexander and sweat and cinemas. Sometimes, it's just about fashion.

* * *

I avoid Jenny for a couple of days, but in the end, she begs to meet up and as the play's about to start, I can't really say no. Jenny doesn't have too many friends at school because lots of girls don't really know how to behave around someone who's been in a blockbuster movie and on a TV chat show and who's 'best friends' with the girlfriend of a Teenage Sex God. (The answer is 'normally', by the way, but that doesn't occur to them, whereas 'meanly' often does.) And Edie's usually busy doing clubs or telling people not to buy clothes, so if I don't talk to Jenny, there's a danger nobody will.

We make our usual date at the V&A café on Saturday, after Jenny's rehearsal. She arrives in her Vuitton scarf again, and she's taken to winding it round her face so she looks a bit like a copper-haired Michael Jackson. She sits down and I spot two separate tables of people taking photos of her on their mobile phones. For the first five minutes she has to keep stopping to sign autographs. Then she takes the scarf off so she can do proper justice to her smoothie, and people seem not to notice her so much any more. We get the chance to chat.

'I don't want to say I told you so,' she says, so that the words 'I told you so' linger over the table.

I sigh. Might as well get it over with.

'You mean about Alexander?'

'Who else?'

'OK. But he wasn't exactly horrible. He didn't

two-time me or anything. He just wasn't . . .'

'What? Sexy? Interesting? Nice?'

'My type,' I say lamely.

'Oh yeah,' she grins. 'Well, you see what they're like now. Sorry you had to learn the hard way.'

She doesn't look remotely sorry. And I'm not convinced she's right. I don't think *all* men are like that. Harry's lovely, for a start, when he's not teasing me. And my dad. It's not my fault if Jenny's unlucky. But I've promised myself to be nice. The only answer is to change the subject.

'How are you feeling? Are you ready for the first night?'

The colour drains from her face. 'As ready as I'll ever be. Anthony says he thinks we're not *total* disasters.'

Anthony Lyle is the director of *Her Father's Daughter*. Jenny's movie director used to make her miserable by complaining about everything she did, including the way she *looked* at people. From what she's said about Anthony, he's the opposite: he hardly says anything to her at all.

'Has he been any more helpful recently?'

'No, not really,' she mutters glumly. 'He's too busy taking Sigrid through her lines and making sure she's happy with her water and asking whether Joe Yule has texted recently. He let us go early today so he could stay behind with her and sort out something that was bugging her. He usually does. I have to rely on Jim to make sure I'm doing everything OK.'

Jim is the one playing the dad character. He and Jenny have formed the SIRTQOE society, which stands for Sigrid Is Really The Queen Of Evil. So far they're the only members. They don't dare ask anyone else, in case they mysteriously have to 'spend more time with their families', like Caroline – the woman who originally had Sigrid's part.

'I'm sure you're brilliant,' I say loyally.

Jenny smiles a sad, wistful, actressy smile. 'I hope so. I want to be. I mean, it's lovely on that stage. I really enjoy it. It's just the audience bit that worries me. You know . . . after . . . everything.'

She means after being compared to dining room furniture the last time she performed beside a Hollywood star.

'Anyway,' she sighs, 'here are the tickets. You can see for yourself on Wednesday.'

She hands over an envelope and I can feel the tickets inside it. For a moment, I feel vaguely sick myself. The last time someone gave me tickets it was my soon-to-be-ex-boyfriend and we all know what happened next.

'Looking forward to it,' I lie, while my insides scrunch themselves up on Jenny's behalf.

'Yeah,' she says, sighing. Then she puts her Michael Jackson outfit back on and we slink through the museum, past the Queen of Evil Oscar dress in its shiny display case, and out into the early spring rain that captures our feelings exactly.

Chapter 27

Wednesday comes. I'm expecting paparazzi everywhere, but amazingly there are only a few. This is partly because the play is on in one of the smallest theatres in London. Also because a big new musical is opening tonight on the other side of town. And because none of the major critics are going yet. They're waiting until *Her Father's Daughter* transfers to the West End, where most of the audience will see it.

This is just how Jenny wants it. It also helps that Sigrid has told Joe Yule to stay away for now, so she can get the chance to act in a bit of privacy. When Jenny told me, it was the first time I heard her talk about that girl without sounding as though she was about to cry. For once, they were just two scared young actresses, doing their best and hoping people would like them.

Until Sigrid decided to celebrate their opening night by presenting everyone involved in the play with a boxed set of her and Joe's movies on DVD, and a signed photo of them both in a silver frame. So now it's one scared young actress and one CRAZED CELEBRITY and we're back to normal.

I've never been to the Boat House Theatre before. It's down a little alleyway that you think will just lead to a dirty bit of river, but in fact leads to a tiny square, with a rickety half-timbered building at one end. There's no room inside for people to mill about, so the square – which has been hung with fairy lights – is full of theatre-goers drinking out of plastic cups and chatting excitedly about the play.

Because it's the opening night, lots of the audience are family and friends. I've come with Mum and Harry and we quickly catch sight of Jenny's mum, looking incredibly nervous and drinking too fast out of her plastic cup. We go over, and Mum tells her how fabulous Jenny will be and how proud she must be of her talented daughter. Mum is SO good at this stuff. Jenny's mum looks totally grateful and starts sipping slower.

When we get inside, the theatre is what Mum would call 'intimate' and Harry and I would call 'cramped'. It's not much bigger than our school hall. Everything is painted black and there's no curtain. Or opera glasses. Or space. There's only about two hundred of us there and we're all perched on top of each other, in practically vertical rows. The seats are hard – many of them are just benches, really. But the whole effect isn't miserable. It's actually quite jolly. It's as if everyone enjoys suffering a little to see what their friends can do on stage and to share the experience. I wouldn't be surprised if someone started a sing-along while we were waiting.

Then the lights go down. My tummy is the size of a pea, in sympathy with what Jenny must be feeling right now. Honestly, with the amount I've been through recently I'm surprised I can even digest.

Luckily, though, Jenny's friend Bill isn't known as a brilliant playwright for nothing. When the play gets going it's surprisingly funny and, after all the conversations about line-hogging by Sigrid, Jenny has more to say than I expected. Everyone on stage seems to be enjoying themselves and they should be. So are we.

As they take their bows, Jenny looks happier than I've seen her for weeks. Almost as happy as she did before Sigrid joined the production. The colour's back in her cheeks and she's soaking up the applause, which is loud and long and enthusiastic. I'm glad she decided to do the play. Hopefully she can rebuild her confidence after the *Kid Code* disaster. She deserves to. I know I'm her friend and I'm biased and everything, but she was great and I'm totally proud of her.

Next day, Edie, Jenny and I go back to my room after school and trawl the papers and the internet for news about the play. There are, of course, loads of pictures of Sigrid arriving at the theatre, and leaving it, with her sunglasses and her 'I'm an authentic actress, please no pictures right now' face on. But, with most people waiting for the West End version, there are only four tiny reviews.

All of them are about six lines long, but are very complimentary about the play and everyone in it. Everyone points out how stunning Sigrid is in the flesh. And a couple of people also mention what a surprisingly good actress Jenny is 'for a sixteen-year-old'. She's obviously better when movie cameras aren't involved.

'What d'you think?' I ask.

Jenny beams happily. This is exactly what she hoped for.

We even check on Twitter.

@sigsantorini was totally awesome, says Joe Yule, as if he was there. He forgets to mention the play, or any of the other people in it, but then, he's not going out with them.

By now, Jenny has to head off for her next performance. Her phone goes and it's a text from Sigrid. 'I'm with Crow. The mom says ur here. Wanna share a car?'

This is a bit creepy. When you're Googling someone famous on the internet, you don't usually expect them to be downstairs in your friend's house, texting you. But then we remember – a dress fitting. She must have been trying on the sea-goddess dress for Crow. We troop downstairs and there she is, in the hall, wearing jeans and a jumper, her hair scraped back, but looking, as Joe would say, 'awesome'.

I congratulate her on her performance last night, as

you do. She gives me a breathless 'thank you', without recognising me from last year, when she PRACTICALLY RUINED MY LIFE. Or Edie, who's standing, frozen, beside me. Crow and Jenny get squealy kisses, however, before Sigrid trips daintily out of the house and down our front steps, where a white Bentley is waiting to take her to work. I'm not sure how 'authentic actress' this is, but from the grin Jenny gives us over her shoulder as she follows Sigrid into it, she's happy to give it a go.

Crow comes to stand beside us and wave them goodbye.

'How's the dress?' I ask.

She smiles. 'It's OK, I think. So far, anyway.'

We all go to take a look at it, half-finished on its tailor's dummy, which has been adjusted to Sigrid's precise proportions for when I'm not around to do my 'house model' thing. Even now, you can tell it will be stunning. It's the most over-the-top, complicated, deluxe, gorgeous creation Crow's done yet.

By now, she's constructed the bodice, with its inbuilt corset that would probably stop a tank. She's in the process of finely pleating several lengths of ultramarine silk for the skirt, until they look as if they could float away on a puff of wind. The results will be embroidered by the woman who lives outside Toulouse, before Crow hand-sews the waiting jewels into place, one by one.

I know I shouldn't, but I ask Edie what she thinks of it.

Edie peers hard at the bodice, and the pinned-on

jewels and the metres and metres of silk. 'It looks very heavy,' she says doubtfully, after a long pause to think about it.

Heavy? HEAVY?

I'm just glad she's not writing for *Vogue* right now. That's all I'm saying.

Chapter 28

Jenny's lucky to have something to take her mind off exams as we hurtle toward the end of term. For four weeks, she heads off to the theatre with her duffel bag over her shoulder, moaning about revision and looking as bouncy and happy as a teenage Shirley Temple.

Edie's absorbed with her 'Cheap Clothes Cost Lives' campaign and researching Mumbai like it's some sort of extra GCSE. I've got my textiles project to think about, but although it's fun, it isn't exactly on the same level as organising a collection. And I'm trying *not* to think about Mumbai, because if we don't sort things out there, I'm probably out of a job. Which is why I spend far too much time in the workroom with Crow, watching the sea-goddess dress come together while making sure I don't come into contact with spillable stuff of any kind.

Sigrid stops by for more fittings, and spends most of the time on her phone, complaining about the London weather and gossiping about the *incredible* party she was at last night, before the *other* party, and how difficult it is being a working actress in this town.

The dress goes to Toulouse and comes back, looking even more incredible. And Crow just keeps working silently, adjusting, pinning, rethinking, until the fit is so perfect it's impossible to imagine Sigrid in anything else.

One afternoon, an editor who works for *Elle* calls to say she's heard a rumour that Crow's designing something truly exceptional for Sigrid to wear to the Elysée Palace, and that they'd love to do a photo shoot featuring it afterwards, and would I like to suggest some of Crow's other designs they can use?

That night I go to bed imagining page after page of Crow's dresses on a beautiful model in *Elle* and remembering why I love working in fashion so much, despite the occasional stressful moment. It's hard to be grateful to the Queen of Evil for anything, but I suppose I'm going to have to give it a try.

The Elysée Palace do is at the end of term, just after the play ends at the Boat House and before we head out to India. Crow and I have agreed that I'll go to Paris with Sigrid and help her with her outfit. This is almost better than organising dresses for a photo shoot at *Elle*. I only have to miss one afternoon of school and I get to stay overnight with Dad. And I'll be travelling on the Eurostar with a couture dress in my luggage, which is THE MOST ROMANTIC THING IN THE WORLD.

Sadly, Edie isn't jealous, because of her whole I-don't-get-fashion thing, and Jenny isn't, because it isn't to do with the theatre, and Crow isn't, because she just isn't. Crow is too cool to be jealous.

So I'm completely thrilled when Granny comes up to London on a shopping trip and she's *totally* jealous.

'You'll be like something out of *Funny Face*,' she says. I look blank. 'It's a film with Audrey Hepburn, darling. A classic. God, you're so *young*. Anyway, *il sera ravissante*.'

Which is not only painful to hear, it's also ungrammatical. One doesn't correct Granny's grammar, but I try to look like my Eng. Lit. teacher does when I talk about Shakespeare. It's mildly disappointed bordering on annoyed. Granny doesn't notice, of course.

I'm in the middle of this look when I get a text. For a minute, I flinch, wondering if it's Alexander. He hasn't contacted me since the whole horror-movie kiss scenario, and I've been hoping he won't, but you never know.

However, it's not Alexander. It's a number I don't recognise. It says: 'No need to go to Paris. My stylist's coming. Just give her the dress. S xoxoxoxo'.

Granny sees the look on my face. The new one.

'Bad news, darling?'

I try and show her the text but she hasn't got her glasses on, so I read it out, including the xoxoxoxo.

Granny says a rude word, in English, perfectly pronounced, that you wouldn't expect to hear from someone her age.

'*We* call her the Queen of Evil,' I tell her.

'I can understand why.'

I'm still half hoping that the text is a joke by Jenny or Edie, not that I could imagine them doing it. Or even Harry. But it's not.

Next morning, Sigrid's stylist appears. She is small, Italian and dressed in head-to-toe Louis Vuitton. Not just the scarf, but the top and skirt and boots and bag and everything. She's on her mobile and the whole time she's with us, she doesn't speak a word of English. She just chats away in Italian down the phone and mimes to us what she wants.

She mimes the dress. We take her down to the workroom and show it to her. She nods. She mimes putting it in its bag, supported by acid-free tissue paper, which we do and it takes ages. All the time, she's still sorting out whatever Italian problem she's got. Then she mimes us giving her the bag, which she has to hold high above her head so the bottom doesn't drag on the ground.

Then she goes. That's it.

First Paolo, and now whatever-her-name-is in Vuitton. What is it with me and Italians? Have I done something?

Oh, no. I look down. I'm wearing the leggings with the swearwords on that my pen pal Marco taught me. Great. So I've probably managed to deeply insult her without even saying a word to her.

Fabulous.

Chapter 29

I don't tell anyone about the leggings moment. Luckily. Because I don't think it was my fault this time. I really don't. Well, I'm pretty sure it wasn't. Probably. It's just that Sigrid is the Queen of Evil and THE DISASTER was destined to happen. Our only mistake was not to see it coming.

Harry and Crow join me to watch every news channel we can find for hours and hours, looking for coverage of the Elysée Palace event. We're all so excited. It's like the Oscars all over again, but better, because this time we're not nervous. Eventually, an entertainment show on Sky has a clip of all the famous people arriving.

French famous people. Italian famous people. English famous people. American famous people. Other famous people I don't recognise. All the women are beautiful and all the men are Johnny Depp-gorgeous. It's as if they had to pass some sort of beauty test before they were invited.

Every designer has gone to town. The women

shimmer and flutter and glitter and glow, depending on what version of 'incredibly stunning' their chosen designer has gone for. We're just congratulating ourselves that Crow designed something so difficult and dazzling and EXPENSIVE when I spot Sigrid. She's with a man who looks vaguely familiar. Jenny squeals. It's her director, again. He looks as if he's died and gone to celebrity heaven.

Sigrid, as always, looks magnificent. She is one of the most beautiful people there, which is saying something. She has an extra-special glow to her, as if she's spent the whole day in a spa, being covered in gold leaf, which I wouldn't put past her. But her dress isn't blue, it's pink. Dolce & Gabbana pink satin, with a black cummerbund as wide as my geography exercise book, and a single black cuff for jewellery. I'd like to say she looks like a liquorice allsort, but she doesn't. She looks incredible. Possibly because I still can't believe what she's wearing.

The sea-goddess dress is nowhere to be seen. Presumably still in its bag in some chic hotel, like a Cinderella who never got to go to the ball.

We should have guessed. Of course we should. But what with the dress being SPECIALLY ORDERED FOR THE EVENT and everything, we stupidly didn't. Even with Sigrid involved. We just never learn.

Harry makes a snorting noise and turns off the TV in disgust. Crow looks shell-shocked and her fingers are trembling. My ears are suddenly full of that ringing noise again. Harry goes straight back to his room and puts on the Russian folk music at full volume. Mum takes Crow and me into the kitchen for smoothies and popcorn and hugs.

The phone goes. Mum hands it to me. It's Andy Elat.

'What happened?'

'She had a stylist,' I say. 'I guess the stylist knows Dolce & Gabbana.'

'*Stylist*? You should have *told* us!'

'But the stylist came to pick up Crow's dress!'

There's a pause while Andy decides whether to shout at me any more and obviously decides not to.

'Well, enjoy India,' he mutters and ends the call. I'm not sure he said it in his most cheerful voice. I get the impression he wouldn't be too devastated if we all *did* get a bug of some sort.

Why did I go into the fashion business? *Why?* I know there have been times when it seemed like a pretty good idea, but I must have been mad.

Next morning, I'm supposed to be packing for our trip, but I'm too depressed. Mum suggests revision, which is just pure sadism. Harry's still listening to Russian folk songs, which make it worse.

I realise that there are only two places that can make me vaguely happy. The first is the V&A, but that's where I'll find the last dress Sigrid used to make my life a misery. The second place is Oxford Street. You can't pack until you've bought a few things to go in your suitcase. This is what I tell myself. And it might be a bit mad, buying clothes to take to India when the place is FULL OF GORGEOUS, CHEAP STUFF, but you never know. It pays to be safe.

Edie would be horrified. I really should be sticking to charity shops and my sewing machine. But today I can't face them. I need to do something fun and frivolous. I need fashion.

I take the bus to Oxford Street and my first stop is Miss Teen. I like their latest styles, but I find I can't concentrate because I keep remembering Crow's launch, and how terrifying it was, and picturing the wooden boardroom upstairs, and how terrifying *that* was, and it doesn't put me in the mood to choose tee-shirts.

Then there's a whole range of shops all the way down to Oxford Circus. I can't help looking at the designer collections and realising how extremely difficult they are to do. In fact, the more I look, the less I feel like buying anything. Fashion is a scary business. I'm not sure I'm made for it after all.

Finally, I get to Topshop. It's impossible to do an Oxford Street fashion adventure without including Topshop, so I go down the escalators and hope that the sheer quantity of amazing clothes will cheer me up.

They don't. They simply prove that there are hundreds of designers out there who can do high-street collections – really good ones – and we can't. We just got lucky with the first one. Out of sheer habit, I load myself up with things to try on and join the queue for the changing rooms. Which is where I am when I suddenly hear my name being called out.

I look up. An eight-foot goddess is approaching me, all smiles. Actually, it's Svetlana in a jumpsuit and strappy heels.

She gives me a big kiss. 'I haven't seen you for ages! How are you?' she asks.

'Fine,' I lie.

Then she turns back. 'Lulu,' she shouts, 'come over! See who it is.'

My first thought is how sweet Svetlana is. I'm pretty certain, thanks to all the Russian folk music, that things are wobbly between her and Harry at the very least, but that doesn't mean she feels the need to avoid me in shops. I think that's really brave and amazing and I like her even more than I did before, which was a lot.

My second thought is 'Oh. My. God.'

Lulu is Lulu Frost. And she's not just here with her model pal, she's here with her off-again on-again BOYFRIEND. I see him look up from about three racks away and his face freezes. So does mine.

'Hi,' says Lulu, coming over. 'You must be Nonie. Svetlana's told me all about you.'

Oh no, I hope not, I think madly to myself. But then I realise I haven't seen Svetlana since I got that first call from Alexander. She might not know that we ever met up.

He approaches slowly. His face is blank, except for a polite smile that doesn't reach his eyes. I can't tell what he's thinking, but I know what *I'm* thinking. I'm thinking PLEASE GOD FAST FORWARD THE NEXT FIVE MINUTES OF MY LIFE SO I DON'T HAVE TO LIVE THEM.

'This is my boyfriend,' Lulu says cheerfully. 'Alexander Taylor.'

He holds out his hand. 'Good to meet you,' he says, giving me a long, steady, dead-eyed gaze.

I grasp his cold, confident fingers. Then drop them. I want to say something witty and cutting that only he will understand and that will make him feel like the two-timing evil *toy-er* he obviously is, but I can't think of anything, so I just say, 'Hi, Alexander'. Except it comes out as 'Hggmmphh, Aaruugghdder,' because my voice isn't working properly.

Svetlana says something. I don't hear it because my brain is fizzing with embarrassment, so she has to repeat it. She blushes delicately. Which of course makes her look even more stunning.

'Tell your brother hi from me.'

I nod. I get the impression that this is a sad, wistful 'hope you're OK' hi, not a 'hey, let's get back together' hi.

I don't know why they would have split up. They were so good together. But I bet their break-up was noble and slightly tragic, not totally mortifying, like mine. And it's not as if mine *was* a break-up. According to frozen-face in front of me, there was nothing to break up. We hadn't even met. He was going out with Lulu all the time.

Then, as if by magic, I reach the front of the changing room queue. I say goodbye and practically run into the nearest cubicle and slide my back down one of the walls until I'm crouched on the floor, under a huge pile of clothes I'm never going to wear, wishing I'd followed Mum's advice and invested in waterproof mascara.

Chapter 30

I have the perfect moment to give Harry Svetlana's message. It's on the flight to Mumbai. He's ended up as our chaperone, as he's been here before and everyone else is either too busy (like Mum, with her business, and Edie's parents, who have their teaching jobs and her little brother to look after, and Henry, who has exams) or too worried about sunstroke and ankle-swelling (Granny).

We're stuck beside each other for nine hours. I've been dreading it, because I know it's physically impossible for me to sit near my brother for so long and not tell him all the gory details about Alexander. It was bad enough watching him snigger when we were going out. Telling him about the non-break-up after the non-relationship is going to be worse.

To start off with, we sort of ignore each other. Harry has his iPod and I have FIVE BOOKS OF REVISION, which I'm supposed to read on the trip. As if. There are also magazines to read and movies to watch, and I can sit on the arm of Edie's seat, across the aisle, and chat to her and Crow. But when they serve the first meal, I have to sit back next to Harry with no distractions. I put off the Alexander moment by asking him about Svetlana.

'Is it really over?'

He nods.

'Why?'

He looks at me as though I've lost it. This is quite normal for Harry. Fifty per cent of the looks he gives me suggest my brain doesn't work properly.

'You know,' he says. 'Life.' This is not entirely helpful.

'Did she do something?' I ask. 'Or you?' I sort of gulp this last bit. The trouble is, I can't imagine either of them doing something. How do relationships between two nice people end? I mean, I know there's *Romeo and Juliet* and that was misunderstandings and fake death and suicide, but that's a bit extreme.

'No,' he says at last. 'She didn't do anything. Nor did I. Bad timing, I suppose.'

I have no idea what this means. None at all. There is *so* much about relationships I don't understand.

'At least you ended things with Fancy Pants before it all got stressful,' he adds, searching around his tray for something edible.

I'm astounded.

First, Harry has a pet name for my ex-not-boyfriend. Not a good one.

Second, he thinks there was a time when things

weren't stressful. When? *When?*

Third, he sounds a bit jealous of how quickly it ended.

'Things were stressful, believe me,' I say. I sort of feel as if I need to reassure him of the rubbishness of my love life, to make him feel better. The boy who picked up a SUPERMODEL, just by ASKING HER. He's right: my brain doesn't work properly.

'OK,' he says. 'We've got a few hours left. Tell me.'

So I do. Once I start, I can't stop. The awfulness of the sweaty lip. The windy bench. The horror-movie kiss. The Topshop moment. And he doesn't snigger once. He doesn't even look tempted.

'Mum said I ought to get you to bop him on the nose for me.'

He nods to himself, as if it might have worked.

'There's a couple of guys at college like that. It's all about them. They just use pretty girls to make themselves look good.'

Harry's so sweet. About the 'pretty girls' bit. Although I'm surprised he knows what the boys at college get up to because he's hardly ever there.

Mum has gone beyond sheer terror that he's not going to get his degree this summer. She's just sort of numb now. The trouble is, she can't exactly have the usual 'How on earth are you going to get a job?' conversation, because he's already a very popular DJ and booked up for a lot of the spring/summer catwalk shows in September. And she can't accuse him of not working, because he works at his music all the time. So she just takes it out on me and explains once a week that Harry is an 'exceptional case' and if I don't work hard and get a good degree some day I'll 'regret it for the rest of my life'.

I could point out that she modelled through her teens and only managed one A-level and she's now super-successful in her art dealing career, and that by the way, I ALREADY HAVE A JOB AND I HAVEN'T DONE MY GCSES YET. But I don't. There's a look she does, which is totally logic-proof. It's just not worth it.

'So I was right to dump him, then?' I ask Harry.

He pats the top of my head in a brotherly way. 'You were brave to dump him. Really brave, kiddo. You amaze me, the things you do.'

I amaze myself sometimes, the scary situations I get myself into. It's great to have Harry to back me up. I realise I've missed him *so* much since the first sniggering incident, even though he's been around. Watching somebody mope around the house is different from actually talking to them. And not only that, he now passes his iPod over and puts on a playlist of Bollywood tunes to get me in the mood for our trip.

'What about the Russian folk music?' I ask.

'I've decided to give it up,' he says. 'It wasn't helping. Try this.'

'This' is happy and mad and groovy and wild and makes you want to dance round the aeroplane with your arms waving. It's much better. I try listening to it while attempting French revision and he's right: it helps. It might even make geography bearable, when the time comes.

Chapter 31

People say India is strange, and crazy, and chaotic, and colourful. They go on about the heat and the crowds and how it's like nothing you've ever experienced.

The people who say this haven't run a catwalk show in the middle of Fashion Week.

We get to Mumbai airport and even though it's night, the air is warm and muggy. I see hundreds of people rushing about looking totally focused or completely confused. There's activity everywhere, lots of loud shouting and talking urgently into mobile phones, and every type of outfit from string vests to sharp suits and flowing shawls. There are queues of excited people and other, harassed individuals trying to make some sort of order. This is just what it was like during the shows last year and I instantly feel at home.

I look over at Crow and see the same expression on her face: happy wonderment. We know we're going to have a good time. Edie looks a bit overwhelmed and is sticking as close to Harry as she can. For someone who wants to work in the United Nations one day, she's going to have to get a bit more relaxed about travelling.

We're being met by the man who runs the main factory that makes Miss Teen clothes in India. His name is Mr Patil and he turns out to be rotund, loud, impeccably dressed in a silk suit, and pleased to see us when we eventually make it through. He's brought his wife and children and two cars, so we can all fit in them on the way to our hotel.

While our cases are being loaded in the cars, Mr Patil arranges that he'll take Harry and Crow, while Edie and I travel behind with his wife and kids. The journey isn't quite what I was expecting. While I'm busy looking out of the windows, trying to make out the lights of Mumbai, Mrs Patil decides that now is a good time for a bit of revision.

'Suraj is a maths champion,' she says proudly of her son, who looks about nine.

'Oh, so's Edie,' I say, without thinking.

Edie gives me the Look, but it's too late.

'How wonderful,' says Mrs Patil. 'Let's do a test. What is four thousand and seventy-four divided by seven?'

I assume this is a friendly joke and go back to looking out of the window, but a second later, Suraj says 'five hundred and eighty-two' and Edie looks really annoyed. Mrs Patil does another one and this time Edie gets it first, to her relief. But now the heat is on, and we do maths all the way into the city. Or at least, Edie and Suraj do. His little sister and I keep quiet and look out of our respective windows. Her excuse is she's five. Mine is that I'm saving maths revision till much later in the holidays.

Through my window, I watch Mumbai emerge from the darkness. Some bits are all skyscrapers and swooping freeways. Others aren't much more than tents. Lots of blocks of flats wear little corrugated shacks around their bottoms, like skirts. The traffic is mad, even at midnight, and noisier than Piccadilly Circus, with horns competing for who can beep louder. Even through the car's air conditioning, the air smells sweet and spicy. I try and catch Edie's eye to see if she's enjoying the sights as much as I am, but she's still focusing on long division and her eyes are half-closed with concentration.

As we get closer to our hotel, I wonder if I'm hallucinating. The bits of Mumbai that aren't shacks or skyscrapers look *amazingly* like the V&A. As if its bulky gothic buildings have been cloned and transported to India, replanted by the sea and adorned with bird poo. Will this help in geography GCSE? I'd like to think so, but I doubt it.

When we get to our hotel, the Patils kindly offer to take us out to dinner, but we're suddenly shattered. Edie, Crow and I are all sharing a room. We go to bed and start talking about our plans, but Edie quickly moves onto the subject of mental maths and Crow and I are soon asleep.

* * *

When I wake up next morning, Edie's already on her computer.

'You're not revising, are you?' I ask, blearily. This simply wouldn't be fair.

'No,' she says. 'Just updating my blog. And sending emails. Phil wants to know how we get on.'

I think if we were on a desert island, Edie would be on her laptop, updating her blog and emailing Phil at No Kidding. She's been emailing him a lot recently. And he keeps emailing back. He's really excited about this trip.

Over breakfast, Harry says that Mrs Patil has offered to take us sightseeing and, if we don't mind, he'd like to spend the day at a jazz festival he's heard about, at some venue by the sea.

'Aren't we going to the factory?' Edie asks, looking massively disappointed.

'Tomorrow,' Harry says. 'The Patils thought we'd need a day to acclimatise.'

He catches Crow and me staring at him. 'Get used to the hot weather,' he explains.

'Oh.'

Mrs Patil arrives and Harry heads off. After a round of cheerful hellos, Mrs Patil looks at me and her smile falters slightly. I can sense something is wrong. It's to do with my legs. I look around the hotel lobby and realise that even though it will soon be thirty degrees outside, lace hot pants are not the in thing in Mumbai.

Mrs Patil's in a stunning blue sari, as are a few of the other women. Most are in modern skirts, tee-shirts and trousers, but all of them are what Mum would call 'respectable'. Whereas I look more like something out of a Christina Aguilera video.

I run back up to the room to change. Harem pants will have to do. Normally, they're not my favourite look, but I packed a spare pair for evenings and otherwise my suitcase features hot pants a bit too heavily. Edie, needless to say, looks like a visiting governess and Crow has chosen a gold and purple kaftan that she made in about thirty seconds while I was packing and is gorgeous.

When I get back downstairs, Mrs Patil waves me quickly through the front doors. Her driver is waiting outside and can only pause briefly before the traffic jam he has caused gets nasty. Once we're in the car, she turns round in the front seat and says, 'Now. Sightseeing. Mumbai has many interesting and fascinating buildings. Also galleries and museums. The zoo is excellent. The harbour also. Where shall we begin?'

We all look at each other. I twist my fingers around the folds in my harem pants and we say nothing. Edie can't choose between all the options and Crow and I SO don't care. Crow will do anything, as long as it involves watching people and getting ideas. There's only one thing I want to do and I don't dare mention it.

Mrs Patil sees our faces and bursts out laughing.

'I'm teasing you. I take girlfriends round Mumbai all

the time. I know what you would like to do. And that is shopping. Yes?'

YES!

Sometimes in life, even when your rubbish ex-not-boyfriend pretends not to recognise you in public, and your *Elle* shoot will probably be cancelled because of the Queen of Evil, and you have exams coming up, you get given special moments of pure happiness. One of these is sitting in a fabric shop, drinking tea, watching your designer friend choose length after length of incredible, rainbow-coloured sari silk for 'research purposes', while you know for a fact that most of your school friends are back at home, doing revision.

Even better is standing in a bazaar, with a freshly-bought embroidered bag full to the brim with cheap jewellery and souvenirs, eating mango ice cream from a stall and discussing which *other* shops and stalls to visit. Endless types and sizes of them, from marble-tiled malls playing Bollywood hits to street vendors selling flip-flops, and Mrs Patil seems to be an expert on them all.

Even Edie gives in and starts bargaining for some scarves that catch her eye. She draws the line at mango ice cream, though: 'It's from a stall! You've no idea what might be in it!'

I don't care. She has no idea how delicious it is. So much more fun than the bottled water she's sticking to.

Crow's back in her trance, just like she was in France. If the Paris Métro kept her eyes busy, the overcrowded streets of Mumbai, with the heat and the dirt and the smoggy blue sky, and the colourful stallholders and beggars and busy professionals and endless traffic, are enough to keep her going for a lifetime.

Only two things make life less than perfect. One is the stares from some of the men and boys. Mrs Patil tells us to ignore them and we sort of do, but I'm REALLY glad I didn't go out in hot pants this morning. The other thing is the begging. It's not being asked for rupees – that's fine, we've got loads. It's the children who do it. Barefoot and eager. They have the same look in their eye as Miss Teen shoppers on a mission (although that's all they've got in common) and whatever we give them, they seem desperate for more. Mrs Patil shoos them away but they keep flocking round us. Edie is positively upset.

'They're so young! And so thin! Who's looking after them?'

Mrs Patil laughs. 'Nobody! They're just part of the city. You'll get used to it.'

She nods to Crow, who's letting an astonished little girl feel her super-curly hair, which by now is adorned with a couple of pinwheels from a market stall. Mumbai is a city of many sights, but even here, Crow's unusual.

Edie gives Mrs Patil her polite smile, but I can tell she doesn't *want* to get used to it. She'd take every child home, if she could, and give them new clothes, reading practice and a decent meal. As it is, she empties her wallet and then tries to ignore their outstretched hands and cries of 'beautiful lady'. She's super-relieved when Mrs Patil suggests lunch and points us in the direction of a café with lots of bug-free food to concentrate on instead.

The afternoon is more markets and malls. By late afternoon, Edie and Crow are completely shattered again and even I'm wondering if I can manage *another* sari shop. Mrs Patil decides it's time to call it a day. She takes us back to the hotel.

'Tomorrow, the factory,' she says. 'My husband will send a car to pick you up at seven.'

Seven? That's a bit early. It sounds like work, not holiday. Then I remember, it *is* work. We nod and agree to get an early night.

Harry's waiting for us upstairs.

'How was the festival?' I ask.

He grins. 'Fantastic. Heard about twenty people. They want me to come back in October for Fashion Week.'

'They have a fashion week *here*?' Edie asks.

Harry nods. It's slightly odd to have a brother who's as up on the fashion world as you are, but then, he is going out with a supermodel. Or was. A pained look flashes across his face for a second, then disappears. I want to hug him, but obviously I don't. We catch each other's eye and say nothing.

He's nice enough to ask us about our day, and even though it was pure shopping, he manages to look interested. We lay out all the things we've bought on our beds.

Reds and pinks and yellows and blues; silks and cotton; simple scarves and a gold brocade coat that I will probably wear for the rest of my life.

'It's research,' I say, gesturing at Crow, who helpfully nods. 'For the label.'

'Yeah, right,' Harry says. 'If that's what you want to call it.'

My last thought as my head hits the pillow is that, surprisingly, I haven't seen Crow pull out a notebook since we got here. So different from Paris. She's thinking about something. Worrying about something, probably, if it's stopping her from drawing.

Yvette? The street children? How to design for teenagers? I think her trust in Edie and me is wearing off and I start to worry about her worrying, but the next thing I know I'm tobogganing down a mountain of mango ice cream on a carpet of rainbow silk and I have a sneaky feeling I might be dreaming.

Chapter 32

At seven, we're waiting in the hotel lobby for Mr Patil's car to come and pick us up. At first, I wondered why we couldn't just take a taxi, but it turns out that when they say the garment factory is 'in' Mumbai, what they mean is that it's in an industrial area a two-hour drive from our hotel. When you've got a city big enough to hold twenty million people, a two-hour drive away counts as 'in'.

I'm really hoping that the driver hasn't brought one of his children so we can do fun maths tests again. Luckily, he hasn't. Instead, he's accompanied by Rakesh, the 'Manager for Closures' (which turns out to be zips, not shutting the factory down) – a young man who doesn't stare at us for a second and spends the whole two hours telling us about his fabulous city, and how wonderful it is, and how it's the best at producing movies, playing cricket, building skyscrapers, starting new businesses and creating delicious food.

'And shopping,' I add.

'Oh, yes, shopping,' he says. 'The best in the world for shopping. There is no doubt about that.'

'And ice cream. Mango especially.'

He looks round at me, impressed that I've already discovered so many important things about his city. Then he says something in Hindi to the driver, who smiles and looks round too. This is slightly dangerous, as he's being overtaken by lorries on both sides at the time, but we don't crash, so I assume he knows what he's doing.

Gradually, the countryside changes from flat and brown to green and slightly hilly. There are lakes. Fewer flats and more factories. The road is still crammed with cars and taxis, buses, vans and lorries, bikes and bright yellow rickshaws. Most of them are heavily laden with bags and boxes. Stuff is being carried backwards and forwards in enormous quantities.

A few months ago, some of the boxes would have held the first consignment of Crow's collection for Miss Teen. It's amazing to be here and to think of their journey, past the lakes, up across the ocean (which one? Still no idea) and into the heart of London, where they would have felt right at home in the seething crowd and the clamour and commotion of launch day.

We come to a grand set of white gates with slightly peeling paint. Beyond them are palm trees and car parks and huge buildings. It looks like how Jenny described the studios in Hollywood when she was making *Kid Code*, except with smaller cars and more people in bright pink saris.

The driver takes us to the biggest building of all, which is so long it would take you ten minutes to walk from one end to the other, and Rakesh announces that we've arrived.

This is where the collection was made. This is where we'll find out the truth about how it was done. This is where we'll discover who was mistaken: Andy Elat or the No Kidding people. We all take a deep breath and squeeze each others' hands. Then Rakesh guides us through the heat of the car park to the air-conditioned oasis of Mr Patil's textile empire.

There's a small reception area with plastic garden chairs, where we wait while Rakesh makes a call. Two minutes later, a stunning girl with black hair halfway down her back comes in and gives us a welcoming smile.

'This is Alisha,' Rakesh says. 'She's your guide for the day.' After all the chatting in the car, he is suddenly a different person. He gives Alisha a shy nod, hunches his shoulders and heads quickly for his desk. But the girl makes up for him in warmth and confidence. Especially where Harry is concerned. When she shakes his hand, her smile grows, her eyelashes flutter and she somehow manages to rearrange her hair like a black waterfall over her shoulder. This is a typical Harry effect. He doesn't seem to notice and gives her his usual friendly smile.

Alisha asks us to follow her. She does it in a perfect

American accent, although she looks completely Indian to me. I'm guessing she's already been to Harvard or somewhere. I happen to spot Edie looking grumpily at her. Whether it's the long, black hair, the American education or the Harry effect, I can't tell.

We walk through a delivery area, where there are enough cardboard boxes to build a small city. Everything is carefully stacked and labelled and there's a conveyor belt to deliver ever more boxes to the stacks. This should give me a clue as to what's coming next, but it doesn't.

From the moment we walk into the main building, I'm stunned. I'm not exactly sure what I was expecting, but it wasn't this. I think maybe I pictured a room about the size of our school gym and a few women busy at sewing machines, chatting to each other like an overgrown knitting circle. I didn't picture the largest indoor space I've seen in my life – one that you could easily fit our whole school inside – and enough high-tech equipment to launch a space shuttle.

All the offices are on an upstairs level, overlooking the massive factory floor. The floor itself is rubber and shiny, reflecting the very bright strip lights hanging from the ceiling. It's marked out with lines showing the areas where different stages of production happen, and there are dozens of these, filled with machines and rails and boxes and noise and people. The sewing machine racket is the most amazing thing. It sounds like there's a non-stop hailstorm going on, but nobody seems to notice it. I guess they must be used to it by now.

Alisha leads us up the stairs to the offices. In a little meeting room that smells distractingly of curry, she sits us down and shows us a PowerPoint presentation of the factory and the work it does for Miss Teen and other big fashion retailers. I try to be really, really interested, but PowerPoint presentations are not my most favourite thing and I find myself thinking more and more about mango ice cream. I hope there isn't going to be a little test at the end. Luckily, there isn't.

'Watch out for anomalies,' Edie hisses loudly as we head back down the stairs. She's like something from a spy movie.

I try and ask her what anomalies are, but by now she's chatting to Alisha, so I give up.

'Watch out for anomalies,' I hiss to Crow, doing my best Bond girl impression.

Crow ignores me. We're heading for the pattern cutting section, and now that it's not on a PowerPoint slide, it's actually quite interesting. As well as tables and tables of people cutting fabric with scissors, like you'd expect, there are also massive laser-guided machines that can cut several layers at once. Crow spends ages watching each machine, following its careful path as it traces the lines of the pattern and transforms the fabric underneath into pieces for the factory workers to sew.

Finally, we understand why Crow's fiddly designs would be so 'undoable' here. Each part of the process is done hundreds of times over, and then the results are taken to different workers, doing different processes, in a different part of the building. Pieces are constantly being moved around on giant racks, in vast quantities. If anything is too complicated or detailed, there's a chance that something will go wrong.

Crow doesn't seem to mind that the tour is proving how her latest designs won't work. Instead, she's fascinated by how the clothes are made. We watch the workers cutting, sewing, checking, pressing, hanging, folding, labelling, packing. We watch little scraps of fabric gradually turn into tee-shirts and trousers and dresses and tops. Thousands and thousands of them.

When Alisha leaves us for a moment to make some phone calls, Edie leans forward, still doing her spy-girl thing.

'Have you noticed anything?' she asks eagerly.

Harry considers. 'Did you see how many of the machinists had iPods? That sewing machine din must drive them crazy.'

'They could make the pleated dresses hang better if they cut the pattern differently,' Crow adds.

'Whoever ordered the green satin-effect tracksuits is going to regret it,' I point out.

'I mean, about the CHILDREN!' Edie growls. 'Anything unusual? Any young workers? Any rooms we're not being shown? Trap doors? Phil says they can hide them in all sorts of unusual places.'

'No,' we say. 'Have you?'

No, she has to admit, she hasn't. The shiny rubber floor doesn't look as though it could contain trap doors down to secret basement locations. The whole place feels like an enormous warehouse. The few rooms inside it are glass-walled and contain managers and computers, not children. Everyone here seems older than us, and healthy, and . . . normal. In fact, Alisha's been telling us that the factory helps to sponsor a local school, so if anything, children are doing quite well out of it being here.

When Alisha comes back, we ask if this was definitely the factory where Crow's collection was made.

'I wasn't here last year,' she says. She was probably getting her American degree. She is SO Edie in about five years' time. 'But I've heard about the collection. People were really excited. They knew about that girl at the Oscars. Joe Yule's girlfriend – you know. They were thrilled to be a part of the story. I'll show you some pictures.'

She does. They have a whole scrapbook of photos of pieces from the Jewels collection being made. We all look at each other. We feel really guilty for ever doubting them. Edie most of all. We stay on until the end of the day, but at no stage do I spot an anomaly. Nor does Edie. Nor does Crow. Harry finally notices how pretty Alisha is, but that's about it.

* * *

In the evening, Harry takes Crow to see a Bollywood movie. I can't go because, even though I'm in one of the most exciting, crowded, fascinating cities in the world, I HAVE TO REVISE FRENCH GCSE. Life is *so* unfair. Edie is busy on email again. She spends about an hour describing everything to Phil. Then she reads out an email from Jenny.

'Sorry to say goodbye to the Boat House. Just started rehearsing in the new theatre. It's massive! We got through loads of scenes because people weren't busy getting warm water for TQOE. Joe Ew-l decided she was working too hard, so he's taken her away for a few days. To Venice. Watch out for the photos. Bill's busy on a new project, but he came in to watch rehearsals and he liked my scenes!'

Etc. Etc. I wait for the bit where she asks us about what it's like in India, but she doesn't. I mean, how interesting could it be on a foreign continent, compared with rehearsing a play you've already performed night after night for four weeks? At least she's happy, though.

I ask Edie if she's decided what to do about her website.

'Are you going to take down the "Cheap Clothes Cost Lives" stuff?'

Edie looks shocked. 'Of course not! But I guess I'll have to put up some sort of apology to Miss Teen. So will No Kidding. Phil says he doesn't understand it. The person who gave them those photos of the children was a reliable source. It makes them look stupid. Phil's worried that next time they do a campaign, people just won't believe them. I've sort of made it worse for them by getting involved.'

Her shoulders sag. She's clearly not happy about letting down the No Kidding people. Edie hates letting people down. Even people she's never met who've done nothing but make her life stressful and complicated.

I decide it's time to change the subject. 'So, what's happening tomorrow?' I ask. Now that we've seen the factory, I'm assuming we can just relax.

Edie's in charge of the schedule. She loves that sort of thing and cheers up immediately. She's put it on a spreadsheet, which she brings up on her computer.

'Free morning. Then we need to pack for the train to Agra in the evening.'

'Pack?' I vaguely remember people mentioning that we were catching a train to another town at some stage, but I didn't realise it would involve packing. 'Why do we have to pack?'

'Because Agra's a long way away. It's a twenty-hour journey.'

I snort with giggles. 'You know, for a minute there, I thought you said twenty hours! Hahaha!'

Edie looks at me sternly. 'I did.'

I stop giggling. '*What?* You can't mean we're going to sit on a train for TWENTY HOURS? Why can't we fly?'

'Because there aren't any direct flights to Agra and by

the time you've gone to Delhi and caught a cab, it takes about as long.'

'So why on earth are we going? What can POSSIBLY be in Agra to make it worth twenty hours? Nothing is worth twenty hours.'

Edie smiles at me. 'Oh, I think this is.'

God, I wish I was better at geography.

'OK, put me out of my misery,' I tell her. 'What is it?'

She grins, delighted.

'Even you've heard of this one, Nonie. How about the Taj Mahal?'

'You mean like the hotel down the road?'

'Not *that* Taj Mahal. THE Taj Mahal.'

'Oh,' I say, finally getting it. Actually, that does sound rather wow.

Chapter 33

I'm still not completely convinced that twenty hours is an acceptable length of time to travel *anywhere*, frankly, except possibly Australia, but standing in the station the next evening, surrounded by the bustle of excited train-goers, I have to admit I'm getting used to the idea. Mum once did a photo shoot at the Taj Mahal and has always droned on about how 'simply magical' and 'uniquely inspirational' it is. I shall now be able to shut her up by going 'when *I* was there . . .', which will be very annoying for her and mega-fun for me, so I'm looking forward to that bit already.

Also, I have loaded up on new DS games and magazines and should have enough to keep me busy for the whole journey without once needing to resort to French grammar, which is good. Edie is insisting that we spend most of our time admiring the incredible scenery and 'getting to know the heart of India'. But I'm totally planning to admire my new fashion show game and see how many models I can send down the DS catwalk in record time.

The train is enormously long and just, well, enormous. There are lots of different classes and, with the help of the Patils, we're in one of the best ones, which means air conditioning and a compartment with seats that turn into beds. When we get to the platform, I'm expecting hundreds of people to stream all over the carriages and tie themselves to the roof, like they do in movies. It's quite disappointing when everybody behaves like they do in England, except dressed more colourfully, and gets on normally through the doors. Except they do it in such large, bustling numbers that I'm not sure how we're all going to fit inside the train.

It takes ages to find our seats. Everyone we ask confidently tells us they're somewhere they're not, and I'm beginning to wonder if they really exist at all when finally, Edie shrieks and beckons to us and we all pile in after her, just as the train starts moving.

Cocooned in our compartment, Harry soon loses himself in a memoir by a photographer he likes who travelled in India a lot. Crow gets busy making a dress using some fuchsia pink sari material and a travel sewing kit she's brought with her. Edie surrounds herself with revision books, guidebooks, water and bananas, which is pretty much all she dares consume in case Something Horrible happens to her tummy. She then has to pile the whole lot into her lap when an Indian family comes in to join us and takes up all the other seats.

The train heads out of Mumbai. My plan to read and play DS games is quickly interrupted by the Indian family, who are desperate to chat. They want to know where we've come from, where we're going, whether we'd like to try some of the delicious potato cakes and spicy things they've brought to keep them going on the journey, what my favourite sights in Mumbai are, and whether I've met the Queen. I'm tempted to say I've been compared to her a couple of times by my ex-not-boyfriend, but decide he's not worth bringing into the conversation, and the family are very disappointed when I have to admit I've only ever seen her on TV.

Next thing I know, the daughter of the family, who's about ten, is sitting beside me and 'helping' me with my DS game, while her mother 'helps' me with my magazines, by flipping through all of them and laughing loudly at several of the outfits. I don't mind, because the food she keeps feeding me from the big bag at her feet is so incredibly delicious I'm probably eating more of it than her husband and children put together.

Long after darkness falls, they reach their station and pack up their belongings, leaving me with enough delicious food to last till morning. I'm very sorry to see them go, and amazed to see that four hours have gone by already and it's time for bed. I'm starting to think twenty hours isn't so crazy for a train journey after all. Not only that, but even turning our seats into bunk beds is fun, and there's something very soothing about being rocked to sleep by the sound of the wheels speeding along the tracks, carrying us further and further towards Agra.

I love sleeping on trains, as it turns out, and, unlike Edie, I'm not constantly in fear of being attacked by bandits. This is the advantage of not reading too much historical local literature.

The morning is a bit of a shock. Not the train itself, but the fact that every time I look out of the window, I seem to spot a naked bottom, squatting near the track. Are we travelling along some kind of thousand-mile loo? And, frankly, why don't they teach you about this in geography? It would be so much more interesting than the population of Alaska, which is not a fact I plan on ever needing to know.

I could look out of the window all day. Not at the bottoms, but at the people and animals constantly at work in the fields, or building shacks dangerously close to the railway, or just standing, looking and not doing much at all. However, I don't get much of a chance as a new wave of passengers arrives wanting to know all about us. So it's not until after lunch that I can finally get stuck into the magazines I bought. I'm in the middle of an article on Mumbai Fashion Week when Edie starts.

'The Taj Mahal,' she says grandly, out of the blue, 'was finished in 1653.'

We all look up, nod briefly and go back to what we're doing.

'It took twenty thousand labourers and a thousand elephants to build it and it is rumoured that Shah Jahan had all their hands cut off when it was finished so that nothing so beautiful could ever be built again.'

'Elephants don't have hands,' I point out. 'And by the way, ew.'

Edie looks at me crossly. 'They say the architect was killed,' she goes on, 'but—'

'Shhhhh,' I say. 'We're busy. And as I said, ew.'

'But you need to know this information. Otherwise you won't—'

I cut her off. 'I'm reading about Mumbai Fashion Week. I really don't need to hear about hands being cut off, thank you.'

Crow giggles. Even Harry looks up and smiles.

From then on, about every half hour, Edie tries to tell us something important about where we're going and we take it in turns to shh her. Even when she just tries to start a normal conversation, we shh her in case she tries to sneak in some useful information. The other people in the carriage think this is a hysterical English game and join in too.

Finally, she gives up. Harry, Crow and I get bored with what we're doing and have a conversation about the markets we've seen, and the factory, and what else we want to do before we go back to England, but Edie doesn't join in. I notice she's gone a bit white. I feel sorry for her, but it's her own fault. We do not want to spend our holiday with a walking guidebook. She pulls out her extremely fat novel by Rudyard Kipling and buries herself in it.

Eventually, it's teatime and the train pulls into Agra station. I can't believe the twenty hours went by so quickly. And that I'm going to miss my train seat, and the food and the conversation.

The taxi ride from the station in Agra to the hotel is death-defying and takes four times as long as it should, but that's all part of the fun. Best of all, our new hotel has a pool and we eat supper beside it (Edie's starving by now), and our rooms are inlaid with bits of marble, which gives us a taste of what's to come.

We set our alarms for the early hours of the morning, because apparently 'you have to see the Taj Mahal at sunrise'. They certainly make it hard work, visiting this place.

When I get back from the bathroom, Crow has laid the fuchsia pink silk shift dress she's been making on my bed.

'For me?' I ask.

She looks up from her pillow and nods. 'I hate those harem pants,' she says sleepily.

I give her a hug and crawl into bed without trying the dress on. It will fit perfectly, I know. Crow's things always do.

Chapter 34

It turns out they're right.

You *do* have to see the Taj Mahal at sunrise.

And it isn't like London Fashion Week, or the V&A, or even Buckingham Palace, or anywhere I've ever been. It's incredible. It's glorious. It actually makes me want to cry, just to stand there and watch it, glowing pinkly in the early morning light.

It's better than just an excuse to shut Mum up. It's AMAZING.

We're standing just inside the entrance gatehouse, listening to birdsong, trying to identify the distinctive smell (which Crow eventually pinpoints as 'sweaty trainer') and looking along the waterway leading up to the marble building with its famous onion dome and tall towers in the corners. It looks like an out-of-control Disney jewellery box, except it's real.

'Who did you say built it?' I ask Edie.

She doesn't answer. I look at her more closely and

realise that she's holding back tears. This isn't a total surprise, as it's that sort of place, but I notice that her lip is wobbling too. I put my hand on her arm and ask if she's OK but she just shakes me off like I'm one of the people asking if they can take our photo.

This is odd. I find Harry, who's standing a few metres away from us, awe-struck, and tell him.

'There's something wrong with Edie, but she won't tell me what. Can you talk to her?'

He looks concerned and nods. Then he puts his arm around her and leads her a few steps away, while Crow and I just stand and stare.

'Is it a palace?' Crow asks. 'Or a mosque? It looks a bit like one, with those towers.'

I realise I don't know. But Edie will. She's been reading about it for days. She'll explain.

Except she won't.

Harry comes back while Edie, red-eyed, hangs back slightly. He explains that she was really hurt by the way we teased her yesterday. More than we thought. She can hardly talk now, she's so upset.

Even when we apologise, it doesn't make any difference. And we can't face buying a guidebook, because that would be too rude after all the teasing, so we end up having to go round the place without really knowing anything about it.

When you're used to having Edie explaining stuff to you the whole time, or Mum, or Granny, it's weird not knowing what you're looking at. I'm pretty sure that's Islamic writing engraved into the marble, which is also inlaid with precious stones. But then I'm stuck. So I just focus on how much I love the arched windows and doorways everywhere, and the delicate stonework, and how much Mum would approve of the minimalist approach: white, white and more white.

I expect Harry to be taking photographs the whole time, which is what he usually does when he isn't listening to music, and often when he is, but he hasn't even brought his camera this time.

'I just want to look at it,' he says. 'And hear the sounds. People talking, the birds, the water. I just want to *be* here.'

This sounds very profound and Indian and I am impressed. Crow is so busy just *being* here that she doesn't say a word. I can tell she's drinking in the pure white surface of the marble.

'Amazing, isn't it?' I say, going up to her.

Her shoulders stiffen slightly, in a way that means 'Back off, I'm drinking in the pure white surface of the marble,' so, without anything better to do, I have to just *be* here too. I start to see the detail through Crow's eyes. I notice the delicacy of the inlaid carvings and the clever way you get to see beautiful bits through the gaps in other beautiful bits and before long I just want to take it home with me. It's perfect. I could stand at wonder at it all day. I *wish* I knew what it actually was.

As we make our way back towards the gatehouse, I

give it one more try.

'Edie, you were right, I love it. *Please* tell me who built it. And what it's for.'

Edie still looks sad and tearful. But she takes a deep breath.

'It was built by an emperor called Shah Jahan. For his wife, who died. It's her tomb.'

Wow. This makes Romeo and Juliet look pretty small fry and uncommitted. I now have about fifteen other questions to ask, but I can see that Edie needs a quiet sit-down and a good cry in private before she can tell me anything.

We take her back to the hotel, where she 'has to redo her makeup', and promise ourselves we'll come back tomorrow, when we know what we're looking at.

Chapter 35

It doesn't take Edie long. By the time she comes to join us by the pool at the hotel, she's almost back to her normal self, fussing about whether her water bottle has a tamper-proof seal and double-checking that the lunch we've saved for her doesn't include salad.

We all say sorry again. Harry and I just say it, but Crow also draws it in her notebook – a full-page SORRY made out of wistful dancing girls in saris that would probably sell on eBay for thousands.

'I'm sorry too,' Edie says, in her Edie way. 'I was just over-reacting. It's just, you know . . . travelling.'

We nod. Whatever she wants to call it.

From the hotel, we can see a big, orange-coloured building on the horizon. Edie points to it.

'That's Agra Fort,' she says. 'We should go there at sunset. That's where Shah Jahan was imprisoned by his son so he could see the Taj Mahal and constantly be reminded of his dead wife, but never visit her.'

What?

This is the story that we've been begging Edie *not* to tell us? No wonder she's been tearful with frustration that we didn't want to hear. So we let her get it out of her system and she tells us about Shah Jahan's beloved wife, Mumtaz Mahal, dying while giving birth to their fourteenth child (so not just a teenage romance, then) and his plans for the most beautiful monument in history to house her (big success) and the feud with his son and imprisonment (not so good) and the reputation of the Taj Mahal as the world's greatest monument to love. The few bits that aren't marble are amethyst and sapphire and jade and crystal and turquoise. Like it wasn't wow enough already.

Edie feels much better after that. We all feel weird, though. There's a lot to think about. It certainly puts sweaty kisses and windy benches in their place.

Early next morning, we set out again. We feel like regular visitors now. This is our second day, after all. We make our way through the gatehouse and watch the familiar outline of the Taj appear through the pale grey haze, like a mirage. Crow has her notebook with her and gets busy sketching at last. Harry and I pause with Edie while the sun rises and the marble turns from blush pink to creamy white.

We imagine Shah Jahan watching it from his prison in

the Fort, still pining for Mumtaz Mahal. Then slowly we approach it, as he was forbidden to do until his son finally buried him there.

It seems different to me now that I know it's a sort of love poem in marble. I make the mistake of trying to imagine some boy one day feeling about me this way. It's so NEVER going to happen. Mumtaz Mahal gets a monument. I get frozen-faced, cold-fingered handshakes in Topshop. It's a karma thing.

Harry has such a tinge of sadness to him today that I can almost hear the Russian folk songs in his head. Edie can't be thinking about love – she's never had a boyfriend for longer than four days – but there's something about this place that appeals to her too. She's probably working out the cubic capacity of the main onion dome. Or calculating the number of man-hours it took to build the place. Whatever.

Crow is in a world of her own. Several pages of her notebook are already covered in sketches. Yay! Something's going on in that soul-singer head of hers, I can tell. She doesn't talk to us but she isn't ignoring us. She's just thinking and she's sort of forgotten we're there.

Chapter 36

By the time we get back to Mumbai, Crow has filled up both the notebooks she brought with her and is desperate for more paper. She's even drawing in the margins of Edie's Rudyard Kipling.

I've tried to get a look at what she's doing, but for once she won't show me. When I do eventually manage to get a brief glimpse, all I see is onion domes and filigree marble carving. Please please please may she *not* be thinking about architecture when I really need her to design a doable summer collection so I can keep my job. However, I don't say anything. There's no point rushing her. Her brain works at its own pace, in its own way. I just have to cross my fingers and hope.

We have two days left in Mumbai before our flight home. We've spent most of our money and couldn't fit even another hair clip into our bulging suitcases, so serious shopping is out. Over breakfast, we agree that we'll each think of a cheap thing to do to fill in the time. Harry makes a list and works out a schedule for the day. He's a lot more organised than he looks in his frayed tee-shirt, torn jeans and hair that should have been cut a month ago.

Ever since we got here, Edie has been dying to visit the Gateway to India, so that's top of the list. Outside the hotel, the streets are hot and dusty. I wrap one of my new cotton scarves round my neck, à la Jenny, and clutch my bag close to me. Without Mrs Patil beside us, the city feels big and a bit scary and we realise just how new to it we are.

Immediately, several boys and young men come up to us. Do we need to change dollars for rupees? Do we need a guide? Would we like to be extras in a Bollywood movie? As we move forward, they stay clustered round us, shouting out and waving their arms. I get a brief feeling of what it must be like to be Sigrid Santorini or Joe Yule, if they make the mistake of stepping out without a body-guard.

Luckily, the Gateway to India isn't far away. It's a big, old monument shaped, not surprisingly, like a gateway, and I might be more impressed if I hadn't just seen the TAJ MAHAL. As it is, we spend about ten minutes looking at it before Harry, thankfully, ticks it off our list.

Now it's Crow's turn.

'It says "beads" on the list,' says Harry, with a question mark in his voice.

Crow looks apologetic. 'I know it should be statues and things, but Mrs Patil said there was a bazaar where they sell every kind of bead and crystal you can think of. I've been wondering about it for ages. What if they've got types that you can't get in London or Paris?'

Edie gives us her 'not more shopping' horrified expression, but Crow sounds so worried at the thought of never seeing this place that we can't say no. Harry finds a taxi driver who seems to understand where we're talking about, and after another hair-raising, beep-filled journey, we find ourselves in a part of town that's the total opposite of the modern shopping malls – ancient and crumbly, dirty and smelly, and completely fascinating.

This isn't a market for tourists. It's where local people come to shop and they bustle past us, laden with bags and boxes, pausing just briefly to stare at the tall boy, the white girls in their scarves and the black girl with the pinwheels in her hair.

We wander around for ages in the dust and heat. There are shops everywhere we look, packed with everything from flip-flops to little statues of gods and goddesses. No bead shops, though. And whenever we ask people about them, they just try and guide us into *their* shops, which sell anything you can imagine *except* beads. So we say no to them, and everyone seems shocked and devastated that we're not interested. I've never felt so guilty for *not* shopping before.

On we go, further in to the maze of alleyways, trying

not to admit to ourselves how lost we feel. Suddenly, we're in a big sort-of courtyard with a concrete floor and a roof, and the most incredible smell my nose has ever encountered. Not in a good way. More of a thousand-mile loo sort of way, crossed with the kitchen bins at school. The place is full of animals, mostly in cages, not all of them alive. I'm not sure if they're supposed to be pets or dinner. Or maybe both. Underneath our feet, the floor is wet. I keep trying not to look down, because I don't think I want to know what I'm standing in. The animals are bleating and cheeping, barking and clucking. Edie, who can't bear it if Jenny forgets to feed her cat, is looking distinctly queasy. Harry spots this and tries to get us out of here as quickly as possible.

And next thing we know, we're in a quiet alley, feeling shocked and dizzy, and there's a bead shop, right ahead of us, and another, and another. A whole lane of them. With another one leading off it. We're in Bead Central. A man comes forward, beckoning us into his bead emporium. Finally, we can say yes and go inside. However, it's been quite a journey to get here. For the first time in my life, I'm surrounded by trays of beautiful, colourful, irresistible beads and crystals and stones and I don't want to buy the lot and make a thousand necklaces. I just want to sit down. So does Edie.

Crow is made of stronger stuff. She darts from tray to tray, choosing exactly what she wants and getting Harry to hold it all for her, piled high in baskets. Tiny red ones.

Huge gold ones. Multicoloured ones the size and shape of jelly beans. Sparkly blue-green ones the colour of peacock feathers.

Edie and I clutch each other for support, like the arches of the Taj Mahal. It's the middle of the day and totally hot. We're dusty, hungry and a bit overwhelmed. The owner notices how droopy we are and offers us tea. They don't do *that* in Miss Teen. Edie's about to say no, but I point out that the water is boiled, and she's so tired and desperate that she finally gives in.

It's the most delicious tea we've ever tasted. The owner magics us cushions to sit on from somewhere and we could probably stay there all day. Except that at this precise moment, Crow suddenly darts out of the shop without warning.

What happened?

Harry dumps the trays and chases after her. And we have to dump our cups in a hurry and follow them both before it's too late.

We run fast down the alleyway, dodging cars, bikes, animals and people. We spot Harry going off to the right (lucky he's so tall) and run fast after him. Edie's much quicker than me. She hasn't done five years of running club for nothing. I'm worried I'm never going to see any of them again. Then the stitch that started in my side about ten seconds after I set off finally feels like it's cutting me in half and I have to stop.

I crouch down, panting and wondering what to do.

People step over and round me, as if I'm not there. I'm alone in the middle of a maze of shops, with no clue where to go or how to get there. I feel like I'm in one of my DS games, but without the option of quitting. Actually, I'd really like to quit just now. Instead, I have to stay where I am, telling myself it will all work out OK.

After a few minutes, Edie appears back round the corner. I've never been so glad to see her. She looks relieved too, and very dusty. She flops down beside me, panting, and offers me a drink of bottled water. For once, I'm grateful.

Then Harry and Crow return together, looking hot, tired and disappointed.

'What was that about?' I ask.

'I saw something,' Crow says. She grabs the water off us and takes a long drink.

'What?'

'The Svetlana dress.'

'Seriously?'

Edie looks at us, bemused.

'The Svetlana dress,' I explain. 'The gold embroidered dress Svetlana wore at the Miss Teen launch. It was the best piece of the collection. I mean, if you saw it at a party in New York you'd think, yeah, sure, she found it on eBay. But here? Who would wear it here?'

'I saw it on a boy,' Crow says, between sips of water. 'He was in the bead shop, picking up a package. I only saw him for a moment. He was wearing the dress under an old shirt, but I recognised it straight away. I had to follow him.'

See? Crow has super-vision. The boy could probably have worn it under a spacesuit and she would have spotted it. But why was he wearing it at all? How did he get hold of it?

'Did you find him?'

Crow shrugs and Harry shakes his head.

'There are so many alleyways here,' Harry says. 'He just disappeared.'

We spend half an hour wandering through the lanes, getting vaguely lost again and looking out for a boy in a dress. No joy.

In the taxi on the way back to the hotel, Edie says, 'You know the pictures Alisha showed us of all the clothes being made in the factory?'

'Ye-es,' I say.

'Do you remember seeing the Svetlana dress then?'

Come to think of it, I don't. And it's odd, because it was the star piece. The embroidery on it was incredible. The closest you can get to the sort of thing they've got on show at the V&A, but at a Miss Teen price point.

'We could ask Mr Patil about it,' I suggest.

Edie thinks for a minute, then shakes her head.

'I should really talk to Phil first,' she says.

I groan. She always needs to talk to Phil these days.

'Phil?' asks Harry.

'He's her internet friend,' Crow explains. Then she and Harry exchange glances and Edie goes pink and nobody says anything for the rest of the journey back to the hotel.

Chapter 37

'What does he say?'

It's late. Edie is back on her laptop, updating her blog about Culturally Significant Sites in Mumbai and messaging Phil about the boy in the dress.

Her suitcase is neatly packed on her bed. Beside it are the clothes she'll wear to travel in tomorrow and her washbag. Also the books she's set aside for the flight. She hasn't actually arranged them in alphabetical order, but I wouldn't put it past her.

I'm standing on my suitcase, which probably wouldn't close if we sat an elephant on it. There are only so many new slippers and scarves and souvenirs you can fit in a suitcase before it gives up even trying to hold them, and I reached that point long ago. And I've just remembered my only clean pair of knickers is right at the bottom. Great.

Crow is simply looking at her bag, as if watching it will make the contents smaller. It reminds me of a treasure chest, with all the jewel-coloured silks and gold embroidery peeping out from inside. A very full treasure chest that isn't going to close any time soon, however much Crow stares at it. I think it's 'undo-upable'.

We're both keen to know what Phil thinks about the boy in the dress.

'He says we can try asking in the bead shop,' Edie says. 'But they almost certainly won't tell us anything. These operations are totally illegal so everyone's very secretive about them. It's like asking a drug dealer where he gets his drugs from. And about as dangerous. Oh.'

'Oh what?'

'He's changed his mind. He's asking us not to go back. Begging us, actually. He says there are some nasty people mixed up in this business. If there's really child labour being used, we could be in big trouble if we get too close. He says he'll get some people he knows in Mumbai to have a look when we've gone.'

'They won't find anything,' Crow says. 'They won't know what to look for. Only I know.'

She sounds very sure about this. And she's probably right. Only she can spot one of her designs being worn under a loose shirt by a fleeing child. It's this X-ray fashion vision she has.

Edie's still reading Phil's message. 'Anyway, he says it could all be a mistake. Even if the dress is the Svetlana dress, it could have been stolen from the big factory, or it could easily be a fake. Styles are ripped off all the time.'

'So basically we don't know anything,' I sigh. 'And he doesn't want us to find out more.'

Edie nods. 'Basically, yes. If we want to stay safe. He's saying he's sorry for getting me – I mean, us – into this.'

'It's a bit late now.'

When I think of how miserable he made her with the hacking he did on launch day, he'd have to be *very* sorry to make up for it.

'What's he saying now?'

'Oh . . . stuff.'

She's gone all vague. Very un-Edie. I wander over to get a peek, but she covers the screen and shoos me away. This is even more intriguing. Watching me hover, she gives up on the messaging.

'Look, if you're so interested in the computer, you use it.' She quits what she's doing, gets up and sits on her bed with a book.

Well, I'm not going to get my case shut tonight, so I might as well do some Googling and check my emails.

Crow's stuff is still selling well on eBay. In my inbox, there are nine invitations to fashion events and parties. Three people want to interview us. Two friends want to know how I'm getting on with French revision. Oh, and Amanda Elat says we'll be 'relieved to know' that Sigrid has agreed to wear the sea-goddess dress after all, and she's in the process of having it altered.

ALTERED?

She doesn't like the length, apparently, and wants it shorter.

I tell Crow, whose jaw drops. She comes over, so I can show her the line where it says that. Then we stare at each other in horror. This is the design equivalent of buying a Ferrari and getting someone else to cut the roof off so you can use it as a convertible. IT'S NOT DONE. IT'S RUDE. It's totally normal for the Queen of Evil, though.

There's more. Sigrid wants the dress for the after-show party for *Her Father's Daughter*, when it opens in the West End. She needs something unique, to reflect her new profile as a serious stage actress. And she's sure we'll understand that, in order to emphasise its uniqueness, this means Crow can't design anything for Jenny to wear at the same party. But she's happy for her stylist to find something suitable for her. She's heard great things about this new guy, Pablo Dodo, for example.

Pablo Dodo, who dressed Jenny for her movie premieres as a *cherry tomato*, a *condom in a boa*, and a *telephone directory*. NEVER IN A MILLION YEARS.

I read this bit out to everyone and for a while we're all so stunned that we forget about the boy in the dress.

'You can't let her do it,' Edie says, as if life were that simple.

'Can't we pretend we didn't get the email?' Crow asks.

I shake my head sadly. ''Fraid not. Andy pays us. Sigrid knows we can't say no to him. That's why she asked the Elats, not us.'

'But what can Jenny wear?' Crow asks. Her eyes are saucer-wide and she's looking at me imploringly.

It's hard to ignore her when she looks at me like that. I wish I was Super-Nonie. I wish I could just come up with a clever idea to . . . oh.

Just for once, I think I might have one. Just for once, it might work out. It will be Project Jenny. I need to think about it more and I can't talk about it yet, but that's OK. They see the smile on my face. Edie smiles back. And Crow's grin reminds me of the Taj Mahal at sunrise.

Chapter 38

We spend the first half of breakfast all agreeing that we should DEFINITELY NOT go back to that bazaar. Too dangerous. But while we're thinking of something else to do, Crow mentions that she forgot to pick her beads up from the shop. So we spend the second half of breakfast agreeing that we'll just pop back, quickly get them and spend the rest of the day doing something safe and touristy.

I'm worried at first that we won't find the shop again, but Harry guides us there quite easily. This is a boy who's used to finding his way through the tents at Bryant Park in New York, and the madness that is Milan Fashion Week, so a few alleyways in a market are nothing to him.

However, when we get there, the plan goes wrong and it's entirely my fault. I forget we're supposed to go in and out and keep our heads down. Today, I have the energy to do my usual thing in bead shops, which is GO CRAZY, and that's what I do. I can't help falling in love with everything. I'm picturing the necklaces I could make, the pencil cases I could embellish, the tops and dresses I could transform. I'm not picturing my suitcase, which Harry had to close with a strap this morning, because we don't trust the zips. Nor am I picturing my wallet, which is empty. I'll have to owe Harry.

There are also trays full of gorgeous bangles that I didn't spot yesterday. They come in the brightest colours. Neon pink and electric blue, grass-green and a vivid shade of orange that only exists here in India. My suitcase may be full, but my arms are empty. They're very cheap and Harry agrees to lend me some rupees. I choose twenty.

The others should be hurrying me up, but they seem grateful to linger. Edie has her eye on the curtain at the back of the shop, which is where Crow said the boy appeared from yesterday, and Crow and Harry are watching the street outside. But none of us mentions the boy in the dress out loud. Phil's right. If there's something going on, the shop owner might be a part of it. It's like buying jewellery in a drug den. I'm nuts. The bangles are really lovely, though.

Eventually, it starts to look strange that we're hanging about so much. We haven't spotted anything and my arms are now jangling like temple bells. It's time to pay up and leave, so we do. Except, this time, Harry isn't concentrating. We take a wrong turning and instead of heading for the hotel, we end up going down alleyway after alleyway that we don't recognise. We twist and turn randomly, hoping we won't get so impossibly lost that we never find our way out of here. Maybe I should have left a trail of beads and bangles. Too late now.

Then suddenly, the shops and stalls stop and we're on a bare strip of land near a railway line and some decrepit flats ringed by rows of little shacks. For once, the sky isn't blocked by buildings and satellite dishes. A few cows and goats are nosing through the scrub and rubbish-filled drains, looking for something to eat. At one end, several street children are playing a game of cricket in the muggy heat. The earth is scattered with animal poo, but we really need to sit down for a moment. Harry manages to find a spot that's less pooey than most. We grab a drink of water and catch our breath.

Crow says 'Look!' and points at the game. The children are using a block of wood for their cricket bat and a ball made out of rolled-up packing tape. They can really hit it, though.

A few years ago, Harry had to babysit me for the day and he took me to watch some cricket team play at Lords. Most of the time it was extremely boring, but every now and again one of the players would do an amazing run-up to bowl, or a stunning swing of the bat, or a balletic leap to catch the ball, and these kids are exactly the same. Totally focused and beautiful to watch. It's easy to forget where we are, until one of them slips over in a cowpat and the rest collapse with laughter.

At this point, they notice us and a crowd of them come over, holding out their hands and touching our clothes. Some beg for rupees. Others say 'school pen, school pen', although I'm guessing they don't go to school that often. Crow lets them touch her hair again. She's getting used to it. She has some rupees left and hands them over. Harry even gives them a paperback he has in his pocket.

One of the boys stares at Harry and shouts, 'Freddie Flintoff!'

Harry laughs and says 'Sachin Tendulkar!'

The boy grins back.

'What does that mean?' Edie asks.

'It's the international language of cricket,' Harry explains. Then he runs off a list of cricketers to the boy – Indian and English ones – and holds up his fingers. 'I'm comparing runs. Their guys are doing better at the moment.'

This would be why the boy is grinning so much. He motions for Harry to stand up and points across at where they're playing the game. Next thing we know, Harry's got the bat and is facing some demon bowling with the packing tape ball. Nothing he can't handle, though. The children cheer as the ball sails over the heads of the fielders and lands in a drain.

Meanwhile, Crow and Edie and I are surrounded by girls. We're used to the street children coming up to us, but this is the first time we've ventured into their world.

We feel like guests, glad that they don't mind us being here, happy to let them admire our bags and laugh at our clothes. It's hot and dusty and dirty, but I don't feel as unsafe here as I did five minutes ago. Actually, I realise I'm having a good time.

The match progresses. Harry is put in to bowl. It gets hotter. We share our water with a couple of the girls. An older boy wanders over and I get a frisson of nervousness. Although he's small and thin, like all of them, he seems strong and athletic and somehow in charge. If he doesn't like the look of us, we could be in trouble.

Instead, he says, 'Los Angeles is a very glorious city.'

We look at each other. What are we supposed to reply?

'Actually, we're from London,' Edie says. 'You speak very good English, by the way.'

'Oh yes, isn't it?' says the boy proudly. 'I am Sanjay. I work on film sets. Bollywood. People come from Los Angeles. Very glorious city. Do you know Walt Disney?'

'Not exactly,' Edie admits. 'I know *of* him.'

'Very famous man,' the boy says, puffing himself up. 'He is good friend. Very good personal friend. I help him. I help everyone. Whatever you need, I can get it. Anything. I know everyone.'

'Do you know a boy like this?' Crow asks suddenly. She's scrabbling in her satchel for a new sketchbook and she quickly draws a picture of the boy in the dress. Just like she'd make a good witness at a crime scene, it turns out she could also be a police artist, doing e-fits, if she wanted. The sketch takes her about ten seconds. She hands it to Sanjay and looks at him pleadingly.

Sanjay looks at the picture for a while and says nothing. Then he shouts out to a couple of children, who leave the makeshift cricket pitch and come over. Sanjay is obviously the sort of boy you don't say no to round here. After a quick conversation, the children run off. Before we can ask what's happening, Sanjay says, 'I am excellent batsman. Watch, please.'

He marches up to the wicket and demands the bat from the little boy who's holding it. After a short debate, the boy hands it over, and Sanjay misses the next six balls with a flourish, smiling broadly at us every time.

By now I'm getting pretty hungry and wishing I'd worn a sun hat. Some street food and a nice, cool ice cream would go down perfectly. The bridge of Edie's nose is going dangerously pink. Crow is used to the African sun from childhood and doesn't seem bothered, but I'm starting to miss the shady spaces of Kensington. We ought to go back, but we're waiting for something, even though we're not sure what.

Then Sanjay's messengers come running back. With them is a little girl. She looks about five or six, but holds herself like a much older child. I remember Mrs Patil saying that street children usually look a lot younger than they really are. This girl is thin and barefoot, like the others, and wearing something that used to be a dress a long time ago, but is now merely the ghost of one – a few scraps of cranberry red fabric and some seams. There is something badly wrong with her hair and face. Edie grabs my hand and squeezes it, shocked, but by now Sanjay is bringing her over, so we let go and smile politely.

'This is Lakshmi,' Sanjay says to Edie, as if that explains everything. He notices that we seem confused. 'The sister,' he continues. 'Of Ganesh.' He points to Crow's sketchbook, which is lying open on her discarded satchel. Crow holds up the picture of the boy in the dress.

'Ganesh?' she asks.

They all nod. And it seems Sanjay wasn't joking when he said he knew everyone. In a city of twenty million people, he knows the boy we're looking for. He asks Lakshmi where Ganesh might be. She explains in rapid Hindi, her face alight with excitement. Then Sanjay sends his messengers off again and motions to Lakshmi to sit near us. She comes close gradually, like a little bird slowly gaining confidence, and picks a spot about a metre from me.

Edie notices Lakshmi's hand, which is damaged, like her face.

'What happened?' she asks Sanjay quietly, gesturing at the girl.

He smiles and half-nods, half-shakes his head. Whatever it is, he doesn't want to tell us.

Edie smiles back at him. 'I understand. We're just strangers. It's OK.'

She goes back to watching the cricket and funnily enough, this makes Sanjay change his mind. He seems to prefer it when she's hanging on his every word. He looks round and chats rapidly to some of the other boys. Gradually, they start clustering round us more closely. One boy starts shouting and others join in enthusiastically. We realise they're telling Lakshmi's story for her, while Sanjay translates.

The cricket match is quickly abandoned. The circle grows. The story is this.

Once upon a time, there were two children who lived in the countryside. They can't remember exactly when, but one day they left their parents' home with men who brought them on a long train journey, here to Mumbai, and put them to work in a small room. The men explained that it had cost money to take them on the journey, and to look after them in the small room, and it would take the children years to pay it back. They didn't know why they were paying, when they didn't want to be here in the first place, but they worked. From first light until bedtime. Ganesh was fast and strong and did what he could to protect his sister from the worst of the beatings, and to make sure she got extra food whenever he could steal it.

They were hidden away from police and 'busybodies' in rooms created between the floors of buildings, or in basements, moving every few months. They were taught embroidery and they became very good at it. But as he grew older, Ganesh was given a new job. He became a messenger and courier for the bosses.

Last year, he was out collecting a parcel of new thread when there was a fire in the room where Lakshmi was working. Fires were common. One of the bosses cooked meals in a corner of the room and the stove got knocked over. The door was locked and there weren't any windows. It took a while to escape the flames.

Which is why Lakshmi has only half her hair, and only one eye, and why the skin on her face and neck is scarred and two of her fingers are fused together. It's why she can't really sew any more and was sent out to beg instead. She was seven.

While the story is being told, Lakshmi edges closer to me. Why she picks me, I have no idea. Usually, people notice Edie or Crow. But by the end, she is sitting in my lap and I am stroking what's left of her hair, which is long and silky. She's playing with my bangles. I take several of them off and put them on her wrists. Her arms are so thin that they slide easily over her elbows and up to her armpits. We laugh. I take my scarf off and wrap it round her neck.

'Beautiful,' I say.

She turns round to look at me, surprised. 'Beautiful' is one of the few English words she knows. She must use it a lot to try and persuade tourists to give her money, but I don't think she's had it said to her before.

She's very beautiful, though. Tiny and strong. The

eyelashes on her remaining eye are long and curved – like the fake ones I used on the First Kiss Disaster Date, but less unreliable. Her features are small and delicate. Her smile reminds me of Crow's: sudden and blinding. It feels very natural for her to be sitting in my lap. I don't want her to go.

A shout goes up. Ganesh is here. A tall boy compared with some of the others, with the body of a skinny ten-year-old and the wary eyes of a grown-up. He's still wearing his dress as he approaches, watching us all unblinkingly, especially when he sees me with his precious sister.

Sanjay talks to him rapidly, indicating me and mentioning the word 'beautiful' and laughing. Ganesh seems slightly less wary after that. He joins the group and Sanjay translates for us as we ask him about what happened last year.

Did he see children making the dress that he's wearing now? Is it a fake, or a real one? What happened?

At first he doesn't want to answer, but the other children beg and plead with him. After all, they've told us the worst of it. Slowly, Ganesh agrees. He lets Crow examine what's left of the dress and she's convinced it's too well made to be a fake. He lifts his shirt up to point out a mistake on the embroidery, which is why it was discarded. Then he explains how the panels for the dresses were made last autumn, after the rainy season, in a building not far from here. They were the last clothes

Lakshmi worked on before the fire. Ganesh thought they were some of the most beautiful things he had seen and was thrilled to get this one, despite remembering the beating of the boy who made the mistake with the embroidery. At the same time, some tee-shirts were brought in to be finished. They had crystals sewn on them to make English words.

Edie groans. '"Less Fashion More Compassion". My first slogan.'

We hear spluttering behind us and turn round to see Harry grinning sheepishly. 'You have to admit, it's ironic.'

Sanjay spots Harry grinning and giggles without knowing why. The other children join him. They've told the story about Lakshmi the way I might describe an evening doing a difficult geography project. Not the most fun thing in the world, but hey, life goes on. At least they're out here having a nice game of cricket and a chat with the funny, sunburned people and the girl who can draw.

'Where does Lakshmi live now?' I ask.

Sanjay looks surprised. 'Live?'

'Spend the night. Where is her home?'

He laughs and points beyond the railway tracks. 'There are some old train carriages there that are OK, isn't it? When they find us using them, they will beat us. We'll find different ones. Five star!'

A couple of years ago, I might have asked why Lakshmi and Ganesh didn't try and return to their parents, but then I got to know Crow and now I understand that some things are more complicated than we can guess. Crow couldn't go back home because her parents' life was too dangerous. And now she stays because London is her home. Maybe Lakshmi's parents can't afford to look after her. Maybe they think she's living a good life in Mumbai and that's why they sent her away. Maybe she just doesn't know where to find them. Her story will be different from Crow's, but whatever it is, I know I can't just click my fingers and make everything better. I wish I could, though. I really do.

The kids are still bubbling with curiosity, keen to find out everything about us. Lakshmi has sidled up to Crow and is examining the seams of her sari-fabric dungarees. Despite everything, she still can't help being interested in the way beautiful clothes are made.

I picture her working on the Svetlana dress last autumn – and us having no idea she even existed. Crow looks across and catches my eye. I know what she's thinking. We have to help them somehow. We have to do what we can.

We also have to catch our flight.

I spot Harry looking at his watch and we both realise that if we don't go soon we're not going to make the airport in time.

What do we do now?

'Wait here,' Harry says. Using Sanjay as our translator, he persuades Ganesh to take him to the building his bosses are currently using to house their slave children. Ganesh is clear. He'll point it out from a distance, but he won't let Harry go close. There have been a lot of raids recently. If the bosses think they're being watched, there will be trouble.

We watch Harry go, then sit in silence while the children go back to their cricket match. I'm playing with the bangles on Lakshmi's arms, making her giggle and trying not to think too much about anything. Crow's sketching a boy leaping gracefully to catch a ball. Edie's restless and doesn't know what to do with herself.

Eventually she says, 'This is all my fault.'

'No it isn't,' I tell her automatically. I realise I'm shivering, despite the heat, and try not to.

'It's good,' Crow says quietly. 'It was important to know this. But I hope Harry comes back soon.'

We all agree. Time passes. Someone scores a six.

And then he's back. He's looking very serious, but the main thing is, he's safe. Now it really is time for us to get out of here.

Before we go, though, Harry gets his phone out of his pocket. The children cluster round and admire it. I half wonder if he's going to give it to them, but he doesn't. Instead, he takes their pictures. He starts off with Sanjay and Ganesh and Lakshmi, but soon they're all insisting on posing for him. Then he tells Sanjay the name of our hotel and instructs him to go there in a fortnight.

'There will be an envelope for you. And this picture of

you will be attached, so the people will know to give it to you. Inside, we'll tell you how we'll help you. Get someone to read it for you. OK? Someone you trust.'

Who, I wonder. Walt Disney?

Sanjay looks at us all and shakes his head in the yes-no Indian way. I'm not sure he believes Harry. After all, what can four tourist kids who suddenly show up out of nowhere do? But Sanjay is obviously someone who likes to think that things will turn out well. And someone who likes going to big hotels on important missions.

'Yes, sir,' he agrees. He repeats the instructions. 'This is very easy job. You can count on me, sir.'

We leave at last. I can hardly bear to say goodbye to Lakshmi. I hate the thought that I'll probably never see her again. I wonder what else I can give her. Then I remember I'm wearing a gold chain Mum gave me ages ago. I quickly take it off and hand it over. Maybe she can sell it to buy a decent meal or something. I hug her and she hugs me back. Her arms are so light I can hardly feel her.

On the way back through the market I hardly notice the alleyways, the noise, the smell, the heat. Crow sticks close to me. I think she knows I need her comforting arm to hold.

'What was your plan, by the way?' Edie asks Harry.

'Plan?'

'Yes. Your plan for that envelope. The one Sanjay's going to collect.'

'Oh, that. No idea. What should we do? I was hoping we could have worked it out by then. Maybe your Phil guy can help us think of something.'

My brother. I love him so much. And now I know my habit of winging it is in the genes. I'm so glad it's not just me.

Chapter 39

'So, how was your trip to Agra? You didn't call me again! Have you been OK? I want to hear *all* about it.'

I'm in the car with Mrs Patil, suddenly wishing we were doing mental maths.

We'd all forgotten that the Patils would be driving us back to the airport. And we'd certainly forgotten that they'd want a full report about what we've been up to. Of course, it's worse for Harry and Crow, because they're travelling in the other car with Mr Patil. And we simply don't know if he knows about the slave children. It seems impossible to imagine that he does, having seen him in his shiny factory with all his happy, healthy, grown-up workers and his high-tech machinery, and having met his own cute children, with their amazing maths ability.

Maybe it was someone else who decided that the Svetlana dress was too complicated to make cheaply at the factory. Maybe it was some junior manager who spoke to Ganesh's bosses, arranged the deal and pocketed the profits. Maybe it was someone we've never met. Maybe if we tell the Patils what we've seen they'll be horrified and get the bosses put in jail.

But maybe they won't. One thing we're sure of: we don't know what we're doing and we don't know who to trust. It's better if we say nothing until we get back to London. Then we can use Edie's network of charity friends to help us out.

So I spend an hour talking about bangles and DS games and ice cream and sound like the ditziest teenager ever to visit Mumbai. Edie helps out with ten minutes on the fabulousness of the amazing architecture. When we get to the airport we practically fall out of the car in our eagerness to get to passport control, and safety.

It's not till we've taken off that Harry manages to tell us about his trip with Ganesh.

'You know the worst thing?'

No, we don't.

'The building he showed me . . . it was just a normal apartment block. Nothing special at all. There are thousands of them in Mumbai. If you're looking, where do you start?'

Harry doesn't say much more after that. He loses himself in his book. However, I do notice that he gives Edie a funny look, as if he's finally realised that her saving-the-world obsession is actually more than just a teenage hobby. I'm glad she doesn't catch him looking at her. She'd be doing that waterfall thing with her hair, if she did, and going an intense shade of pink. Instead of REVISING FOR GEOGRAPHY, which is her chosen activity.

Why does she bother? What can she possibly have left to learn?

Chapter 40

I'm back in my room, in my Hello Kitty pyjamas, writing a list of Scary Things Happening Soon.

Two months until Harry's degree show. His problem, not mine, but nevertheless, scary.

Forty-two days until geography GCSE. I still don't know the difference between the Atlantic and the Pacific Ocean. And there won't be a single question on India. Not one. Sadly, there are no garment factories that I'm aware of in the Arctic Circle. Although with global warming going the way it is, there might be soon.

Eleven days until Sanjay will show up at our old hotel in Mumbai (assuming he does), to collect the letter telling him how we're going to help. Still no idea what will be in the envelope. Nor has Harry. Nor has Edie, but she's checking with Phil and her other save-the-world blogging friends.

Eight days until Jenny's first night at the Biggest, Scariest Theatre in the West End.

Seven days until our next meeting with Andy Elat, when Crow has to magic up a new high-street collection and Edie has to say absolutely and positively that she's happy with the way Miss Teen clothes are made in India. Which, of course, she isn't.

One day until I see Granny, to put Project Jenny into operation. I can only hope that Granny's been busy over the last couple of days, because if she hasn't managed to do the thing I've asked her, I'm sunk.

Henry has just called to say he's picking Crow up from the workroom downstairs, to take her home. I check the clock on my laptop. It's 10.35 pm. She should have gone home hours ago, but she's been too busy to notice the time passing. It makes me think. Sure, we're kids and we work a lot, sometimes. But the difference between us and Lakshmi and Ganesh is that the grown-ups in our lives interrupt us from work to make us go to school and sleep. Not the other way around.

When I checked on Crow earlier, she was taking all the Parisian feathers and lace and tweed and trimmings off her pinboard and packing them away in a big cardboard box. I asked her what she was going to replace them with. She indicated a pile of stuff on the worktable, but all I could see were cheesy postcards from Agra, some plain A4 paper, a white hanky and a couple of cheap gemstones.

I was expecting to see all the bags of beads and her treasures of coloured silk and gold thread. Possibly sequinned slippers and jewelled notebooks and keyrings with Indian dolls on – all the things we've been collecting on our trip. I thought the pile would be psychedelic by now, but it isn't. Quite the opposite. Has she lost it entirely?

I've no idea what she's up to, but I do know that she's not blocked any more. For months, the creative part of her brain has wanted to make complicated couture and the practical part has been trying to design something simple. And neither part really wanted to do anything while we were worrying about slave children.

However, something has happened. Her frustrated look has gone. Her fingers are constantly twitching with sketches again, even when she has no paper. She's back to her old self. Unfortunately, her old self tends to get on with things without talking about them much, so I'll have to wait to find out what's changed. And hey, checking my list, we have a whole week for her to get something ready to show Andy Elat, so no pressure. NOT.

I try not to think about it. Thank goodness I have Jenny and her first night party outfit to worry about instead.

Granny meets me in the lobby of the Ritz the next day and I'm relieved to see that she's accompanied by a very large box.

'Guard this with your life, my girl,' she says. 'You have absolutely no idea what I had to do to get it.'

Actually, I do have an idea. I imagine Granny had to suck up to one of her old friends for a solid morning, which is something she would find almost unbearable. I give her a huge hug of gratitude, which crumples her Issey Miyake jacket. It's designed to be crumpled, though, so she doesn't mind too much.

We park the box with the hotel concierge for a while and Granny takes me to the Royal Academy so we can Do Art and I can tell her all about India. It already feels as if we've hardly been away.

Afterwards, I meet up with Jenny and Crow at home for Project Jenny. I feel guilty about this bit. Crow should really be totally concentrating on the Miss Teen collection, but I need her to spare a few hours to help us battle the Queen of Evil. Luckily, when she sees what's inside the box, she can't wait to get started.

'It's beautiful.'

We have to wait for a few minutes while she runs her hands delicately over the fabric, like it's a sacred relic or something.

Then she looks hard at Jenny and cocks her head to one side. 'This will be easier than I thought,' she says.

I know what she means, and this worries me.

Crow's thinking about measurements. She's mentally redesigning seams and adjusting fabric. What she's pleased about – from a purely practical perspective – is that there's a lot less of Jenny than there was a couple of weeks ago, when we last saw her. I admit that this will make Project Jenny simpler to complete, but it also means that my friend has been losing weight at an alarming rate. From a friendship perspective, this is very bad.

'Are you OK?' I ask.

'Fine,' Jenny says, in a strangled voice that means 'Not fine' in friend-speak.

'What's happened? How are the previews going? They haven't cut your part, have they?'

She shrugs and shakes her head.

'Oh, it's not Sigrid, is it? Don't tell me. She wants Joe Yule to play your father.'

Jenny shakes her head and giggles.

'She wants you to curtsey whenever she comes on stage?' Crow asks, getting into the spirit.

Jenny smiles. But instead of answering, she asks, 'Can I show you something?'

I say yes. Crow has loads of work to do, so we leave her to it and Jenny takes me on the tube to Covent Garden. For a moment, I'm worried that we're heading for the Royal Opera House, home of my ex-not-boyfriend and not somewhere I particularly want to be any time soon. But instead she takes me down a side street and I realise we're going to the Big, Scary Theatre, where previews started a couple of days ago and huge, electric signs are already spelling out *Her Father's Daughter* in lights.

There's some sort of last-minute technical session going on. The place is full of people wearing black tee-shirts and headsets, looking busy and making notes and squinting at bits of equipment. They know Jenny, so they don't mind us standing quietly at the back.

'What do you think?' Jenny whispers.

I look down past the rows and rows and *rows* of seats. This place is vast. It makes the Boat House Theatre look like a ticket office. You could probably get two thousand people in here. If I was standing on that stage, so far away, facing such a massive audience, I'd be scared out of my mind.

'It looks *great*!' I say. 'Totally amazing. You must be so excited.'

Her face crumples like Granny's Issey Miyake. She nods. I can tell she's lying, and she must know that I was.

'It's like something out of *Star Wars*,' I admit. 'I've never seen anything so huge.'

'Oh, Nonie!' She sits on the nearest seat and I just hold her for a while.

'It's not Sigrid any more. To be honest, I think she's as scared as I am. But something's gone wrong since we started rehearsing here. And last night was terrible. No-one's really talking about it, but you can see these people having secret conversations. Anthony looks positively ill most of the time.'

As if on cue, Anthony, the director, appears at the side of the stage and shouts at one of the technicians, who makes more notes. He does indeed look ill. Sunken-cheeked and unshaven. Definitely not the same man as the one who accompanied Sigrid to the Elysée Palace in her DOLCE & GABBANA. An older, more haggard version.

'Why?' I ask.

Jenny's voice almost disappears. 'It's me.'

'*You?*'

She nods. Tears fall silently. Jenny really must do a part that requires major crying one day.

'What have you done?'

'It's what I *can't* do. I've heard the rumours. They're trying not to tell me, but you always hear them in the end. I just can't fill this space. With my voice, I mean. I'm trying my best, but I'm only sixteen. I haven't got the vocal power. That's what they're doing now: desperately trying to fix the acoustics so it doesn't sound so bad. They tried miking us up, but it didn't work. They're being nice about it, but it's so humiliating.'

I try to comfort her that nobody will notice, nobody will mind. But we both know that in a few days, theatre critics from England *and* America will be sitting in the front rows for the official first night, and they *will* notice and they *will* mind. And they *will* tell everyone.

In the end, Jenny sighs.

'It's not as though I haven't been through it before.'

She even manages half a laugh. If being 'wooden' in a major blockbuster has prepared her for anything, it's prepared her for this. All I can do is remind her about Project Jenny. At least the first night party won't be a total disaster.

On the way out, we notice two burly men standing at the stage door, their arms full of bowls of orchids.

'That'll be for the star's dressing room,' Jenny says. She sighs. 'They got me a nice cactus. It's very sweet. I've painted a smiley face on it.'

When I get back home, a parcel has arrived. Crow shows it to me. In it is the bottom half of the fabric from the sea-goddess dress that Sigrid won't be needing any more, because she HAD IT CUT OFF.

Crow and I just look at each other. God, we hate that girl.

Chapter 41

Crow is madly busy. I'm not sure if she's sleeping at all now. On the rare occasions I see her, she looks hungry and is busy stuffing down a sandwich before going back to her workroom for another session. She's finally let me see what she's doing and I personally think it's brilliant, but also EXTREMELY RISKY. It's certainly very different from the undoable designs she was working on before we went to India.

Will the Miss Teen people love it, or think she's having a laugh? And more to the point, what will Andy Elat think about all the *other* ideas we've had since we got back from Mumbai?

While Crow's been busy working, Edie, Harry and I have been busy thinking. About how to help Sanjay, who made everything seem so easy when just finding enough to eat every day must be a struggle. And Ganesh, who was so desperate to look after his little sister, whatever it took. And most of all, about Lakshmi, with her shy smile and her fused fingers and her fascination with beautiful sewing, in spite of everything that's happened to her.

I have one of Harry's pictures of Lakshmi on my phone, after he sent it to me from his. I can't help looking at it. I can't bear that she's so far away and it should be me, somehow, who's looking after her. She chose me. I chose her back. And right now only Crow, Harry and Edie understand exactly how I feel.

Edie wants me to go over to her house, so that we can talk through our Miss Teen strategy. Now that she's involved, we don't wing things so much any more. We have strategies. We are SO grown-up and organised.

When I get there, her laptop is on as usual, and she's looking at someone's Facebook page. I look a bit closer.

'Wow! He's gorgeous! Who's that?'

'Oh, that?' she says, as if she hadn't noticed. 'That's Phil.'

'THAT'S PHIL? *That* is Phil?'

Phil from No Kidding is not at all the nerdy communications guy I'd always assumed he was. In fact, he makes Joe Yule look like a hobbit. He has surfer-blonde hair, gorgeous blue eyes and a jawline that you just want to run your fingers over, to check if it's real. Phil from No Kidding is SUPER-CUTE.

'You never said he was hot.'

'Oh,' she says again, vaguely. 'Is he?'

'Yes,' I point out slowly but firmly. 'He is.'

She goes a shade of pink that I've never seen before. It would make a good lipstick colour.

'Anyway, there's a children's charity based in Mumbai that can provide schooling for the kids if we can get some funding and encourage them to go. And it can also find them jobs so they're not reduced to begging and they can find somewhere safe to sleep.'

'How do we get them in touch with it?'

'This is where your brother's plan comes in. We can put it all in the letter. The address for them to go to. A note to the charity about their background, and how we'll raise money to help look after them.'

'By selling tee-shirts?' I ask cautiously. Edie's tee-shirts are OK, but I'm not sure they could fund an education.

'Whatever it takes,' Edie says firmly. 'We've raised money before. We can do it again. We just will.'

I love the way she says 'we'. She's very sweet about not taking all the credit for the amazing stuff she does. And she's right, of course. We just will.

'And we'll find a way of staying in touch. I'm missing them already, aren't you?'

I instantly feel my eyes welling up, Jenny-style. YES, I *am* missing them despite only seeing them that one, hot afternoon. YES, of course I want to stay in touch. YES, my friend is incredible for assuming that we even can, what with them being five thousand miles away (I know the distance, yay!), and not having a home, never mind a phone, or being able to read or write or MINOR

DETAILS like that. But minor details don't bother Edie.

I nod, and there's a bit of a huggy moment, until something occurs to me. I can't help it. I pull back.

'Did Hot Phil tell you about this charity and the jobs and everything?'

'Look, he's just a friend, OK?'

I give her the look that Crow shared with Harry in India when she was explaining about Edie's 'internet friend'.

'A friend that you email and message on a daily basis, even when you're *literally* – check out my geography – on the other side of the world.'

'He's just very nice,' she protests. 'Very charming and caring. He was so worried about us when we got lost in that market. He was ringing people up all over the place, trying to get them to check up on us that last day, even though it was the middle of the night in California.'

'All of us?' I ask. 'Or one of us in particular?'

Lipstick-pink again.

'D'you want to know what the strategy is for the meeting with Mr Elat, or what?'

Actually, I do. And she tells me. And it's a good strategy. I like it very much. Almost as much as I like the look of Hot Phil.

Edie tries to make me promise not to call him that any more, and to stop teasing her about him. I promise to stop.

I'm lying.

Chapter 42

We're standing in the King's Road, staring at a blue front door. It looks like nothing at all – just any old front door of any old flat in London – but to me it's like something out of a horror movie. What lies behind it is VERY SCARY INDEED.

What lies behind it is Andy Elat. Well, actually, not him right now, because he's already texted to say he's going to be late for our meeting, but his flat. Or his lair, as I like to think of it. When I think about what we've come to say to him, I can feel little beads of sweat forming on my forehead. This reminds me. I check my upper lip. Sweat-free, luckily. I would so hate to take after my ex-not-boyfriend.

I look across at Crow. She looks tired and grumpy, which I happen to know means she's secretly mega-nervous too. She looks across at Edie, who straightens her shoulders and rings the doorbell. Edie is a class prefect. Edie chairs the debating society. Edie eats scary things for breakfast. Not literally – she likes Weetabix – but you know what I mean. Edie is the sort of friend you want to have right now. Crow and I sort of cluster behind her, wishing we were invisible. Which would be easier if I hadn't decided that my neon pink legwarmers and bottle-top Converses were appropriate for the occasion.

The door opens. It's a man I've never seen before. He introduces himself as 'Mr Godbold' and looks like the headmaster of a posh school, dressed up in a perfectly-fitted, handmade suit. Turns out he's Andy's butler. Cool! Although it adds to the whole horror-movie effect. He guides us across a little lobby to a lift and presses the button for the third floor. We arrive in another little lobby and Mr Godbold opens a heavy front door, plain wood this time, and leads us through a wide hallway to a large room with rooftop views. Suddenly here we are, in Andy Elat's home.

I've been picturing this place for a long time. Andy Elat has famously lived in a flat above the King's Road for the last forty years. He arrived soon after Twiggy drove her Mini down it on the way to modelling shoots. He was here when Vivienne Westwood and Malcolm McLaren started selling punk tee-shirts and trousers held together with safety pins. He stayed as the posh shops started arriving and it turned from a little, independent, quirky place into one of the main fashion high streets of London.

What style has he gone for? Will there be waterfalls

cascading from the roof? Or wall-to-wall granite? Or gold-leaf ceilings? Or plasma TV screens on every available surface?

I've braced myself for pretty much anything, but what I haven't braced myself for is a sitting room that looks like an old-fashioned junk shop, with sofas. I look around in astonishment. So do Edie and Crow. I'm not sure this place has been redecorated since around the time Twiggy started modelling. No plasma screens. No gold leaf. Just lots of pictures of fishing boats and a collection of coloured glass ashtrays that screams anything but chic.

Amanda Elat comes in, looking more tired than I've ever seen her. There are rumours that Miss Teen hasn't been doing as well as normal recently. And all the press coverage from Edie's website can't be helping. However, when she sees our faces, she gives us a wan little smile.

'I know. Strange, isn't it? When Mum died, he couldn't bear to redecorate.'

'Oh,' we say.

I'd known that Andy Elat was single nowadays, but assumed he was divorced and leading a crazy, millionaire, bachelor lifestyle. Not widowed, pining and living in an old-fashioned flat. The more I know *about* him, the less I feel I know him.

'You're privileged,' she goes on. 'He doesn't usually agree to see people here. But he thought the headquarters at night-time would be a bit scary.'

We all laugh politely, as if the thought of being scared

by Andy Elat *anywhere* is simply ridiculous. How could anyone be so silly?

The reason we're here this evening is that it's the only time he could fit us in before he goes on holiday, which is first thing tomorrow morning. I grump about having the odd meeting on a Saturday morning. Andy Elat seems to have them all day, every day, seven days a week. No wonder he needs this holiday. And I hope Amanda's going with him. She looks as though she really needs one too.

Looking even tireder than two minutes ago, she leads us through to a dining room, where we arrange ourselves on mahogany chairs around a super-shiny mahogany table. Andy definitely has a thing about wood.

We order drinks from Mr Godbold, who serves them in coloured glasses on a silver tray. When he's done it, Amanda starts off the meeting with a deep sigh. 'Dad told me to get going. Otherwise we'll be here all night. So. Tell me about Mumbai.'

I'm sitting opposite Amanda, with Crow next to me, then Edie. Part of our strategy is that I'll go first and they'll help me out when I need it.

'It was fine,' I start, nervously. 'Sort of fine. The factory's great.' I try to sound enthusiastic, but Amanda's not here to hear about how great the factory is, and she knows it. I take a breath and just go for it. 'We found the children who embroidered the Svetlana dress.'

She sighs even more deeply, but she's not surprised. 'Yes, I've heard. It turns out that the factory occasionally subcontracts work that's too expensive to do in-house. It's against the contracts. Completely illegal. I don't know how they managed to fool our inspectors. Anyway, it won't happen again.'

'How can you be sure?' I ask. 'I mean, you already had people visiting. We've talked about it, and Edie can't change her website until we're certain that everyone's doing what they say they are. At least for Crow's new collection, anyway.'

'*If* she makes one,' Amanda points out, and I know she's thinking about undoability. I would be too, if I were her.

I carry on regardless. 'We think someone we trust must be at the factory all the time, checking how every piece is made. And making sure it's possible for them to make each piece properly for the price they say.'

Amanda's lips form a hard line and she really doesn't look like anyone's favourite aunt at all right now. 'It's more complicated than that, Nonie. Business is a complex world. We can't control everything. How could we? But you can be sure we're doing what we can.'

Edie looks across and catches my eye. She gives me a tiny, encouraging smile. I go on.

'I'm sorry, but it's not enough,' I say. 'I mean, you're right about it being complicated and everything. But we feel responsible for each piece that Crow designs. There's this little girl who . . . anyway.' I pause and collect myself. 'We can only put the "Crow" label on pieces we absolutely *know* are made fairly – because we've checked.'

I know there's other stuff too, but my brain has suddenly gone completely empty. I think it's something to do with the look Amanda's giving me. Crow senses me struggling and steps in. I'm starting to like the idea of having a strategy.

'Plus we want labels that warn people to check how their clothes are made,' she adds. 'Because if we all keep buying cheap stuff without thinking about it, there are people who'll keep forcing children to make it cheaply, too.'

By now, Amanda's lips are such a hard little line that they've almost disappeared. I think it would be a good idea to stop here. But Edie doesn't.

'And we want some of the profits from each piece to go towards rescuing child labourers and giving them a proper life,' she says firmly.

Amanda raises one eyebrow.

'Is that it?'

'Pretty much,' I admit.

She looks at Edie. 'And this is all your idea, I assume?'

Edie's about to say something, but I butt in furiously.

'No, it's not! It's what we all think. I mean, Edie's the one who discovered the problem, but we're agreed. Aren't we, Crow? This is what we want. All of us.'

Crow nods. 'All of us.'

'Well, it's nice to see you're all such good friends,' Amanda says, 'but I'm afraid you girls are in no position to dictate terms like this to Miss Teen. If we like the designs, it's up to us how we produce them. And there's no guarantee that we *will* like them, of course.'

She gets up and starts striding around the room, sipping Diet Coke from her glass and explaining how we're still children, and just because Crow has done two collections it doesn't make her Giorgio Armani, and we can't really tell anyone how we want things done.

'Of course, we'll bear your ideas in mind,' she adds. Then her phone goes. It's a text from her dad. 'His meeting's over. He'll be here in five minutes,' she says. Then she sees our faces.

'Oh, don't tell me you're going to walk out again! Grow up, girls. This is the real world.'

If this is the real world, I don't like it. None of us do.

'I'd be sad not to work with Miss Teen any more,' Crow says in a tiny voice. 'It's been great. You've helped me so much. So has your dad. But if I have to go back to just making a few dresses for clients by myself, that's OK. It's how I started.'

I nod. I grab her hand and squeeze it. Edie grabs the other one and squeezes it too.

'There's something I don't think you realise,' Amanda says coldly.

I can feel the stillness of the night. The quietness of the room. The darkness outside. The tension in Crow's shoulders. But also her stubbornness. It used to drive me crazy, but now it's one of my favourite things about her.

'Miss Teen owns the "Crow" label,' Amanda continues. 'We own the name. If you go on your own, you'll have to find another one.'

Crow does a sort-of hiccup. Edie gasps. My mouth goes dry. No, we hadn't realised this.

We look at each other in shock. Of course, Crow could always use her real name, but 'Elizabeth Lamogi' doesn't have quite the same ring to it, and it would take up a lot of space on labels.

I can see tears welling up fast in Crow's eyes. Then I remember that it was her brother who chose her nickname, before he was kidnapped. For five years, while Henry was forced to fight in a rebel army and she didn't know if he was alive or dead, her name was the only thing she had that he'd given her. It's more precious to her than her sketchbooks, her life in London, even her ability to sew.

Crow pauses, willing the tears not to fall. I'm thinking of little Lakshmi sheltering in a railway carriage, her scarred face, her fingers that don't work any more, and the way she hugged me with those arms that were hardly there. I know what I'd do. But it's not my name that's at stake.

'You can keep it,' Crow whispers to Amanda. She gulps. She was going to say more, but she can't.

We have nothing left. Amanda is right. We're only children. There's very little we can do in this complicated business of fashion. And this seems to be it.

I open my mouth to say something to back Crow up, but I can't talk either. Edie is silent and white-faced. She's trying to catch Crow's eye and I know she'd tell her not to make such a sacrifice for her sake, but Crow's ignoring her. She knows what she wants to do and she doesn't want to be talked out of it.

Amanda sits down, looking more exhausted than ever and we stay there in silence until the door opens and Andy Elat comes in, quickly followed by Paolo the PR man in his wraparound sunglasses. (It's totally dark outside.)

'Blimey, I'm glad that's over!' Andy says cheerily. 'Worst meeting of my life.' Then he sees us all sitting there. 'What's happened? Cat died?'

I get my voice back from somewhere.

'No. But I'm afraid I don't think we can do the collection. And Edie can't change her site.'

Andy sits at the head of the table, with Paolo opposite. His mood has changed instantly and all the cheeriness has gone.

'Spill, kids. What's the story?'

We explain our terms if we go ahead with Miss Teen. Amanda joins in occasionally, underlining things or mentioning bits we've missed.

'Right,' Andy says, when we've finished. He laughs once, loudly. 'No wonder there was an atmosphere.' He looks at Crow. 'Better show us your designs, young lady. After all the trouble you're causing, they'd have to be bleeding incredible.'

Finally, Crow unpacks her satchel and spreads out her mood board and the little pile of sketchbooks in front of Amanda and starts to go through the designs. For once, I don't have to do the talking. I just sit back while she explains her inspiration and what the collection is about.

'It's called White Light,' she says. Her voice is quiet and still full of stress from our conversation just now, but she goes on. 'I got the idea when we visited the Taj Mahal. It's made entirely of white cotton or silk, for summer. It's inspired by love, so it's romantic. It's layered and full of curves, like my original work, but there's hardly any embellishment, apart from a couple of pieces that will use these little stones. And we know of some really good workshops in India that could do them.'

Edie nods hard at this point. She's suddenly an expert on international embroidery and she knows that Indian workshops – manned by grown-ups – can be some of the best.

But Crow hasn't finished yet. 'For this collection, though, it's really all about the cutting. They have the most amazing cutting tools at the factory. I think they could do this.'

Amanda, Andy and Paolo huddle over the designs, listening to every word and flipping backwards and forwards between pieces. In just a few days, Crow has produced designs for tops and trousers, dresses and skirts, tunics and leggings. More than half the pieces they would need, and all giving a strong idea of her vision for the clothes.

I hear them muttering things like 'architectural' and 'sculptural'. Their faces are very serious and it's impossible to tell what they're thinking. Besides, I'm still in shock from the idea that someone can take your own name away from you. I didn't know it was possible, but we must have signed up to it in a contract somewhere. I must read those things more carefully next time. If there ever *is* a next time.

'The pieces look more complicated than they are,' I add, trying not to sound too desperate. 'Once you get the pattern right, they're actually quite simple to produce. We think. We made some of our own samples to check, and they worked out OK. I mean, the patterns would probably look pretty weird but Crow's a bit of a wizard with cutting, ha ha, and you'd get these incredible waterfall effects, like here, or the billowing sleeve, here, which is inspired by a dome, and then you get these cut-outs and you can see the other layer behind them, and that's white too . . .'

I'm jabbering. I stop. Andy looks at Crow and me and everyone falls silent.

'Let me get this straight,' he says. 'You want me to produce these designs. And in return for Edie saying I'm not some evil slave-driver, you want total control on how they're made. *Plus* how I run my staff based in India. *Plus* labelling. Have I missed anything?'

'Er, yes,' Edie adds. 'A percentage of the profits to help child labourers in India. And preferably other countries too.'

‘Oh sorry,’ he adds sarcastically. ‘I forgot. *And* how I spend the profits. Paolo?’

He turns to the PR guru. Paolo has removed his sunglasses to examine the designs in detail. Underneath, his eyes are pink and puffy and I can quite understand why he quickly replaces the shades. Then he sits up to his full black-polo-necked height.

‘There is only one word to describe this collection,’ he says decisively.

He pauses for effect. We wait, silently.

‘GENIUS!’

He looks around the room triumphantly. ‘Sheer genius! I LOVE LOVE LOVE it! These girls are AMAZING. The clothes are FANTASTIC! Who would go to the most colourful country in the world and produce something that is totally monochrome? It’s INSPIRED! It’s CHANEL! But it’s so NEXT YEAR! Miss Teen girls will ADORE it!’ He grabs the nearest sketchbook and kisses it.

Andy’s face doesn’t move a muscle.

‘I’ll get back to you later, kids,’ he says. ‘We have some talking to do. But we might be able to do a deal.’

Chapter 43

I can still hear his voice in my head the next evening. I'm sitting in Jenny's dressing room, which she shares with Megan, the actress who plays her mother, trying to read *Vogue*. Mum suggested maths revision. I don't think so.

So far, six people have walked past the open door with massive bouquets of flowers for Sigrid. Or maybe it was the same person six times. Impossible to tell behind about four thousand flowers.

Whatever Joe Yule has bought for her to declare his love requires two bodyguards to hang about in the corridor, taking up space and getting in the way of the stagehands. It may be my imagination, but I'm starting to wonder if there might be other members of the Sigrid Is Really The Queen Of Evil Society.

Tonight is the first night of *Her Father's Daughter* in its new location. Actually, it's not. It's the eighth night, but the others were previews and don't count. Jenny wouldn't let us come to any of them. She was too nervous and said we'd make it worse. She's been losing so much weight that they've had to take her costumes in.

Crow's been working madly on Project Jenny to keep the fit perfect. What with that and getting her White Light designs ready, she's totally exhausted, which is why she's at home, fast asleep, and not in the audience tonight. She'll have plenty of other occasions to see the play.

Assuming she wants to. Tonight is the night the critics come. What they write tomorrow will make or break the production. Not the sales – it's nearly sold out – but whether people come to watch a car crash or a smash hit. Jenny should be worse than usual and I've been half expecting her to self-combust with tension, but, bizarrely, tonight she's better than she's been for ages.

It's just like the Boat House again. Now that she's got a proper audience to perform to, she can relax and do her thing. And theatre *is* her thing. You can tell. She has exactly the same look in her eye that Crow has had since we got back from the Taj Mahal. This is what she was born to do and I'm not sure even the critics can ruin it for her this time.

I don't know how Sigrid feels about it, because when she heads for her dressing room, past the Gift Guards, she keeps her head down and her eyes on the floor.

'We've been instructed not to talk to her,' Jenny says.

'Press night nerves. She needs her space.'

She's certainly got it in that dressing room. Jenny says it's the size of all the others put together. And Sigrid has had it entirely decorated in her favourite shade of ivory, with Jo Malone candles, five humidifiers and three antique mirrors 'for atmosphere'. Well, it's created an atmosphere among the cast and backstage people all right. Not necessarily the one she wanted, but definitely an atmosphere.

I'm not just here for moral support. I'm also a bodyguard of sorts. An Outfit Guard. There's a clothes bag hanging on a screen beside Jenny's (old, but not antique) mirror, with Project Jenny inside. If anything happens to it, I've been reliably informed by Granny that bits of me will be fed to the lions in London Zoo. The contents are going to have to compete with the sea-goddess dress, which isn't easy, but that one's been cut off at the knees, literally, so I think we'll be OK.

When Jenny comes back to get changed after the final curtain, she's flushed from the standing ovation that the performers have just received.

'That sounded good,' I say encouragingly.

'Better than good,' Jenny answers, her cheeks flushed. 'It was perfect.'

Megan, the actress sharing the dressing room, nods vigorously.

'How long till the reviews come out?'

I know I shouldn't ask, but I can't help it. They check their watches.

'About seven hours. The online ones may be sooner.'

The next thirty minutes are very busy. I'm trying to get Project Jenny into perfect working order with a borrowed steamer, but people keep interrupting me by bursting into the dressing room and telling Jenny how fabulous she was. And occasionally Megan too. It's a bit like it was after Crow's first Fashion Week collection. All your friends come clustering round to support you. It's really nice and almost makes all of the stress and hassle worthwhile.

An hour later, we're driving up to a posh club in Soho, where the press night party will be held on the top floor, with dancing under the stars. The place is surrounded by enough paparazzi to open their own online camera business. I remember the first time Jenny got out of a limo, in her cherry tomato dress, feeling as if the world was about to swallow her up. Now she slides out of the car and faces the camera flashes like a pro. She's still on a high from the performance and she quite possibly knows how good she looks, which is very. I slide out behind her in my gold brocade coat, copying as best I can.

Sigrid and Joe are just disappearing through the doors, having posed for several pictures already. Joe looks as yummy as ever. Totally Sex God-ish, as he flashes a final smile. Sigrid seems anxious to get inside. I catch sight of what's left of her ultramarine skirts swinging around her knees. They look fine. More puddle-goddess than sea-goddess, though.

'Oi, Jenny,' someone shouts out, 'are you wearing Crow too, then?'

Oh, my goodness. Just how fashion-conscious are these people? Next thing, they'll be asking if my sculpted shorts are by Chloé (which they're not – I made them – but they're *inspired* by Chloé).

'Actually, this dress is Givenchy,' Jenny says.

'It was worn by Audrey Hepburn,' I add. 'Around the time she was filming *Breakfast at Tiffany's*.' I've already tipped the press off about this. It's another thing you learn how to do when you work in fashion.

Good old Granny. As well as her own stuff, she has friends who collect couture. Some of them are really, really rich and obsessed with old movie stars. Some of them don't mind one peach-pink bouclé cocktail dress ('Just one, dar-leeng – I am *nevair*, *nevair* doing zees again – and mind ze seams') being temporarily adapted by a respected designer to fit a budding new actress, who isn't exactly Audrey's size, even when she's thin. There aren't many outfits that can outdo Crow on a good day, but anything once worn by Audrey Hepburn can.

Jenny's shoes are vintage Roger Vivier, in case anyone wonders, but nobody does. After the Audrey Hepburn moment, the shoe moment becomes a bit irrelevant.

Inside the club, Edie, Crow and Jenny's mum are

already waiting for us. Mum offered to come and help monitor my champagne consumption, but after the London Eye episode with Alexander, I don't really feel like it any more. Tonight I'll be exploring the delights of lemonade and fruit cocktails.

Jenny spends the party being congratulated by theatre types. So does Sigrid, when people can get past her Gift Guards (this time it's a heart-shaped yellow diamond the size of a Cheerio) and Joe. Nobody mentions the stress of the last two weeks. Nobody mentions the critics and the press night reviews. Everybody is really just waiting for them, though.

Finally, a few hours past my bedtime, Anthony, the director, comes in, clutching a print-out.

'Here's the first one!' he says. Everyone perks up and stops talking. 'I haven't read it yet, promise. I'll just say it as it comes. Here goes . . . "London theatre has found a new star in the making. A striking young talent who lifts *Her Father's Daughter* from light comedy into high drama. I urge you to beg, borrow or steal a ticket to see this play for the startling performance by . . ." Oh.' He pauses. '". . . By Jenny Merritt. But that's not all. There's another not-to-be-missed turn."' Anthony stops and smiles. 'Ah, here we go. ". . . If you haven't seen Sigrid Santorini on stage then you simply must, if only to find out for yourself how . . ." Oh.'

He stops again. He puts the piece of paper down and sort of pretends it's not there. He bustles over to Sigrid and Joe and starts loudly ordering another bottle of champagne. Jim, the actor who plays Jenny's father, picks up the review and carries on the reading for the crowd who are still listening.

'". . . if only to find out how awful a performance can be when delivered by someone with the vocal range of a fruitbat. Whatever was director Anthony Lyle thinking, putting an actress with such poor diction and projection into one of the largest theatres in London? The poor woman may look a million dollars on screen, but she mangles her oversize part in this play to rising hysteria from the audience. It is only the stunning performances of her fellow cast-members that prevent this comedy from quickly descending into farce."'

I look up to see how Sigrid is handling it, but she's gone. These Hollywood stars seem to have a sixth sense for back entrances and quick exits. No sign of Joe either, or Anthony, or the Gift Guards.

'Poor Sigrid.'

I look up. It's Edie speaking. Only Edie.

'How's she going to face everyone tomorrow?'

'She's going to have to act,' I say. 'Act happy. Like Jenny did when Sigrid stole Joe.'

'Aha!' says a deep voice behind me. It's Bill, the playwright, who has his arm around his new star, shining in her vintage Givenchy dress. 'Would that be Jenny Merritt, the "striking young talent"? I'm sure she made an excellent job of it. She's just been telling me she thought it was *she* who had the voice problems. Silly girl. Of course it was Sigrid. But Anthony would have killed anyone who admitted it.'

Jenny is looking the way her cat Stella does when you tickle her under the chin. I'm not sure she isn't actually purring. For a girl who has GCSEs in less than a month, it's amazing how happy she seems.

On the way out, I spot a Robert Pattinson lookalike sitting on a squashy leather sofa, with a famous teenage rock princess on his knee. She's on the receiving end of the horror-movie kiss. I grab Jenny and point.

'Oh my God! *Nonie!*' She grabs me back, stunned.

He's got his same old scarf on, and the too-tight jeans. Funny that I used to find him so attractive. Next to Hot Phil from No Kidding, he's really just pushy and ew. I check my insides and I have to admit, they're not being totally loyal. They're still doing the odd jeté and half-hearted arabesque, but it's getting better.

'Let's go,' I say.

'Isn't he still going out with that model?' Jenny whispers.

'Who knows? He probably doesn't even know himself.'

We go home and I sleep like a baby. I don't dream about Alexander, or spiders, or horror movies of any kind. My insides may be taking a while to catch up, but my brain has definitely moved on.

Chapter 44

Over the next few days, I work my way through the biggest pile of revision in the history of the universe. I lock myself in my room and only come out for meals, *Project Catwalk* and *Gossip Girl*. Not only that, I only allow myself one hour a day Googling and messaging. How strict is *that*? So it takes me a while to find out the following things.

1. Jenny is being called 'the new Judi Dench'. Judi Dench is very famous, has an Oscar and is in the James Bond movies (although not Harry Potter, surprisingly – perhaps she was busy), and is a Dame, like Vivienne Westwood, so this is good.

2. Sigrid has tried to pull out of *Her Father's Daughter* 'for medical reasons' (not having big enough vocal cords, I guess) but isn't allowed to because of all the money they've spent on the Big, Scary Theatre, so sometimes even starlets can't have everything they want.

3. Harry has somehow managed to get a signed photo

of Freddie Flintoff to put in the envelope of information for Sanjay. Jenny's also donated her picture of Sigrid, just in case he's interested. Funnily enough, we're all feeling a bit sorry for her now.

4. Crow's White Light collection is already the talk of Miss Teen. Facebook and the fashion blogs are full of people saying how amazing it's going to be.

5. Edie's 'Cheap Clothes Cost Lives' tee-shirts have completely sold out, but one of the retail chains has asked if they can make and sell some more. Ethically, of course. Edie really *is* beating Crow and me to becoming a fashion supremo. All profits to charities that help street children in countries with big garment industries.

6. Little Suraj Patil has found out about the slave children through reading Edie's blog and wants to know how he can help.

7. *Vogue* want Jenny to write an article (I say 'write' – I mean talk to a journalist) about being a successful teenage actress *and* doing GCSEs *and* wearing jaw-dropping Givenchy. Jenny has tried to point out that she's too busy actually doing all of these things to talk to someone about doing them, but in the end she can't resist. It'll be in the September issue.

8. Svetlana Russinova, the supermodel, is rumoured to be going out with a New York-based photographer called Zanni, who did the pictures for her last *Elle* cover. There is, apparently, a queue of models waiting to go out with her ex-boyfriend, Harry Chatham, the

rising fashion show DJ.

9. On the subject of models, Lulu Frost has announced her split with Alexander Taylor, who was recently seen romancing a teenage rock princess at a posh London club.

10. Miss Teen will shortly be making an announcement about a major new PR initiative.

I call Edie to see if she knows anything about this initiative, because I certainly don't. But she's as much in the dark as me.

'I just got a call from someone in Paolo's office saying they'd be sending me a press release on the twentieth of May.'

'*Press* release?'

'I know. I've never had one before. I did check they'd got the right person, but they said yes, they definitely had. They even said they liked my blog.'

The twentieth of May is emblazoned on my heart. It's geography GCSE. What on earth is going on?

Well, it sort of makes sense. When the day comes, Edie sends me the Miss Teen press release and it turns out to be geography-related. It's about a new strategy called 'Fashion Holds Hands'. As a business manager, I understand all about strategies, of course. I use them all the time, you know. And the more I hear about this one, the more I like it.

Andy Elat's on the news that evening, talking about it. First of all, he explains, there's going to be a Fashion Holds Hands team, who will work full time checking how clothes are made in every factory they use. There will be funky new labels on every garment saying 'Check me out' and giving details on where it came from. Then there is the Miss Teen Fashion Fund, which will help thousands of children who've been made to work in the garment industry. Finally, Andy wants to set up a special committee of all the major high-street brands, with himself as chairman, to help everyone come up to the new standards.

In the conversation that follows, Andy hints at other ideas to come, and suddenly everyone is talking about Miss Teen, waiting to see what happens.

Edie gets a bouquet of roses from the No Kidding team that's seriously worthy of Joe Yule.

After our geography papers, life doesn't seem too bad. I almost start to enjoy the summer for about a week, but then I bump into Lulu Frost in the West End, and life goes back to being excruciating for a while.

Crow and I are back in the Big Scary Theatre, to see Jenny doing her thing in *His Father's Daughter* ('Beg, borrow or steal a ticket . . .'). It's my seventh visit and Crow's third. They give us cheap tickets and squeeze us in somehow and I've discovered they use the same ice cream supplier as the Royal Opera House, so the interval is yum.

We're queuing up for our usual supplies, when someone taps me on the shoulder and it's Lulu. What *is* it about this girl and queuing?

'Hi,' she says smiling nervously at us both. 'Oh, Nonie, you look exhausted.'

Gee thanks. So would you if you were in the middle of revising for science and English. Thank goodness Crow's persuaded Henry to help me with Eng. Lit. He's an amazing tutor. I think I might even get a B.

'Oh, I'm fine,' I lie. 'You look great.' Also a lie. She looks rubbish. But YOU DON'T SAY THAT.

'Thanks.'

Lulu smiles nervously again and fiddles with a tassel on her handbag. Oh no. She wants me to ask her something. Why do people do this? Why does it always have to be me who thinks up the conversation?

'I'm sorry to hear about Alexander,' I say.

Crow pats me on the elbow at this point and disappears back to her seat. She may not seem to be paying attention half the time, but she certainly knows her stuff when it comes to relationships. And she knows how much I want to discuss this one with Lulu. NOT.

'Right,' Lulu says. 'Thanks. Well, he's history. There was that kid at the club. And, well, there were rumours about someone else. Someone he was really smitten with. He denied it, of course.'

She looks at me long and hard. I concentrate on looking exhausted. Merely exhausted.

'Poor you,' I say. I suppose I should say 'I'm-sorry-I-snogged-your-boyfriend-I-didn't-know-you-were-still-going-out-isn't-he-rubbish?' But I'm just not that brave. I find the whole 'gosh-I'm-exhausted-I-don't-know-what-you-mean' approach much simpler.

But smitten, huh? Smitten.

I cheer up slightly. 'Lulu,' I say, 'd'you mind if I ask you a question?'

She looks even more nervous. But she says yes anyway.

'It's about Harry. My brother. And Svetlana. You're a friend of hers. Do *you* know why they split up? Because he won't say and it's been bothering me for ages.'

Her look changes from nervous to relieved.

'Oh. *Harry*. Well, Svetlana said it was all about her apartment.'

Her apartment? I don't remember that bit in *Romeo and Juliet*. Or the Taj Mahal story.

'What d'you mean?'

'Just that Harry assumed he'd move in with her when he graduated. She's got this cool little place in TriBeCa for when she's working in New York. And she thinks he's great and everything, but she thought they should keep their own places. And it just sort of spiralled.'

And that was it? They split up because they couldn't agree whether to SHARE A FLAT? All this time I've been worrying about broken hearts and Shakespeare scenarios and it was about living arrangements? I completely give up with relationships. Thank goodness I only have

GCSEs to worry about.

At this moment, a voice comes over the speakers, telling us all to go back to our seats for Act Two.

Lulu says a hasty goodbye and I head back to my seat, where Crow's waiting for me. I tell her about the flat conversation and she doesn't seem surprised.

'Besides,' she says, as the curtain rises, 'there's always Isabelle.'

Isabelle? *Isabelle?* Isabelle who?

'Isabelle who?' I whisper loudly.

But Crow simply shushes me and points at the stage, where Jenny's got a big speech coming up. And grins silently when she sees the look on my face.

Chapter 45

Oh, *that* Isabelle.

GCSEs are finally over. Harry's set up a projector in the kitchen and Mum has let him take down about twenty framed photographs so he can show us his finished degree project on a wall. He's extremely nervous. Partly about what the viewing public at Central St Martins will say, but mostly about what Mum will say. Mum adores Harry, but he drives her nuts. And he and I both know that when it comes to art, she's the hardest person to please. If she likes something, you're walking on air for the next week. And if she doesn't, you just want to dig a little hole and bury yourself in it.

Harry originally set out to be a great painter. Or possibly a great photographer. But we all know that really he's a great DJ, and doing an art degree probably wasn't his best decision. Although if you can even half draw (unlike me) and have Mum for a mother, an art degree is pretty inevitable. Anyway, he's managed to find a compromise. His degree project is made up of three videos and, guess what, they've got a major instrumental soundtrack. We know he spent most of the time perfecting the music and only a small amount on the videos, but luckily he had a friend to help.

Isabelle.

The videos turn out to be a series of shots of her walking down a catwalk, wearing wispy, ghostly outfits (designed by Crow, of course, which is how they met), and with her long blonde hair flowing behind her. The clever bit is that one of the videos is run backwards, and in another one she's *walking* backwards. They love this sort of thing at art school, apparently. They don't have to try walking backwards in spindly stilettos.

Isabelle makes it look easy, though. And mysterious. The background is mostly dark and she seems to be walking out of nowhere (or into it), her feet resting on a gentle mist. Mum nods knowingly at this, as if it's totally artistic. I nod knowingly at this, because it's totally cheating. It means no props, no expensive outfits, no backdrops, no complicated lights, like I needed to organise last year. All you need is a smoke machine. And a very pretty girl with a good sense of balance.

Isabelle is a *very* pretty girl. Isabelle is Isabelle Carruthers. *Lady* Isabelle Carruthers, to be precise. She's nineteen, pale, ethereal and lovely. She's famous for her almost waist-length, ringletty hair, grey-green eyes, pale, freckly skin and sultry lips. She recently postponed doing her degree in English at Oxford so she can BE AN

INTERNATIONAL COVER GIRL. She's also famous for being the muse of two designers, one in Paris and one in London.

She could walk down a crowded Kensington High Street in a bin liner and Harry's videos would still be sensational. As it is, Harry's videos are *totally* sensational. Mum has tears pouring down her cheeks by the end.

'You don't deserve it, darling,' she says, hugging him. 'God knows, you don't, after all the classes you've cut. But they're wonderful. Ridiculously wonderful.'

He looks slightly relieved at this, but still surprisingly nervous. He turns to me.

'What do you think, Nonie?'

This is odd. Why should he care so much what *I* think? I'm only GCSE girl, after all. Then I realise. He's not asking me about the videos. He's asking me about Isabelle. He knows I always really liked Svetlana. But from the look in his eye, I know that the new thing with Isabelle must be serious.

How does he DO it? He's just skipped from one supermodel to another, even more incredible supermodel. How come he got all the sex genes and I just got all the two-timing, rubbish-kisser genes? *And* he's tall and I'm short. Life is *so* unfair.

'I think they're great,' I say, which is my code for 'I forgive you about Svetlana.'

Now he looks properly relieved.

* * *

Summer holidays come at last. With Harry's permission, Edie puts all three videos on her website. It crashes again, naturally. I'm starting to wonder if Edie is *quite* as much of a technical genius as I thought. She still gets straight As in her GCSEs, though. And I get two – in French and textiles. Yay! Which kind of makes up for geography. Oops.

Edie's site is becoming essential viewing for anyone wanting to know how to update their wardrobe without destroying the planet or causing children to work sixteen-hour days. It's packed with ideas about vintage shops, charity shops, swapping parties, knitting circles, dress patterns and ethical clothing companies. As the weeks go by, the ideas develop and people send her new ones. But that doesn't mean the site is all bobble hats and pinafores. Quite the opposite. In addition to Isabelle, it still features Crow's party dresses (which we *know* are made fairly, because we watch her do it) and lots of the latest high-street trends.

It also has a new section, which is extremely popular. Children from one of the charity-run schools in Mumbai take it in turns to blog about their lives. Edie pays for them to use a local internet café and one of the charity workers is happy to type what they tell him. It's a mixture of stuff. Sometimes it's about cricket. Sometimes it's about trying to find a job. Sometimes it's about what they learned in school that day. Sometimes it's a list of questions for the rest of us: What is London like? Is it true that everyone in America is a millionaire? Does Africa have more elephants than India?

Edie doesn't have to write the replies. Comments flood in from around the world, eagerly providing the answers. I imagine little Lakshmi on the fringes of a group of kids clustering around the computer to hear them read aloud. I'm sure her face will be bright with excitement.

Sometimes, she talks to me about them. Every Sunday, she messages me at breakfast time, with the kind help of Mrs Patil and Suraj, who types for her on the family's home computer. She calls me 'Special Auntie Nonie'. Mostly, though, she doesn't ask about millionaires or tigers. Just the collection, and how the samples are going, and what Crow's currently working on. I ask about school and her job selling books to passing motorists (as you do) and get the usual 'oh fine' you'd get from any eight-year-old, which makes me feel very good.

Lakshmi is learning to read and is surprisingly good at mental maths. I think Suraj gives her extra coaching on Sunday afternoons. She's not particularly thrilled about school, but she loves the time she gets to play with her doll collection. She has four dolls, like Crow's sister Victoria in Uganda, and Crow and I – as well as lots of Crow's designer friends – have great fun making clothes for them all and producing serious fashionista wardrobes. It's become a bit of an addiction. Edie's started blogging about that too.

Over the summer, we've been making dolls' clothes to

auction for Miss Teen's 'Fashion Holds Hands' campaign. But the auction's just the start. Andy Elat is in the news almost every week, announcing some new ethical initiative. Sales are rocketing. Lakshmi calls him 'Mister Hero'. This is because one of the papers has started calling him the High Street Hero, and it's stuck. He always looks slightly embarrassed when people say it to his face and says stuff like, 'Oh, I'm just doing my job for the planet,' but you can tell he absolutely loves it. Especially when he's nominated for his first award for ethical retailing.

Interestingly, he never mentions how he got his ideas. He's very quiet on the subject. Some people think it's just his natural genius for fashion. Several people 'in the know' say it's down to his amazing PR guru, Paolo Perugino. A few people think it's his daughter.

'I think it's totally outrageous,' Jenny says, when we're back at school, starting our AS-levels (and we thought GCSEs were bad). 'He never even called you about it. He just went ahead and did it and took every scrap of credit. Why don't you say something, Nonie? Why doesn't Edie?'

Well, for a start, Edie's too nice. Also, Edie has noticed, like me, that Andy has given us everything we asked for and much more. He's not exactly the sort of man to grovel to a bunch of teenagers. This is his way of making everything right. And it's a good way. We're not complaining.

Also, I'm thinking about small print. It's another thing

you do (eventually), when you work in fashion. I read Crow's latest contract for the White Light collection very carefully. Without telling us, Andy had put in a line saying that 'all rights to the name of CROW when used as a fashion label pass solely and without prejudice to the Designer'.

Which basically means that Crow gets her name back. Without asking. Which means that underneath it all, Andy Elat is our hero too and we really like him.

I pointed out that line to Crow, and explained it to her. She said nothing, of course. But through one of Granny's friends she got hold of a very old, very beautiful Edwardian velvet smoking jacket and relined it with patterned silk, which she hand-embroidered with hearts and soaring birds.

Andy's 'thank you' was very gruff when she gave it to him. He wore it to collect his ethical retailing award. He looked great.

Chapter 46

It's nearly Christmas. Jenny is wearing a white cotton dress with exaggerated, billowing sleeves, and high-heeled sandals that have been designed especially for her by one of India's top shoe designers. The dress is slit at one side, to reveal a damask tunic underneath and white leggings, beautifully cut to make the most of her calves and ankles. The people at the factory double-checked when we said we wanted size 14 samples, instead of the normal peanut-sized ones they make for professional models. But luckily Jenny is back to her normal shape now that the Queen of Evil has returned to Hollywood. She looks healthy and her face is glowing, the way it does when she's really happy.

I think Andy is slightly scared of me now, because when I suggested that this time Jenny really *should* be the face of Crow's White Light collection, he looked at me thoughtfully and said, 'You might have something there, kid.' Instead of 'You *are* joking?' which is what he said last time.

Jenny's standing in front of the Taj Mahal, posing for the camera, and surrounded by laughing street children, whose tiny frames make her look about eight feet tall. The sleeves aren't the only things billowing; the photographer has to keep stopping because the Taj Mahal is billowing too. Sanjay is running around frantically, trying to find someone who can attach the canvas it's painted on more successfully to its scaffolding frame.

Last week, this set was being used as the background for a major Bollywood musical number, and the canvas was painted to look like the Gateway to India. Which is a bit mad, as the real thing is only a few miles down the road in Mumbai. (I am SO good at Indian geography now. When people hear I failed GCSE they will be *shocked.*)

I'm not sure who had the idea of us coming to Bollywood to create the publicity shots for the White Light collection. There was a brainstorming meeting (in the Miss Teen boardroom – getting used to it) and we all agreed that India would be great, but some people were saying Mumbai, and others were saying the Taj Mahal itself, and then we all gradually realised that we could sort of do both. Andy asked his team if they had any contacts in Bollywood, and they were all shaking their heads and looking gloomy, and then suddenly I realised. *I* did: Sanjay.

Andy gave me the strangest look. 'Is there anything you can't do, Nonie Chatham?' He said it quite severely, but Amanda was grinning, so I assumed he was being nice. Even Paolo looked quite impressed.

Ever since, Sanjay has been having the time of his life, telling us who all the important people are, and how Bollywood works, and how he, Sanjay, needs to be involved in *everything*, and preferably in charge. I suspect he's younger than me, but in his head he practically *is* Walt Disney by now. Anyway, he's been offered a job as a runner on a movie here in the new year, instead of just emptying bins like he used to, so maybe he will be the Indian Walt Disney by the time he's finished.

We've been here a week. The crew on the shoot will be going back tomorrow, but we're staying on for a mega-holiday. Mum's coming. Granny's already here. Andy Elat persuaded her to brave her fear of swollen ankles and booked her into a presidential suite in the best hotel in Mumbai, so she's coping. Harry's coming out with Isabelle and a cricket bat signed by the England team for Sanjay. Edie's coming over with her family. And her BOYFRIEND.

Hot Phil came to visit her in London last half term. I went along to meet him at the airport, and personally, I was disappointed. He looked a bit thinner and weedier in real life than on his Facebook page. He was wearing glasses with thick navy frames that definitely need replacing, and he seemed to be struggling under the biggest laptop bag I've ever seen.

However, Edie didn't seem too worried. She went

lipstick pink the moment she saw him, and the hug she gave him did not say, 'How lovely to meet you after all this time, Philip. Welcome to London.' It said, 'Oh. My. God. Wow! Hold me!'

It took them two days of blushing and fingertip touching before I caught them with their faces glued to each other, like he was trying to retrieve something from the back of her mouth with his tongue. She had her eyes closed and so did he, which gave me a couple of seconds to check her expression for signs of horror. There were none. In fact, she looked quite pleased. Next day, she needed loads of Chapstick. I have a feeling she'll be needing a lot more this holiday.

Out of all of us, how did Edie end up being the first one with a proper, normal boyfriend with acceptable kissing ability? I'd never have guessed it, but then, that girl surprises me all the time.

'How's it going, darling?'

Granny's watching as they stretch the Taj Mahal canvas back over its scaffolding. I'm glad to see her here, as it means she's not shopping. She already seems to have bought most of Mumbai's pashmina collection, and enough embroidered silk and knick-knacks to keep her going for twenty years. Shopkeepers *love* Granny, and she loves them back. 'Everyone here is so utterly charming, darling,' she keeps pointing out. Which they would be, if you were constantly staggering out of their shops, laden with parcels. I think Mum's inheritance is going to be about two pounds fifty by the time Granny's finished.

'Fine,' I say. 'The photographer says he just needs another five shots or so. I'm making sure we cover every outfit, and we nearly have. They'll be done soon.'

The street children are teaching Jenny bhangra dancing while they wait. Jenny's OK for someone who hasn't done it before, but she's still working out what to do with her hips, and next to the local kids her arms look like jerky windmills.

I look for Lakshmi in the crowd. Normally, when she isn't with the other kids she's with me, but suddenly I can't find her. We've hardly been parted since I got to Mumbai and I can feel panic starting to rise. What's happened to her? Where can she have got to on this huge Bollywood set? Is she OK?

Then I spot her, sitting next to a clothes rail with a sketchbook on her lap and a doll tucked under her arm. She's staring intently at Crow, who's sketching beside her. I go over to say hi, and as I approach, Crow looks up at me and grins.

'She's really good,' Crow says. 'Take a look.'

I watch as Lakshmi eagerly copies a couple of Crow's dancing girl pictures for me. Even though her fused fingers mean she has to hold the pen at a crazy angle, she sketches with the same easy grace as Crow. And the results are just as sparkling.

I don't believe it. I've wanted to draw like that all my life and even tiny little Lakshmi is already better than me.

'They're amazing,' I say, hoping she hasn't noticed how totally jealous I am.

Lakshmi gives me her shy smile. She's still wearing the gold necklace I gave her in spring. How she's managed to hang onto it all this time, I can't imagine. I think she's a tougher cookie than she looks – a bit like Crow.

'Maybe I'll go to fashion school one day,' she says. Well, she whispers it, really. I know that whisper. It's the same whisper I used in my head when I thought about my dream of working for a designer. It's the whisper that means 'it's too wonderfully impossible to say it out loud properly, but if it happened it would be the most amazing thing *ever*'.

'You will,' I tell her.

After all, here's me, working in the fashion industry right this minute. Well, not working. Taking a five-minute break and chatting. But I'll be working again as soon as they've got the Taj Mahal sorted. And if Lakshmi's good enough to go to fashion school, I'll make sure she gets there.

I'll have help. Crow has been asked to stay on for an extra week and teach cutting techniques on a fashion course at one of India's best design schools. They think Crow is incredible and they love the idea that they'll be learning from someone who learned from someone who learned from Christian Dior. So there's me, with my textiles GCSE, and Crow is TEACHING the stuff to INTERNATIONAL COLLEGE STUDENTS. You get used to it.

'Right, we're ready!'

The photographer is waving, Jenny's getting back into position and Sanjay is running around, making sure everyone else is doing what they're supposed to be doing.

Then my phone goes.

Normally, I wouldn't answer it at such a crucial moment, but when I see who's calling, I do.

'Hi, Andy.'

'Hi, kid. Everything OK?'

'Totally fine,' I tell him happily.

'Good. Thought you'd like to know – *Vogue* have seen some of the samples from the collection. They want to do a piece to time with the launch in summer. They might use one of the dresses on the cover. And they'd like that friend of yours to model it. She worked well in the September issue. Curves are in this year. Pass the message on, will you? Nonie? Nonie?'

But I'm not answering. I've dropped the phone in shock. Lakshmi rushes over and tries to help me rescue it. We bump heads, scrabbling on the floor, and giggle. She gets to it first and hands it over.

'Yes,' I say, breathlessly, into it. 'Yes, Andy. I'll pass the message on.'

I imagine telling Jenny that in a few months' time she

may be a *Vogue* cover girl. And Crow that Jenny will be in one of her dresses. Then I realise that I really have to learn bhangra dancing, because I just want to wave my arms in the air, and those dancers seem to have worked out the best way in the world to do it.

'Nonie!' the photographer shouts at me. 'Come over here! You have a job to do.'

I sort of dance over to him, with Lakshmi following close behind. He's right. I do.

What can you do?

If you'd like to help children like Sanjay, Ganesh and Lakshmi, you can! You can find out more at www.oxfam.org.uk and www.savethechildren.org.uk. I also support www.soschildrensvillages.org.uk, where you can sponsor a child and help a whole village of children get the food, shelter, healthcare and education they need.

The other thing you can do is write to the owners of the shops where you buy your clothes and get them to check how they were made. If you care, they will care. You are more powerful than you know!

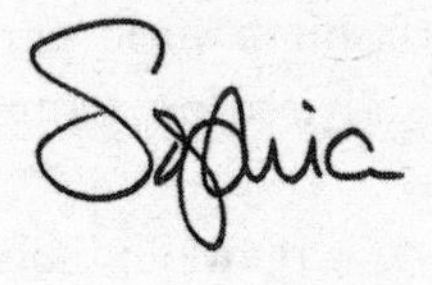

Acknowledgements

Writing this book was such a pleasure. And a big part of that pleasure was getting the chance to talk to old friends, and new ones, in the name of research. If by 'research' you can include having a delicious curry cooked for you and chatting deep into the night about the delights of Mumbai.

I'd like to thank Lola Gostelow (again) and this time her husband Harry, too, for their advice about charities and the theatre. And to Scott Thomson, who read the draft while actually travelling far and wide to help make a difference.

Alison Stratton cooked the curry, and her husband Jake was just as helpful in describing Mumbai. As was my brother, Christopher Pett, who gave me the idea for the cricket match (which he did in real life).

Ann Ceprynski and Modus are my fashion world gurus. Tanielle Lobo designed the cover dress, advised on Mumbai and gave me moral support. Go, Tanielle!

Sophie Lachowsky gave me more moral support and lots of useful advice just when I needed it.

The Longchamps and the Dampierres made Paris a magical place for me a long time ago, and the magic still lingers. *Merci, tout le monde.*

Claire Potter, Katie Rhodes and Anna Linwood were joined by the wonderful Sophie Elliott in advising me on the first draft. Those jobs as book critics are still looking good.

And a big thank you, as ever, to everyone at Chicken House. Barry, Rachel, Imogen, Claire and all of you. It's lovely to be part of a team.

Finally, my family. Without you, it wouldn't happen.

I should mention that I've played with Mumbai's geography for the sake of the story. Please don't use this as a guide book! The train journey is real, though. Imagine! Twenty hours . . .

About the author

Sophia Bennett would have loved to be an artist, fashion designer, or the lady who does costumes for Jane Austen films. However, not being able to draw or sew very well made those careers unlikely. Luckily, she also loves to write. She is the author of the internationally successful *Threads* series, as well as *The Look*, *You Don't Know Me* and *The Castle*, and has written for *The Times* and *The Guardian*.

She lives in London with her family, and is known for her shoes and her writing shed. You can find out more about her on her website: www.sophiabennett.com

@sophiabennett

SophiaBennettAuthor

ALSO BY SOPHIA BENNETT

STARS

The third book in the fabulous *Threads* series.

Best friends Nonie, Jenny, Edie and Crow are close to beginning glittering careers. So why do their challenges suddenly seem so overwhelming?

The girls have choices to make. Who will wait for fame and success? Who will emerge an outright star? Who will fall in love? And who will turn her back on her dreams?

'. . . perfect for teen readers who've grown out of Cathy Cassidy and dream of designing a catwalk collection, or being a Broadway megastar!'

WATERSTONES BOOKS QUARTERLY

ALSO BY SOPHIA BENNETT

THE LOOK

Ted is tall. Freaky. When she's spotted by a model agency, she can't believe it.

At the same time, her gorgeous sister falls seriously ill.

With her world turned upside down, Ted must choose between fame and family. Can she be a supermodel and a super sister? All in five-inch heels?

'. . . one word, BRILLIANT. A difficult topic, sensitively handled.'
CATHY CASSIDY

Paperback, ISBN 978-1-906427-91-7, £6.99 • ebook, ISBN 978-1-908435-16-3, £6.99

ALSO BY SOPHIA BENNETT

YOU DON'T KNOW ME

Me and Rose. In a band. Singing together, all the way to the live finals of Killer Act.

Only to be told one of us must go.

But no girl would drop her best friend in front of millions . . .

Would she?

If this is fame, it sucks.

Everyone's talking about us, but nobody knows the truth.

'. . . her best yet.'
AMANDA CRAIG, THE TIMES

Paperback, ISBN 978-1-908435-46-0, £6.99 • ebook, ISBN 978-1-908435-80-4, £6.99

ALSO BY SOPHIA BENNETT

THE CASTLE

It's not just the bridesmaid's dress that Peta has a problem with – it's the whole wedding. How can her mum remarry when Peta's army-hero dad isn't dead?

When Peta receives clues that seem to prove he's alive, she sets out on a crazy mission. Somewhere across the sea, her father's being held in a billionaire's castle.

Dad would do anything to save her – and now it's her turn to rescue him.

'. . . a fun, frolicking, and increasingly frightening adventure.'

TERI TERRY

Paperback, ISBN 978-1-909489-78-3, £6.99 • ebook, ISBN 978-1-909489-79-0, £6.99